THE MISADVENTURES OF
MAUDE MARCH

—— or ——
Trouble Rides
a Fast Horse

Also by Audrey Couloumbis

Getting Near to Baby

Say Yes

THE MISADVENTURES OF
MAUDE MARCH

or ——
Trouble Rides
a Fast Horse

AUDREY COULOUMBIS

RANDOM HOUSE ⌂ NEW YORK

Copyright © 2005 by Audrey Couloumbis
Jacket art copyright © 2005 by Gino D'Achille
All GreyWolf Free Fonts are copyright © R. Gast, GreyWolf WebWorks.
All rights reserved. Used by permission.
Some jacket fonts copyright © 2005 by The Scriptorium, all rights reserved.
For information on these fonts, go to www.fontcraft.com.
All rights reserved under International and Pan-American
Copyright Conventions. Published in the United States by Random House
Children's Books, a division of Random House, Inc., New York, and
simultaneously in Canada by Random House of Canada Limited, Toronto.

www.randomhouse.com/teens

Library of Congress Cataloging-in-Publication Data
Couloumbis, Audrey.
The misadventures of Maude March, or, Trouble rides a fast horse /
Audrey Couloumbis.
p.   cm.
SUMMARY: After the death of the stern aunt who raised them since
they were orphaned, eleven-year-old Sallie and her fifteen-year-old
sister escape their self-serving guardians and begin an adventure
resembling those in the dime novels Sallie loves to read.
ISBN 0-375-83245-9 (trade) — ISBN 0-375-93245-3 (lib. bdg.) —
ISBN 0-375-83247-5 (pbk.)
[1. Frontier and pioneer life—Fiction. 2. Orphans—Fiction.
3. Adventure and adventurers—Fiction.] I. Title: Misadventures of
Maude March. II. Title: Trouble rides a fast horse. III. Title.
PZ7.C8305Mi 2005   [Fic]—dc22   2004016464

Printed in the United States of America

10 9 8 7 6 5 4 3 2 1

First Edition

RANDOM HOUSE and colophon are registered trademarks
of Random House, Inc.

For my husband, Akila.
My husband is, as ever, my greatest supporter and champion.
Put your feet up, honey,
and let Maude and Sallie bring you a sarsaparilla.

LEGEND

Sallie's track

Maude's track

Marion's track

Sallie & Maude with mule

Sallie & Maude together on horseback

State line

River

Abandoned Cabin

The Rattler!

Grand River

IOWA

MISSOURI

Cleomie's Place

Snow!

The Cougar!

Willie's Gang!

Ben Chaplin's Cabin

Platte River

Missouri River

INDEPENDENCE

Lavender Hotel

Hatmaker

Livery

Restaurant

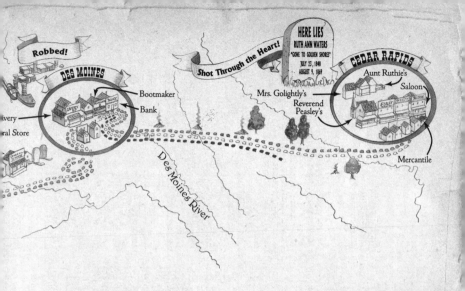

Robbed!

DES MOINES

Bootmaker

Bank

ivery

ral Store

Des Moines River

Shot Through the Heart!

HERE LIES
RUTH ANN WATERS
"GONE TO GOLDEN SHORES"
JULY 27, 1840
AUGUST 9, 1869

Mrs. Golightly's
Reverend
Peasley's

CEDAR RAPIDS

Aunt Ruthie's

Saloon

Mercantile

TRAIL OF THE

NOTORIOUS

"MAD" MAUDE MARCH

AND HER GANG OF

ROBBERS, MURDERERS, AND HORSE THIEVES

ACROSS

IOWA & MISSOURI

-1869-

ONE

THE HEAT WAS AWFUL.

The breeze, when we got one, felt like it came out of an oven. Aunt Ruthie hoped to take our minds off our misery by taking us to town. Even in the dim cool of the mercantile, sweat made our clothing cling to our skin.

My dress was the worst, made out of some kind of muslin that got itchy once it stuck to me. Every two minutes, Aunt Ruthie would say, "Stop scratching, Sallie, it isn't polite."

The shooting didn't start until we'd stepped outside of the mercantile. The screen door whacked shut behind us, and we were greeted by a volley of shots. It was stunning really. Then it was scary. The noise was too great to take it all in at once.

It's strange the way time stretched in that moment and seemed to go on forever. The entire morning passed through my mind, starting when my older sister Maude ate my biscuit with jelly that I had left over from breakfast.

When I complained there were no more biscuits, and that was the last of the black currant jelly, she said, "If you wanted it, you shouldn't have left it laying around." So while Aunt

Ruthie said it was the heat, I knew it was that biscuit that had me squabbling with Maude all day.

As we neared the barbershop, walking to town, Maude pulled Aunt Ruthie toward a stone bench, saying, "You're tiring yourself. Come sit down for a minute," and I dragged on Aunt Ruthie's other arm, saying, "It gets too hot to sit on that rock in the sun. Let's go someplace cooler."

Aunt Ruthie said, "I've had enough of being pulled apart."

In the mercantile, she showed her teeth at us and whispered, "You are to keep your distance, both of you. I don't care to listen to you bicker for another minute." We promised to be good. To this, she said, "Stay over there by the farm goods."

In these aisles, there were only smelly jars of lanolin and herbal salves to examine, and such things as curative oils for ear mites and wireworm to avoid, having nasty little pictures of the ills on the side of the bottles. This bothered me so bad that I pulled a dimer out of my pocket and set to reading it instead.

But Aunt Ruthie was right in sending us there. It was not two minutes before Maude started up again. She told me that Joe Harden, Frontier Fighter, was never a real man. "Those books weren't meant for girls to read, either," she said.

"How would you know?" I said to her. Maude didn't like for me to read dime novels. Sad to say, Maude thought dimers were a waste of learning how to read.

"It's just a made-up name for made-up stories out of books," she said. "Boys probably look up to him, but Joe Harden is just a story figure."

"Like David?" I asked her.

"David who?"

"David who slew Goliath. Is he made up?"

"Of course not, Sallie," Maude said. "What a terrible thing to say. Don't you let Aunt Ruthie hear you talk like that."

I didn't think Aunt Ruthie would care all that much. She hardly ever cared about anything but whether the work was done right. Maude was the one who cared about such things.

Maude and me were orphaned when our folks took sick with the fever. Aunt Ruthie had already started out from Philadelphia to come live with us and teach school. By the time she got to Cedar Rapids, Aunt Ruthie had to take us in. Or rather, we took her in, and she took care of us.

I'm forgetting Uncle Arlen. He was Aunt Ruthie's, and Momma's, younger brother, but he had gone west not long after our folks died, and we had not heard from him in years. So he didn't count as kin. Aunt Ruthie herself said he was as good as dead to us.

She felt he ought to have stayed around to help her raise us, I guess. Around the middle of winter, she felt he ought to have stayed around to chop wood; that was when I heard his name mentioned most often. Aunt Ruthie could hold a grudge second to none.

"David's out of a book," I said stubbornly, "and I ain't never seen any giants."

"That's because he killed them all," Maude told me. "You have to stop reading those cheap stories. Your grammar is atrocious."

"You ever seen any Indians?" I asked her.

3

"Not around here," Maude said.

"That's because Joe Harden, Frontier Fighter, cleared them all out. Single-handed." That's what I said. But down deep, I believed Maude.

"Single-handed*ly*," she said. Maude had in the past year begun to help Aunt Ruthie in the classroom, and she had become quite a stickler. "Kansas is a frontier, Sallie. Iowa is civilized."

"It didn't used to be," I said, but only because it grated on me sometimes that Maude knew just about everything.

Everything except what I had learned from those dime novels. I just knew that if I ever had to survive off the land the way the frontier fighters did, if I had to kill a bear or outsmart a wily Indian, I'd be better able to do it than my sister.

"Ask Aunt Ruthie about Joe Harden then," Maude said as Aunt Ruthie came our way, carrying her purchases wrapped in brown paper that nearly matched her dress.

We'd been orphans for six years. In that time, given the choice between Maude's answers and Aunt Ruthie's, when mulling over the knobbly questions of life, I'd found Maude's to be more to the point.

Maude said, "Go ahead, ask."

"Don't you dare ask me anything." Aunt Ruthie strode right on past us. "Some days it isn't even a good idea to get out of bed," she muttered as we left the mercantile. The screen door slapped shut behind us, and gunshots broke out in the alley between the barbershop and the saloon across the street. The noise was awful.

A stray bullet hit Aunt Ruthie in the heart and killed her dead.

4

"What's happening?" Maude said when Aunt Ruthie dropped like a stone. Although the shots were deafening, I heard this as if Maude spoke right into my ear.

There were several other people on the street who took no notice of Aunt Ruthie at all. They were scurrying madly for their own safety. The shooting went on in fits and starts even after Aunt Ruthie fell. Only Maude and I stood like wooden Indians in those first moments.

There was hardly any blood. On Aunt Ruthie's sacking-brown dress, it looked at first like only a dark wet spot, but still I couldn't take my eyes off it. After another moment I saw the hole in the middle of that spot and then the color, just a rim of blood-red at the edge of the dark wet. I don't believe I breathed, watching.

It's safe to say Maude had not noticed even this much when she dropped to her knees to stuff a paper parcel under Aunt Ruthie's head like a pillow. Maude patted Aunt Ruthie's cheek rather smartly, believing her to have fainted. Yanking off her bonnet, Maude used the brim to ruffle the air around Aunt Ruthie's face.

"Aunt Ruthie," Maude kept saying, scolding really, because she'd told Aunt Ruthie she was tiring herself. Aunt Ruthie wasn't all *that* old, but she'd had a long bout with the influenza the winter before that left her considerably weakened. However, it had not left her with a hole in her heart.

"Maude," I said, and pointed.

Maude screamed and fell over Aunt Ruthie in a faint.

The gunshots stopped then, although probably not because Maude screamed.

Likelier, those stupid cowboys had run out of bullets, or

killed each other. Maybe one of them shot out the mirror again, the way one of them did every so often, and had stopped to think about seven years of bad luck.

"I need help here," I shouted into the mercantile, where everybody now lay on the floor, but not because they were hurt. They were hiding. "Aunt Ruthie's been shot and Maude has fainted dead away."

I tell you all this to make you understand that Maude was an upright young woman who never made mock of the truth or questioned the dark ways of justice until she saw how truth could be mangled to make a shape unrecognizable.

To have you know her for a rightly raised person who never complained about the awful twists of fate that made her life less comfortable than it might have been.

To show you how impossible it was for her to do the things everyone claimed that she did. For this is the true story of how my sister, Maude March, came to be known far and wide as a horse thief, a bank robber, and a cold-blooded killer.

TWO

AUNT RUTHIE DIED THERE ON THE BOARDWALK IN FRONT of the mercantile, and our lives changed overnight. We went out in the morning to choose a box at the undertaker's and came back to find a man from the bank locking our doors.

But I'm getting ahead of my story.

The sheriff came running at the sound of gunshots, and the shooter was arrested. We saw this happening, but again, it hardly seemed real. Maude cried over Aunt Ruthie in a lady-like way that Aunt Ruthie would have approved of.

I cried because Maude cried, that was how I felt right then. The terrible truth was, I was not so sad as surprised. Deeply surprised. Somehow hopeful that the school bell would ring and Aunt Ruthie would stand and say, "That's all the time we have. Put your pencils down."

Reverend Peasley and the undertaker arrived together. The blessing in this was that Maude and I had only to let them take things in hand. The reverend installed us in his buggy. It was a tight fit, being a one-seater, but we lived only a few streets away.

Although it was a very short ride, we were twice nearly

overcome by a terrible odor. The first time, I thought Reverend Peasley must be the guilty party. I kept this notion to myself. The second time, I understood it to be his buggy pony.

Only the sudden gust of a breeze saved me from gagging. "A bit windy all of a sudden," I said.

"Thank the Lord," Reverend Peasley replied.

He took us to the home of an elderly neighbor lady. When she came to the door, Reverend Peasley told her Aunt Ruthie had passed over.

"Oh, poor thing," Mrs. Golightly said. She had to look up at him, as she wasn't any taller than myself. "Did she go quietly?"

We heard all this, the buggy having been drawn up near the door. Maybe Reverend Peasley thought he would only upset us further, because he didn't answer that question. Instead, he asked her if we could stay the night with her, if she would comfort us in the womanly way. That's what he said to her. What was the poor woman to say to him but yes?

I had not expected this, nor had Maude, I could see that. It came home to me in that moment that we were all we had, Maude and me. This time there was no Aunt Ruthie to take us in hand. This time we were orphans once and for all.

He left us there.

Mrs. Golightly did her best. She offered us cookies and cold buttermilk, but we weren't hungry. She suggested a lie-down, but we said, no, thank you. We sat in her parlor for several minutes, all of us silent, until Maude said, "I want to go home."

"And so you shall," Mrs. Golightly said so kindly that we cried some more. The feeling of surprise had left me, but still

I didn't feel my tears were for Aunt Ruthie so much as they were for Maude and me. What were we to do now?

Aunt Ruthie was gone so quickly she hadn't even had time to wonder what happened. The reverend told us she'd gone to a place where no one had need to be scared. I was glad for Aunt Ruthie; I was only sorry that Maude and me had to face this worry without her stern face to guide us.

By the time Mrs. Golightly got around to putting her night things into her knitting bag, some weather had blown in. We had to walk arm in arm with Mrs. Golightly or we might have lost her to the breeze. Not only was she no taller than me, she was strangely lighter, as if her bones had no weight to them at all.

Maude's hair and mine whipped and snapped around our heads, and by the time we got to our house, Mrs. Golightly's hair was doing the same dance. The wind had stolen her every hairpin. We took turns brushing out each other's hair, which got us past the first rush of sadness over coming home without Aunt Ruthie.

Mrs. Golightly made us some hot cocoa to drink. I was none too enthusiastic about this till I realized she'd made it some sweeter than Aunt Ruthie would have. Mrs. Golightly had a free hand with sugar. I had already known that about her, but I appreciated the fact all anew.

She even lit an extra lamp to make us feel more cheerful.

Mrs. Golightly was as kindly as could be, but she was something less than a comfort. Twice during the evening, she asked where it was that Aunt Ruthie had gone. Each time, we told her Aunt Ruthie had passed. Each time, she said, "Poor thing. She went quietly, did she?"

In the morning, Mrs. Golightly went with us to the undertaker's to choose a box for Aunt Ruthie. In this matter, she was very helpful. Even though she seemed to think the box would be for her sister. We didn't know anything about a sister. Maude simply passed Mrs. Golightly a hankie.

"I've been thinking about her stone," Maude said as we stood by the bench in front of the barbershop. The bench had a message carved in the back, REST YOUR WEARY BONES, but something had chopped the center out of the *o* in *bones*. "We ought to say something pretty. She deserves that."

"What do you have in mind?" I asked, although Aunt Ruthie had never cared for things pretty. She liked practical. To her, that was as pretty as things got.

On her stone, we said, HERE LIES RUTH ANN WATERS, GONE TO GOLDEN SHORES. July 23, 1840–August 9, 1869. Over this, Mrs. Golightly needed another hankie.

Aunt Ruthie might have thought it was wasteful to pay for any letters other than her name and dates. But then Maude said the words made her picture Aunt Ruthie as a boat with billowy white sails. That was better than picturing her dead on the boardwalk, and I thought even Aunt Ruthie could see the sense in that.

We went back to Mrs. Golightly's and made sure she knew it was not her sister, but Aunt Ruthie, who had passed. When we left her, we saw that a buggy had drawn up at our house. A man was nailing something to the door. We hurried over there to read the large print at the top: "First Bank of Cedar Rapids." And in red, the word "Foreclosed."

"What are you doing?" Maude asked him. "We live here."

"Your aunt was behind on the payments for this property," the man said, without so much as a glance in Maude's direction. "We need to sell it off to make our money back."

"Aunt Ruthie paid the bank only last week," Maude said.

"That payment covered last year's last payment," the man said, now on his way back to his buggy, with us on his heels. "That still leaves you nearly nine months in arrears." He gave us a doubtful look. "That means you still owe me money."

"I know what it means," Maude said angrily. "I'll make the payments."

The man said, "Where are you going to get the money?"

"I don't know just yet," Maude told him. "But I'll manage."

"Your aunt said the same thing, that she'd manage. And she wasn't any green girl. She knew how to work."

This appeared to strike Maude to the quick. "I know how to work," she said in a nearly breathless voice.

I understood how Maude felt. I was five when Momma and Daddy died, and Maude was nine. We didn't have anyone but Aunt Ruthie, and we didn't know any better than her. But that was the end of childhood as we knew it.

Aunt Ruthie worked hard, and she made us work right alongside her. Despite being a teacher, she didn't seem to know such a thing as a child existed. Just some people were shorter and more able to clean the floor under the table than others.

If someone was to have asked us, well, girls, do you want to work like oxen, give up playing with dolls, and wear brown dresses for the rest of your days, we'd have said, no sir, send us

11

to the orphanage, where at least they'll let us keep our dolls. The sad fact was, Aunt Ruthie thought playing with dolls was foolishness.

She often said to mothers, "Those girls will have real babies soon enough. Let them learn to run fast. Let them learn to climb trees. Let them learn to shoot rabbits." I suppose she would have said, prepare them to work themselves to the bone, if she thought anyone would heed her.

To give the devil her due, Aunt Ruthie was a right fine cook, and she never worked us any harder than she worked herself. She was a stern woman, but she was never a cruel one. I never learned what shaped her that way; she wasn't much for talk once she'd told us what she wanted done.

She taught school the same way. She did not become a friend to her students. They did not love her, although they showed her all the respect she could have hoped for. She arrived with one small suitcase she called her "necessary," and she left this world with even less.

It didn't seem right to hand over all she'd worked for without a fight. "You can't take our house away," I said to the man from the bank.

"It isn't your house till it's paid for," he said, "and you can't pay for it."

"Just give us a chance to bury our aunt," Maude cried, clinging to his coat as he climbed into his buggy. "We'll find a way to pay the bank every penny it's owed."

I pulled her back just in time, for the buggy jolted as the man loosened the horse's reins. It would have knocked her flat.

"I'm sorry, miss," the man said, "but the bank can't wait any longer."

"Where are we supposed to go?" Maude wailed.

"See your minister," the man said, looking ashamed of himself. Then he whipped up his horse and raced away.

I checked the front door. Padlocked, of course.

I walked around to the back and found that door had not been padlocked, but we had locked it ourselves the night before.

"What are you up to, Sallie?" Maude asked me, her face gone pale. She didn't look much more lively than Aunt Ruthie had that morning at the funeral parlor.

"I'm going in," I said.

"You heard the man," Maude said weakly. "It isn't our house anymore."

"Our stuff is in there." The pantry window had a crack in it, but we hadn't yet replaced the pane.

"Oh, Sallie, don't do that," Maude cried as I picked up a rock.

"I am not leaving my dime novels and my one dress with some color in it and my good boots behind."

Most of the glass fell when the rock hit, but I pounded another rock all around the frame to get rid of the last jagged edges. If we got so much as a scratch climbing through, I knew I would never hear the end of it.

THREE

T HE FAMILIAR SIGHT OF AUNT RUTHIE'S POLISHED-TO-A-
gloss canning jars cheered me some.

They were brim-filled with sweet corn, pickled beets,
bright green snap beans, damson plum jam and prune butter,
and strawberry sauce for pancakes.

Not that my mind was on the food stores. I went straight
to my room and tied my dimers into a thick packet with Aunt
Ruthie's saved-up string. I put my clothes into a carpetbag.
Three dresses still hung in the wardrobe when I finished, all
of them made for Maude by our mother's own hands, and
long since outgrown by both of us. I still kept them, not because they held memories but because my eyes could never be
tired of the blue gingham, the rose-figured cotton, the green
calico.

I found myself staring hungrily at them, reluctant to leave
them behind. But there was no room for them in my bag. I
went into Aunt Ruthie's room, once our mother's room, and
found the sewing scissors. I went back to the dresses and cut
big patches out of the skirts, folded those, and stuffed them
into my bag.

Maude looked in as I shut the wardrobe. "I heard you in Aunt Ruthie's room. Saying your good-byes?"

I blinked. I hadn't even thought of it. For that moment that I stood in Aunt Ruthie's room, it was almost as if nothing had changed for us. Yes, I was cutting patches out of our dresses because we were leaving, but there was still a part of my mind that believed I had to put Aunt Ruthie's scissors back where I'd found them. As if she might come looking for them again.

I dropped the scissors into my carpetbag and said, "If you like, we can say our good-byes together."

"This is the only house we've ever lived in," Maude said as we stood in Aunt Ruthie's room. "We were both born in that bed."

I didn't remember that. I only remembered that Aunt Ruthie barely disturbed it when she slept there. Even when she threw the covers off herself in the morning, the greater part of the bed remained made up. Maude tried again, saying, "Momma used to read to you in that bed. With the curtains open and the sunshine falling on your heads."

That memory wasn't mine. I had tried time and again to remember our momma and daddy, but my mind always drew a blank. Maude's words called to something held deep inside me, but it didn't seem to have a thing to do with this bed.

What I noticed now, Maude had taken the quilt and woolen blanket from Aunt Ruthie's bed and stacked them with ours, ready to go. Wherever we ended up, we would not be going to sleep under somebody's old, thin blankets.

We went all around the house, with Maude touching things in each room. This was the great difference between

Maude and me. She had sentimental values. I didn't have them much. I had this in common with Aunt Ruthie.

"You could take some of this stuff," I said. "Not something as big as the rocking chair, maybe, but that china cat on the hearth." Or the fancy candleholder that looked like a frog on a lily pad. I had always admired that.

She shook her head. "It won't mean anything once we take it away," she said.

"It would still be ours," I said. "It won't be ours for long if we leave it here."

We went back to Aunt Ruthie's room and Maude took the Bible. "This belonged to Momma," she said. "And there's something else."

She opened the secretary at which Aunt Ruthie wrote out her bills. She pushed some papers out of the way, pulled out a packet of letters, and set them aside so that she could feel around at the upper back corner. She yanked a panel out, exposing a secret compartment. I saw then it had a little cloth tab for a kind of handle. I had never known it was there.

I glanced at the letters. I couldn't picture Aunt Ruthie being much of a letter writer, but it appeared that someone had taken time to write to her. But then Maude pulled out a thin stack of bills, and I watched as she counted them.

She finished, saying, "Twenty-four dollars, that's all. Too bad Aunt Ruthie did pay the bank. If she hadn't, we'd have more of a bankroll to see us through."

"To see us through what?"

"I don't know yet," Maude said. "We're going to have to live somewhere if no one takes us in. This won't carry us for long."

"Mrs. Golightly would probably take us in," I said.

My thought was, she probably needed us as much as we needed her. Maude shot me a look that said she thought Mrs. Golightly was not suitable even as a last resort. I shot her a look back that said beggars can't be choosers.

Maude said, "Mrs. Golightly is too old. One bad winter cold will see her out. We would soon be back in the same boat."

To this I had no reply.

"There's the egg money," I said, and headed for the kitchen. The egg money was kept in a cracked sugar bowl. That came to something under three dollars.

"This and the two dollars I had saved up, that's all we have in the world," Maude said in a flat voice.

"We have each other," I said, but it sounded a little weak, even to me. I wished I was a saver, but I wasn't, and that was a fact. I spent all my money on dimers.

"This is the only house we've ever lived in," Maude said again. "It's going to seem strange to call any other house our home."

"People do it, though," I said as we left through the back door. "They leave one place behind and make their home in another all the time. They like it fine."

"People do it," Maude said. "I'm not sure it's fine."

I didn't argue with her. But I couldn't help the way I felt. A little sad that Aunt Ruthie couldn't come along, but I was excited too. Like a new life was starting for us. Like we were embarking on an adventure.

FOUR

EEING OUR MINISTER TURNED OUT TO BE A GOOD suggestion. It was not a suggestion that Aunt Ruthie would have made, or followed up on either. Aunt Ruthie often said that in hard times family helped family. What she meant was, don't even ask anybody else.

However, we were fresh out of family.

It was not even a suggestion Maude wanted to follow, which surprised me some. "He already dumped us on Mrs. Golightly's doorstep. Where do you think he's going to set us down now?"

I didn't argue. Maude could take a notion, and once taken, her notions tended to be unshakable. Reverend Peasley had slid in her eyes, and he might just as well have tried to climb a glass hill. But he made a better showing the second time around.

"Miss Maude, and Sallie, dear, I am shocked to my marrow," Reverend Peasley said as we finished telling him about the man from the bank.

I liked Reverend Peasley somewhat, considering I hardly ever saw him except on Sundays. He looked fatherly to me,

18

and he was, in fact, a father several times over. Most times, although not as we sat there telling him our story, he was a smiling sort of man.

I liked smiles, and I liked to think that someday my life would have more of his smiling sort of people in it.

"You will simply have to stay here with Mrs. Peasley and myself until we get your business affairs settled," he added, and won my heart entirely.

Maude broke down and cried pitiful tears. She had cried before, of course, but she had not been so broken in spirit until that man from the bank got finished with us.

Mrs. Peasley and I patted Maude's hands and soothed her and made her lie down with a cold cloth on her forehead. But all the time, in the back of my mind, I heard the reverend's voice saying, "—until we get your business affairs settled."

Something deep inside me stood up and cheered at the notion of myself having business affairs. That they were a complete mess bothered me not at all. I had come to this house a homeless waif, and I was not here for half an hour before I was a woman of means. More or less.

The next afternoon, after Aunt Ruthie's funeral, we sat in the Peasleys' parlor and allowed the church ladies to make us feel better with such remarks as, "I am saddened to hear that your Aunt Ruthie was in such dire straits. I never suspected for a moment."

And, "I suppose you girls could hire out. You know everything there is to know about running a house. Lord knows, I could use a hand. Of course, I couldn't afford to pay you. I have too many mouths to feed as it is."

"Did you hear that the man who shot off that gun and

killed your Aunt Ruthie claims it was an accident?" And then to the gathering at large, "He's not a local. Name of Joe Harden."

At that, my heart rose into my throat. Joe Harden! I pinched Maude at the back of her arm, hard. She yelped and jumped up off the settee like it was a hot stovetop.

"Now, Maude, I never meant to upset you," one of the church ladies said. "I just thought you should know the name of the terrible man—" Maude ran from the room, brushing past Mrs. Peasley, who had been coming and going with little cakes and fresh pots of tea. The lid on the teapot rattled and a spoon fell to the floor, but Maude did not turn back to pick it up. "—who shot your poor aunt down like a rabid dog."

"I reckon we're feeling much better now," I said, and stood up, inviting the ladies to do the same. We'd buried our aunt that morning, and it had saddened me more than I had believed it would. These women were not Aunt Ruthie's friends in life. Aunt Ruthie didn't have a good word to say for most people; she'd just as soon shut the door in their faces as say hello to visitors. This had often troubled me, but not just at that moment.

"Maude and I can't thank you ladies enough for spending the day with us." They rose somewhat uncertainly, but I only let my chin jut out as I walked to the door and opened it.

"Aunt Ruthie would have thanked you," I said, and it was probably true. She would have thanked them to leave. We had done our duty by the church ladies and if they did nothing else for us, they dropped that word about Joe Harden.

I had a man to see. I was nearly happy as I shut the door.

FIVE

I STOOD AT THE BACK OF THE JAIL AND SHOUTED OUT HIS name. "Mr. Joe Harden!"

A face appeared in one barred window. The most I could make out was, it was a bearded face, and hairless on top, like maybe he'd gotten himself scalped in one of those frontier fights.

After he'd taken his time to look me over too, he said, "Who wants him?"

I held up a dime novel. "Are you this Joe Harden?"

"What if I am?"

I put my arm down. What if he was? He was still the man who shot and killed Aunt Ruthie. I couldn't be here to shake his hand. "Are they going to hang you?"

He went away from the window but came back again after only a moment. "If this doesn't just turn a man's stomach, I don't know what will," he said. "Shouldn't a girl your age be at home playing with her dolls?"

This struck me to the quick. "I don't have a doll."

I had not had a doll since I was eight years old, when one day a dog grabbed it and ran off. Aunt Ruthie wiped my tears and said matter-of-factly, "You're too old for such things anyway."

"Well, don't you have anything better to do than hope for hangings?"

I said, "You shot my aunt. She was my only kin, but for my sister, Maude."

For a moment I thought he would leave the window again. He said, "I'm sorry, girlie, I truly am."

I stood there, not knowing quite what I wanted from him. I didn't know what I expected, but not this fellow with whiskers.

He said, "If I could undo it, I would."

"You can't, I know that," I said, and walked away. I was sorry I'd come.

SIX

THE REVEREND HAD BROUGHT AUNT RUTHIE'S EGG layers and her little brown cow over to his own place. This was necessary, since we couldn't very well expect these animals to take care of themselves.

He also cleared Aunt Ruthie's pantry on Maude's say-so. On a laundry day, he took the older children with him and brought a wagonload of canned goods and flour and sugar, in addition to hams and part of a side of beef. There was an atmosphere of quiet good cheer about the family as we all helped to fill Mrs. Peasley's pantry to overflowing.

Maude acted as if she'd never seen these things before, as if her hands had never tightened the caps on these jars or helped to salt the ham. She made several trips between the wagon and the pantry without a word said to anyone, causing Reverend Peasley to comment, "Good worker."

If there was one thing the Peasleys could be said to need, it was another pair of hands. What with five children, all younger than me, I guess it would be fair to say Reverend Peasley and his wife were overworked at the get-go.

But there was far more than daily cooking and housework

and wood chopping to be done. The church floor had to be swept twice a week, the pews needed a coat of wax, and wax took a lot of rubbing to make it shine. Two extra pairs of hands could not complain if they were put right to work.

Children were underfoot at every turn, running through the sweepings, dipping their fingers into whatever they were told to stay away from. Mrs. Peasley did not run what Aunt Ruthie would have called "a tight ship."

Maude's voice was deep, which scares small children sometimes, and besides that, Maude tended toward swatting people when they annoyed her severely. I had taken my fair share of swats and stood immune, but the Peasley children had never dealt with the likes of Maude, and in a week's time, they all stood afraid of my sister.

My voice was also deep, but I had the good sense to make it higher when I spoke to little ones, which made me seem friendlier, even if I was scolding. Also, the two oldest were boys, six and eight, and all I had to do to get them to go along with me was to promise to read them a dimer later on. Joe Harden was their favorite hero, and they had both of them concocted an ending for the dimer that quits just as Joe sights a cave where a wounded killer has no doubt taken shelter.

Because she was judged to have little patience with small children, and because Mrs. Peasley was growing round with her next baby, Maude took on the work that needed hours of standing up. She baked cakes and pies for ladies' meetings, for the sick or elderly, and for Tuesday night box suppers.

Mrs. Peasley had gotten a good start on collecting clothing for the poor, and much of that needed ironing, if not a good wash as well. There were socks to be mended and sizes to be sorted. Finally I tied things together with bristly twine as full sets of clothing for the needy.

Just in time to begin the canning.

I worked mostly at preparing the vegetables. I was only grateful I was too short to stand at the stove. That fell to Maude. When she wasn't baking, she was lifting steaming jars from the canning pots. It made me feel bad to leave her with all the work when I went back to school in September.

Maude didn't go, but I had to. A new teacher had been found to take Aunt Ruthie's place. It wasn't that I expected Aunt Ruthie to show up there. I hadn't really thought about it, not out loud in my mind like, but somewhere inside myself I did think her classroom would stand empty, like our house.

I never mentioned it to Maude, who went on baking cakes and pies and doing the wash. If that room stood empty in her mind, that was fine by me. But if I hoped to spare her sentimental values, that was not to be. Once I went back to school, it fell to Maude to tie up the old-clothing parcels.

Aunt Ruthie's clothes made their way into the pile of give-aways. It had given Maude quite a jolt to find one of Aunt Ruthie's few dresses there. She had tied it into the middle of a bundle to hide this fact from me, but I was the one sent to get the clothes when Mrs. Peasley was all set to ride out on an errand of mercy. I spotted the fabric, Aunt Ruthie's practical brown cotton, as I put the bundles in the buggy.

"I see she's given away Aunt Ruthie's clothes," I said to Maude, so she would know the secret was out. "I guess it's too bad for her that Aunt Ruthie wasn't partial to pretty calicoes or tartans."

"Don't bother about it, Sallie," was Maude's reply. But

her mouth was held tight in the way she had copied from Aunt Ruthie.

Mrs. Peasley told us how fortunate she believed herself to be to have all this help with her duties. She said this as she wrote a list of things to be done by Maude and me, and another list of people who needed the balm of her visits to them.

As the days wore on, I wanted something more than a thank-you. It was not that I was not grateful to be taken in, but it did seem to me that we were also taken for granted.

It made me angry that Reverend Peasley would turn a smile on me as I helped to scrub his floors, or wiped up after feeding his youngest child, or peeled the potatoes he would be getting for his supper, and yet he did not think to help.

But he was not the one making up daily lists. I said to Maude, "That Mrs. Peasley doesn't know when to say whoa."

"I know, I know," Maude agreed. "But at least you get away some of the time. If Reverend Peasley calls me an 'answer to a prayer' one more time, I'm going to hit him on the head."

I didn't think this would improve matters much.

I said, "Don't you think we ought to just tell them it's not right to work us from morning till night? Even Aunt Ruthie let us play a game in the evenings. She let us pop corn and read by the fire. We got to visit with the other girls for an hour after Sunday service, instead of rushing back to the kitchen work."

I had never felt such an appreciation for Aunt Ruthie. I understood now; she didn't smile much, but she never used us either. Whatever we did, she did just as much.

"Maybe we should get ourselves taken in by someone who doesn't have so much work to do," I said.

"And maybe we'll get taken in by someone worse," Maude said with a dark look on her face. "They could have separated us."

So maybe I shouldn't have held it against the Peasleys that they made good use of us. But I did hold it against them.

I went in to make up the little children's cots one morning and found they had been, without ever saying one word to us, covered over in Aunt Ruthie's quilts. Worse, these were not her everyday quilts, but the ones that had taken blue ribbons at the fair. I finished my chores with my lips atremble.

When Mrs. Peasley went out for a minute, I brought Maude to have a look. The matter was not lost on her. "She kept those in her cedar chest at the foot of her bed," she said. "They're going through all her things."

"What are we going to say?" I asked her.

"Nothing," Maude said.

It got to the point where Reverend Peasley would smile on me, and I would turn an upside-down smile with lots of teeth back at him. He'd look at me like his eyes couldn't be trusted and make a deliberate smile. "Sallie? You don't look like yourself. Sallie?"

And I would smile back just as nice as you please.

I hoped to wreck his mind.

It surprised all of us, I think, when the Toleridge boy tried calling on Maude. That is, he would call, and she would shut the door in his face, refusing to see him.

The reverend wondered if Maude felt it was too soon after Aunt Ruthie's death to think about marriage. He cleared his throat, then said, "Not that I would have you rush into anything, Miss Maude. But there is the matter of your house. The Toleridge boy…"

Had enough money to buy it back from the bank. Or his family did. That's what Reverend Peasley was too particular to say.

"I don't like the Toleridge boy," Maude told Reverend Peasley. At this, Mrs. Peasley's mouth pinched up like she was sucking on a lemon drop.

"He never was nice to dogs or cats or even little children in the schoolyard," Maude went on saying. "He couldn't be trusted. I would never think of marrying the likes of him."

"Maude, I thought you would do anything to get the house back," I said to her that night. We did most of our talking in the dark, in the few minutes between blowing out our candle and falling asleep.

"I thought so too," she said. "But that boy is too big a dose of 'anything' for me."

"Do you still want the house back?" I asked her, wondering if there weren't some things she'd still want from it. Maude was sentimental that way.

"I do," she whispered. "I want it something terrible. I want Aunt Ruthie too."

I think it soured the reverend on us a little when Maude turned away the Toleridge boy. I'm not sure why. I only know he started to take a firm tone with us.

About that time, Mr. Wilburn took to coming to dinner every Tuesday, Friday, and Saturday evening. At first he brought small gifts to Mrs. Peasley. Then he began bringing them to Maude. An embroidered case for her scissors. A silver thimble. A comb for her hair.

Mr. Wilburn was a grandfatherly sort of man, and I was still of an age when I thought I might like to have a grandfather. Especially one who brought me his already-been-read-twice dime novels, like Mr. Wilburn did, once he learned I liked them. He spared them out, one each week, which was fine by me; it made a Christmas of every Friday evening.

It took Maude till October to figure out that Mr. Wilburn was sweet on her. "I could never marry that old man," Maude said to me. "Why, he could be our grandfather."

I was sorry to have to be the one to say it, but Maude didn't have all that many charms. Not the kind men are said to go for. Maude was good, she was honest and true. But she was plain. Wren brown hair, ordinary brown eyes, and stick thin from neck to foot. It wasn't likely many others were going to come calling.

"Just be nice to him," I said.

Meanwhile, the leaves on the trees had turned yellow and orange and began to fall. The Peasleys were getting fewer and fewer pats on the back for having taken us in. The church ladies had begun to be sorry they hadn't taken us in themselves.

"Those five Peasley children must be a handful for you to look after," one of them said to me.

"They're all right," I said. "They're just little, is all."

I overheard another of them saying, "Mrs. Peasley used to pay me a little to bake bread, as well as all those cakes and pies." I gathered she was feeling the crimp in her coin purse now that Maude was doing the baking.

"We're working harder here than we did at home, with

Aunt Ruthie driving us like sled dogs," I said to Maude as we cleaned up after a Sunday dinner.

"What kind of dogs?"

I'd read about sled dogs in *Wild Woolly, Lost in the Yukon*. There were several Wild Woolly books, I gathered, but I only had the one where Wild Woolly was lost, possibly to die out there in the blinding snowstorm the book left off with. It occurred to me that Mr. Wilburn might have the means to get the other books from somewhere. I desperately wanted to know what happened to Wild Woolly.

I remembered Mr. Wilburn had recently brought Maude a box of writing paper with little flowers painted in the corners of the pages. She had no one to write to, but the paper was so pretty Maude got a little misty at the surprise of it. I wondered if maybe she was softening a little in her opinion of him.

"Unless you get married, we don't have anything to look forward to but working for room and board in this house," I said.

"If you like him so much," Maude said, "you marry him."

"I can't marry him, I'm only twelve years old."

"You're eleven, and you can't expect me to marry him either."

SEVEN

DO YOU REMEMBER UNCLE ARLEN?" I ASKED MAUDE ONE night before we went to sleep.

"I remember he sang songs. He used to dance with Momma because Daddy couldn't dance at all." She stopped there, but I only gave her the look of, and what else? So she dredged her memory and came up with a little more.

"I think he was pretty for a man, but maybe he was only young. I was nine, after all, so I never gave these things much thought."

"You must remember more than that."

"He put sugar in our milk until Aunt Ruthie put a stop to that. He was around the house quite a bit, but maybe he lived somewhere else." She thought for a minute, then said, "That's about it. Not much, I know."

She was right; it wasn't nearly enough.

Even so, I said, "Maybe we ought to try to find him." I fully expected Maude to shoot that idea down. To my surprise, she looked at me like this was the first good idea she'd heard. The next morning, she brought the subject up with Reverend Peasley.

He laughed right out loud. "I can assure you that your uncle wasn't the kind to survive out west. His nose ran all the time. We gave him quite a hard time about it in the schoolyard, as I remember."

He seemed to me to remember this very fondly. I had a sudden picture of the Toleridge boy come to mind.

"Where was he headed? Independence?" Mrs. Peasley said, like she was trying to remember something funny she'd heard. " 'To ride the tail of the Oregon Trail.' He didn't even have a wagon, did he?"

"One mule," Reverend Peasley said in the unmistakable tone of, and good riddance.

"How far to Independence?" I asked. Independence was beginning to sound real good to me.

"It must be three hundred miles," he said, "maybe more."

"How long would it take to get there on a mule?" Maude asked.

"Weeks," said Reverend Peasley. "Far longer, walking."

"I thought you said he had a mule," I said.

"The mule carried supplies," Reverend Peasley said. "Your uncle walked."

"Here, let's stop talking about this," Mrs. Peasley said suddenly. "Independence is no place for young ladies to set their sights for."

"I suppose not," Maude said, and even Reverend Peasley heard the disappointment in her tone.

"He never was the kind to listen to good advice either," the reverend said, beefing up his argument. "He didn't do any planning; just one minute he was doing a little smithing, and the next minute he fancied he could set down his anvil out there in Independence and get to be a rich man. He didn't even leave here with enough food to take him that far."

The reverend allowed Maude to chew on this idea for a moment before he added, "I doubt he got ninety miles before he died of something."

This information might have bothered some. It appeared to bother Maude. But I liked the sound of Uncle Arlen even more than I had liked the idea of him. He sounded like a man of action. I figured I took after him in that way, although it caused me to be thought of as troublesome.

"Uncle Arlen sounds like Joe Harden, as true a hero as I have ever heard of," I said, much to the enjoyment of the Peasley boys. Grins spread over their faces, and there was a great deal of jostling, at least until Maude gave one of them a swift kick.

She knew better than to kick hard, but she put a stop to the fooling around. On the whole, the Peasleys tended to be in favor of letting Maude handle their boys.

Mrs. Peasley said, "It would be an imposition on the man even if you did find him. He certainly couldn't know a thing about raising girls."

Maude said, "I don't need raising anymore, and I can take care of what raising my sister needs."

This was as outspoken as they had ever heard her to be. I was proud of her. But I saw, too, that it unsettled the Peasleys. It had never occurred to Reverend Peasley that Maude might have some backbone.

The very next evening, at Friday night supper, Mr. Wilburn made his move. "I've bought a wedding gift," he said, "for the gal I'm going to ask to be my bride." With those words, he pulled a sheaf of papers, tied with a ribbon, from the inside pocket of his coat.

I'd noticed the thickness there, but I thought he carried a dime novel for me. There was a new issue of *Joe Harden, Frontier Fighter* due to come out. I wanted to know what kind of exploits had gotten Aunt Ruthie killed.

Mr. Wilburn showed us the papers he'd signed for the purchase of our house. The reverend and his wife looked so surprised, I knew they had nothing to do with it. I only hoped Maude wouldn't think I had put him up to it.

In fact, Maude said nothing at first. She panted a little, like a dog. She didn't touch the papers when he held them out to her.

It must've occurred to Mr. Wilburn that his gift might not be enough. Possibly he'd come prepared with the speech he made: "I know you come from a long line of kin who die young, and I'm right sorry for that. But I figger we're a good match, 'cause I ain't going to last forever neither."

Maude's face was writ with regret and sorrow and gratefulness; I saw all that and I reckon everybody else at the table did too. But she couldn't say a word. It was like the breath had been snatched from her chest and she was fighting to get it back.

"You'd like to be mistress of your own house, now, wouldn't you?" Mr. Wilburn asked.

The pressure was on.

Maude still hadn't said a word. She only stared at the pages he held in front of her, her face all flushed and sweaty.

Mrs. Peasley laughed nervously and said, "This is more

than she could have hoped for." The reverend chimed in with, "She's been struck dumb with the joy of it."

"Maudie?" Mr. Wilburn said.

She begged me with a look to say something, to say the right thing. I didn't open my mouth, though, because I couldn't trust myself to say the right thing for Maude. I shook my head.

Mr. Wilburn touched the papers to her hand. Maude seemed to give up on me then. Something behind her eyes broke away, making me wish I had spoken up. But still I couldn't, because what was right for me was wrong, so wrong for Maude, I saw that now.

"My house," she whispered, and two fat tears rolled down her cheeks.

I knew then why she had gone all around the house touching things she couldn't take with her. She loved it. She had known our parents, and unlike me, she could remember them there.

Mr. Wilburn had bought Maude's only home, and now he was asking her if she wanted him to sell it to her.

Maude herself was the asking price.

EIGHT

YOU SHOULDN'T HAVE RUN OFF FROM THE TABLE, Maude," I told her when I found her buried under the covers in our bed. "You never told him a proper no."

"What are you saying?" she asked, lifting the pillow off her head.

"That he thinks you'll marry him."

"No!"

"That's what you should have said at the table."

"I know it," Maude said. "What did the Peasleys tell him?"

"That it was too much all at once: the house and the marriage proposal. To come back tomorrow, when the joy of it all will have worn off some and you'll be able to speak for yourself."

"Why do they want me to marry him?" Maude said. "Don't they like me? Don't I work hard enough?"

"They can't have the church ladies wondering if, between the two of us giving her a hand, Mrs. Peasley has to do anything at all."

Light dawned in Maude's eyes.

But before I could tell her the worst of it, that the Peasleys wanted her married off but planned to keep me there—"You don't need to worry, Sallie, dear," Mrs. Peasley had said to me before I was excused from the table. "I could never part with both of you"—the Peasleys knocked on the bedroom door and came on in.

"You've embarrassed us in front of a guest, Maude," the reverend said. His very tone was so grave as to make me feel like we'd had another death in the family.

Mrs. Peasley's mouth was drawn up like a drawstring purse, but she loosened it just enough to say, "Mr. Wilburn will be joining us after services tomorrow. You will tell him you are honored to be his wife."

"Oh, no," Maude cried, "I could never—"

"We can put off the wedding for perhaps six months," Mrs. Peasley said, like she was doing Maude a kindness, "even a year. To give you time to get used to the idea."

Unless I missed my guess, bread-baking lessons were in my near future. "I'm going to live with Maude after she's married," I told them.

"Oh, now that is just a poor idea," Mrs. Peasley said to me.

"That's what we do in our family," I said.

"You're part of our family now," Mrs. Peasley said more firmly. "I can't allow it, Sallie, dear. It's hard enough to get a marriage off on the right foot without a live-in relative to muddy the waters."

I wanted to tell them I'd show them some muddy water, but I decided to do like Maude, who had gone very still. Everything was out in the open now, clear as a sheet of glass, and the facts were indeed ugly enough to take the breath away.

We sat quiet for a good five minutes once the Peasleys went back downstairs. Even though Mrs. Peasley did mention she could use a hand in the kitchen now that supper was done with.

Maude knew as well as I did, Mrs. Peasley wouldn't lift a hand to do the dishes. She'd taken to having a tiny bit of something in a glass after dinner, sitting in the parlor with the reverend. They looked like they were playing king and queen.

I hatched several plans for revenge. Those Peasleys would rue the day they asked me to wax the pews. Or bake a pie. Or bathe their children. I knew I couldn't bring myself to drown one, but a little soap in the eyes never killed anybody. Mrs. Peasley tended to be real anxious about soap in the eyes.

"What are we going to do?" I asked when it came clear that Maude must have hatched a few plans of her own. She was up and moving about the room.

"I'm running off," she said.

"Maude!" She had never been so daring. "When?"

"Tonight," she said like I'd grown stupid. "Didn't you hear them? They want me to tell that man I'll marry him."

"They won't marry you off tomorrow," I said.

"I can't tell him I'll marry him and then run off," Maude said. "If he really cares for me, that would be cruel."

"Are you telling me you want to leave tonight to spare Mr. Wilburn's feelings?"

"However much they can be spared," Maude said, "yes. If I leave tonight, I'll look ungrateful. But if I lie to the man to buy myself a few more nights of sleeping in a warm bed, he looks like a fool. I can't do that to him, Sallie, even if for no better reason than he was kind enough to bring my little sister a handful of dime novels."

If she was hoping to make me ashamed of myself, she was barking up the wrong tree. I didn't twist Mr. Wilburn's arm to bring me those books. He'd only done it to soften up Maude. Aunt Ruthie wouldn't have apologized for me, and neither would I.

"Just put him off for a little while," I said. "We have to make plans." This was true; we'd starve or freeze to death if we didn't make preparations. Anyone who read *Wild Woolly* knew that.

Apart from that, I admit to wanting mostly to ruin at least one batch of bread, to burn some pies, to oil those pews so heavily no one could sit on them for a month of Sundays. I said, "Maybe we could pretend you have a little fever to buy ourselves some time."

"I can't take you with me, Sallie."

NINE

"IT ISN'T SAFE FOR GIRLS OUT WEST," SHE SAID. "IT'S NOT kindly even to men. And winter's coming on..."

Like a picture flew from her mind to mine, I saw her sitting frozen to her horse in the middle of the plains. I said, "I can't take it, Maude, never knowing what happens to you. I'd rather die frozen to my horse."

"You don't have a horse," she said, getting mad, "and neither do I."

"You can't expect to make it to Independence without one."

"I'll travel light," she said. "Maybe someone will offer me a ride."

Maude was not a stupid girl, but for the first time I wondered if she could make it to Independence without me. "You said it yourself, Maude, you're going west, where Reverend Peasley didn't think Uncle Arlen stood chance enough to make it ninety miles."

Maude rattled off a variety of arguments, each one weaker than the one before. "If you stay, Sallie, you'll be fine here. Losing the house is no bother to you. And the Peasleys will keep you. They'll practically have to."

"Maude, take me with you. I don't want to stay here."

"I don't even have a plan," Maude said on a low, plaintive note.

"Let me do the planning," I said to her as I reached for the candle.

Which is how we came to be standing in the barn when the moon was high, our carpetbags once more filled to bursting. But this time we'd left our dresses behind. My high-top boots too.

Moving silently through the darkness in my nightgown, I'd raided the collection for the poor, hunting up some boys' clothes. Maude and I were outfitted in rough pants, flannel shirts, and lined jackets. We had a change of clothing, should we need it, and even some long underwear—they had holes but I knew I had washed them thoroughly.

I had put on a pair of lace-up boots, the kind farm boys wore. And I'd made a real find of an old pair of riding boots with hard, pointy toes. The leather hadn't cracked open anywhere, and they looked likely to fit Maude.

I tried for felt hats, the kind with a brim like a shed roof, which I knew was a necessary. There were only two, one more battered than the other, but both of them fell so low as to cover the tip of my nose. I figured one of them might work out for Maude. We had cold-weather gear, if we didn't mind holes in the fingertips of our gloves, and if we could bear the scratchiness of scarves that were given away because they'd shrunk to pure ugliness.

While I was busy, Maude had rolled up the quilts and blankets we had brought with us from home and tied them with whatever she could find, from bootlaces to the curtain ties. I didn't mention the quilts we had to leave behind, and neither did Maude. As we dressed, I said, "We have to cut our hair, so we'll look like boys."

Maude wouldn't allow it until I reminded her that she'd told me it wasn't safe for girls. "We won't look like girls," I told her and, making good use of Aunt Ruthie's scissors, hacked my own hair off first.

Maude proved to be more talented in this direction. She smoothed out my edges just right and showed me how to do hers. While I cut her hair, Maude said, "It's good we have such deep voices."

I didn't reply. Such careful work demanded that I keep my tongue clenched between my teeth.

"You can't remember Momma's singing voice," Maude said wistfully. "So clear and high. It always saddened me that neither of us got it."

"Deep voices are what we need now." This was a great deal to say, and it caused me to make a poor cut. But it was at the back, and Maude wouldn't see it.

"There, you're done," I said, and shrugged my shoulders to ease a crick in my neck.

Maude insisted on sweeping the hair into a sack and shoving it under the mattress, in hopes that no one would guess how different we might look. Once the Peasley household was cleared of us, it would be some time before anyone looked under a mattress.

She put our twenty-eight dollars into her pants pocket.

"You don't mind if I carry all of it, do you?" Maude asked me, maybe because I was watching. "Half of it is rightfully yours."

"Fine by me," I said, because she had not raised a stink about making space for my dimers. I couldn't take them all, but I took the seven newer ones that Mr. Wilburn had given me, and three old favorites.

Next we looked through the larder. We emptied burlap sacks of potatoes and rutabaga and filled them with a side of bacon, the makings for flapjacks, oatmeal, two dressed-out chickens, a salted ham, and two loaves of Maude's bread before Maude got anxious. I had to find a minute when she wasn't looking to cut off a wedge of cheese. This led to wanting an apple pie.

I couldn't figure out how I'd carry the pie until it struck me to set two of them top to top and wrap them up tight in a tablecloth. They might not be pretty when we ate them, but I could shove them into the potato sack that way and expect they wouldn't spill all over.

The eggs were the biggest challenge. There were more than a dozen set aside for the next day's use. I finally settled on wrapping them in mismatched socks from the poor collection. I didn't feel bad about taking the food. Most of the eggs came from our chickens. It could be argued that what little food we took with us probably came from Aunt Ruthie's pantry.

The more I packed, and the more I thought about it, the better I could understand Uncle Arlen starting off without enough to take him where he was going. He'd have needed a wagon to carry enough food to get to Independence.

Maude balked at the horses too.

We had to be long gone before anybody was up and

43

around. There was no time to be nice about this. I pointed at the tied-up potato sacks and our carpetbags. "Who did you think was going to carry all this?" I asked her, mean with impatience.

I tossed around the bedrolls and gave them a few kicks. "I should have known better than to take you with me," I said, as if the whole idea had been my own. "You've always been a careful type, Maude, no gumption in you at all."

Maude and the milk cow wore the same indifferent expressions; I could see I was making no progress with bullying Maude. I settled down and spoke more quietly. It was the only way to get anywhere with her.

"I figure we're owed the buggy pony and the plow horse," I told her. "The one is gassy and the other is so old it would have died soon anyway of overwork. Aunt Ruthie's cow is worth more than the two of them put together."

This was only too true. I'd have happily ridden our cow if she could be counted on to run when I dug my heels in. She could be counted on in every other way that mattered, but she wasn't built to run.

I glanced over and noticed the buggy pony was blanketed. Reverend Peasley called her Goldie. A pretty name for a pretty horse, if you didn't get downwind of her. He came out here himself every day to curry and comb that shiny black hide to beat the drum. It was plain to see who was the favorite in this barn.

"Besides, the congregation will help him get another horse to get around with," I said. His new horse might not be such a looker as Goldie, but I figured it would get him where he needed to go.

"You can't know they'll replace his horse," Maude said. Her opinion of the congregation had slid some downward.

"The ladies will feel guilty about talking behind her back when Mrs. Peasley starts buying bread again."

"They hang horse thieves, Sallie," Maude whispered, like maybe God would hear.

"They hang them when they catch them," I said.

Maude looked at my ruined head, then touched her own brush of hair. We'd come too far to turn back now, even she could see that. "Let's hurry up, then."

"You better ride old Flora," I told her, thinking Goldie might be skittish. I figured if one of us was to get thrown, I weighed less and wouldn't fall so hard.

I threw the mule saddle over the plow horse. It wasn't a true saddle but a set of four canvas saddlebags. Maude could slide her legs between the bags forward and the ones back. We put the flour and meal in there and all else we couldn't let get wetted down. The rest of it we tied down with thick, hairy twine that pricked our fingers but was plentiful enough in the barn.

With each additional bit of weight, I kept worrying that Flora would balk. Flora didn't budge, not even when Maude boarded her. Then I had to worry would she move at all.

I draped a lead rope over Goldie's head, and got her halter on her, then the bridle, and soon got her to take the bit in her mouth, sweet-talking her the whole time. "You're riding bareback?" Maude asked in astonishment as I coaxed Goldie closer to the stall fencing.

I didn't see another saddle anywhere, and I figured there was a good reason for that. I said, "This buggy pony is used to pulling, not carrying. She won't tolerate it." To tell the strictest truth, I wasn't yet sure Goldie would tolerate *me*.

I stood on a rail, got a grip on her mane, and threw a leg over.

There were a few dicey moments when she circled and circled in the same spot. I was just about to give up on her, hoping the old plow horse could stand to carry double. Then she settled down with a suddenness that took me by surprise. It was like Goldie said to herself, this is different, but it ain't worse. And she took the lead moving out of the barn. That horse did like to be in front.

"Close the barn door?" Maude whispered to me.

"Never mind," I said. "They're going to know we're gone the minute they wake up and wonder why you didn't get downstairs to start the coffee and biscuits."

TEN

I WISHED WE COULD HAVE JUST STRUCK OUT FOR THE countryside when we left the Peasleys' barn. At the rate we were going, we wouldn't be properly on our way till morning light was coming on.

I hated like the dickens to ride through town. But we had to stop at our house for some things we couldn't rightly take from the Peasleys. We took a shortcut, easing our way between buildings and through backyards whenever we could be sure there were no dogs about.

We had one near misfortune. Goldie had no sooner set her foot into the open road than we heard another rider making his way by moonlight. But he was in a sight more of a hurry than we were, and he galloped past us none the wiser, as our horses stood in shadow. Just as well, because even boys would have to answer for riding out of town in the middle of the night with horses that didn't properly belong to them.

The one good thing I learned, as that rider came at us like a howler wind and disappeared nearly that fast again, Goldie wasn't nervous. She stood her ground. Maude's horse was equally well behaved, but in the plow horse's case, this was no surprise.

"I'm never going in there again," Maude said when we reached the house. "I'll watch the horses."

"Fair enough," I said, and went in through the back door. We'd left it unlocked the last time we were here and so, apparently, had the reverend.

I took a pot for oatmeal and a frying pan, table forks and teaspoons, a long-handled spoon, and a flat turner. I took every good strong kitchen knife we had. I took the ladle from the drinking-water bucket, and after a moment's thought, took the bucket. I padded everything with dishtowels and a tablecloth that must've been too worn to catch Mrs. Peasley's notice. We wouldn't clatter like a peddler as we rode away from town.

I took the medical kit Aunt Ruthie kept in the pantry. This last wasn't planning. The shelves were so bare I couldn't miss it. The reverend had picked up nearly every useful item that would have been there, save two poor candles. I took the coffee pot. I didn't care for coffee, but at that moment I was in the mood to claim that pot.

The picnic basket already held a set of tin plates and forks. I packed it tight with as many of the small items as I thought we could use. The can opener and a potholder were chief among those.

I tried to see the shelves filled again in my mind's eye, to reach for whatever might have been found. A minute of hard thinking sent me after one of the paper parcels Aunt Ruthie had been carrying when she was shot. Inside it were two lengths of clothesline and a box of white-tipped matches.

I took the rifle and the shotgun that mostly Aunt Ruthie had used. She had turned into a fine shot with the rifle, mainly because she hated picking shotgun pellets out of her game. She taught Maude, and Maude was supposed to teach me.

But Maude hated shooting at anything with legs, and she couldn't tolerate skinning in the least. Shooting lessons tended to turn into fishing trips, if we were expected to bring home something for dinner.

So I could load a gun, and I could shoot it, but I couldn't hit much other than the side of a barn. I hoped we weren't going to need the rifles for anything more than popping a rabbit. I hoped Maude could still pop a rabbit. I hoped I could skin it. Or we were going to get mighty hungry when the food ran out.

I remembered the packet of envelopes in Aunt Ruthie's desk. I didn't have enough light to find out whether the letters were a worthwhile thing to have, but I slipped them down the inside of a sack. I figured if Uncle Arlen turned out to be a dead end, we might at least find ourselves a place with an old friend of Aunt Ruthie's we hadn't known about.

Then I searched for the one piece of equipment I didn't believe we could do without. I found the pocket compass Aunt Ruthie once told me belonged to my father. I remembered exactly what she said: "The man had a terrible sense of direction. He could get lost on a trip to the outhouse."

The sad truth was, I didn't do a whole lot better. I'd read about watching the sun to figure out direction. I had tried to do it when we rode out into the countryside for picnics and such. But it seemed to me the sun had two places to be, on the horizon or high in the sky. Now our lives depended on being able to strike a true path west.

I had already written myself into a dimer in my mind, even to the point of seeing my face painted on the cover. It was a story of being lost in the wilderness, a story of courage and wits tested against the brute force of nature. And it would be me, Sallie March, Range Rider, who knew the way.

I dropped the compass into my pocket. I still had a case of tetchiness over the matter of taking the horses and had no intention of letting Maude see that I needed help to find the way. Just as I was fixing to leave, I remembered something more. I dashed back to the parlor and stuffed my pockets with the peppermint candies Aunt Ruthie kept for a little treat now and then.

I didn't blame Maude for staying on her horse. There was something sad and final about raiding the house. It angered me to see how much of it had been emptied by the reverend with less good reason. I left the house filled with fresh resolve.

Goldie went through the circling thing again, now fighting the notion of carrying a bucket and a picnic basket tied together at the handles and hung over her back. She didn't care, either, for the weight of a couple of loaded potato sacks. It took a little longer but she eased into the idea again. We were begun.

Maude fell behind once in a while, because Flora liked a slower pace. But Goldie cured her of that, passing wind the way she would every half hour or so. Flora would get a whiff and pull ahead right smartly, holding her speed for maybe twenty minutes or so—till she forgot why it was she was taxing herself that way.

I had never felt so lonely as I did during those first few hours of darkness on our stolen horses. Even with Maude right there next to me, I felt like we'd left all the rest of humanity behind. I wondered how Wild Woolly stood it, lost out there in the Yukon.

ELEVEN

THE PINK STREAK THAT OPENED THE SKY TO MORNING was never so welcome a sight.

Once I could see her in daylight, Maude looked very fine as a boy. Her thin frame and flat chest had looked a little unfinished for a girl. "If I look half as convincing as you do," I said, "no one will take us for girls."

Maude narrowed her eyes at me. If looks could raise hives, I'd've been itching for days.

"I'm only saying, we'll be able to pass," I told her, but she was not in a forgiving mood.

"Are we going west?" Maude asked grumpily. Probably she believed I'd gotten us lost already.

"I'm trying to stay away from the wagon roads, just in case. But we're headed in the right direction."

"They might not have looked for us at all if we hadn't stolen these horses," Maude said. If Maude's heart was honest and true, she made it a point to be kind and good, but she could be sullen too. Sullen was the mood for the day.

"If we didn't have these horses to ride, they wouldn't have

had to look for us. They'd have found us stranded at the Peasleys' gate with all we're carrying."

"And whose idea was all this stuff?"

"Mine," I said, and I was proud of it. "We have enough to eat for maybe a week if we stretch it. We may get hungry sometimes, but we have rifles to pop a rabbit and matches to light a fire and blankets against the cold, hard ground."

I could have gone on and told her that leaving on such short notice hadn't been my idea, but I thought better of it. Maude wasn't the sort to trifle with when she thought she was in the right, and I had to be satisfied with getting in the last word, even if it wasn't the only word. We rode that first day mostly in silence, probably because we were tired.

Sure enough *I* was tired. We hadn't stopped for more than minutes at a time, and throughout the day our legs grew stiff from sitting the horses. And still we rode. We didn't push the horses hard for speed, but for distance.

"How long do you think this trip will take, Maude?"

"Reverend Peasley said at least three hundred miles to Independence. So let's say we make a hundred miles a week. Does that sound about right?"

I tried to remember anything I'd ever read about making distance on a horse. Nothing came to mind. I thought of Wild Woolly's frozen beard. But I was warm enough so far, so I put on a confident face and said, "I believe we can do it."

Around noon, Maude tore a dishtowel in half to fashion bandannas for our faces, which were already burned red from the wind. The felt hats both fit Maude but were too large for me. A few hours later, I consented to wearing the worst one and peering at the land through a hole where the brim had torn away from the top.

We were of one mind on the subject of short hair: Boys have it good.

Even if we had tied it back, pieces of long hair would have come loose and whipped our faces and stung our eyes. This way, we wouldn't even have to brush it.

Except, of course, that Maude said we did have to. "You can't go around looking like you're wearing a bird's nest, even if I am the only person who sees you."

Our one piece of luck was to find a spring where the water ran fast and clean. There was plenty of graze for the horses. We stopped there for our meal, saying a grateful prayer for the cheese and the bread.

One item had slipped my mind entirely: a canteen. "We're going to have to travel with our noses trained on the scent of water," I said. I did feel a little stupid.

Maude reached over to get a drink. Something jumped out of a patch of weeds and landed on her hand. Maude shrieked and jumped up and all around—swearing loud enough to be heard in Missouri, which was still some distance away—and spooked the horses into jogging a little distance away.

"It's only a toad," I said when I knew for sure. Startling, I'd give her that, but harmless.

"I thought it was a snake," Maude shuddered. "Let's eat on the go," she said, picking up the bread and cheese. Maude disliked snakes something fierce.

A bull snake had once fallen from an overhead beam to land right in her dinner plate, and she had never forgotten the experience. As we walked slowly toward the horses with offerings of handfuls of grass, I blamed that snake for ruining this meal.

"It wasn't a snake, though. A toad can't do you worse than a wart," I said. "*If* it comes back. Let's sit and eat."

"My appetite is spoiled now," she said when we had the horses well in hand.

I didn't much want to get back on that horse. Not right away, anyway. But Maude had her ways. She pinched my shoulder. Pulled my hair. Short hair hurt worse than long, I couldn't say why. So we did go.

It might have been easier on the horses if we'd ridden single file, taking turns at breaking the path. But Goldie wouldn't tolerate walking behind Flora, and Maude couldn't tolerate riding behind Goldie. "That horse has a digestive problem," Maude said, showing some delicacy.

"She does that," I agreed. So we rode side by side. The hours stretched before us as long as the miles, and we resorted to rushing the horses every now and again to feel that we were making distance. But we couldn't rush them long, nor did we want to, for easy riding was what we did best.

"Hey, you know what I picked up?" I said at the first hint of late afternoon light that set a rosy glow over the land. "That packet of letters that Aunt Ruthie had in her desk."

"Those could have been Momma's, you know," Maude said. "It was her desk too."

"Let's just take a look at them when we stop for the night," I said.

So we started to watch for a place to camp, but we happened on a well-traveled road bordered by a split-rail fence. "We'd better find a place a little less popular," Maude said.

We tried, but we found another road shortly and then another. "Awful lot of people must live around here," I said.

We soon found this was true. We pulled up outside a town. Nothing fancy, no boardwalks. Just eleven or twelve weathered gray buildings scattered about, with hard-worn paths running between them. Even though it was fairly dark by then, suppertime on a Saturday, the town was bustling with wagons and horseback riders.

So many windows were lit it looked welcoming. Or maybe I was just tired of looking at short grass and long horizons. "We need a canteen," I said.

"We can't just go riding in there. What if the Peasleys had the sheriff telegraph all over the place? What if they're watching for us here?"

"They aren't watching for two boys," I said. "They aren't watching for one. I'm going to ride in."

"No, you're not," Maude said.

"Yes, I am," I said, not wanting to be treated like a child.

I would have begged and pleaded, but that didn't sit well with my picture of myself as Sallie March, Range Rider. I had packed us up for this trip almost single-handedly, and I was leading the way to Independence, Missouri. Surely I didn't need Maude's permission to buy a canteen.

Maude said, "You can't go in there windburned and riding bareback like an Indian. People will ask questions."

I had not thought of this.

Besides, we needed to find a place to settle for the night. And from the looks of things, that wouldn't be an easy place to find.

TWELVE

HE AIR COOLED QUICKLY ONCE THE SUN STARTED TO GO down. I might have been tempted to wrap a blanket around my shoulders and travel on, but Maude looked weary, and I figured we shouldn't push the horses any harder unless we had to.

Besides, I wanted a look at those letters.

We found a stand of cottonwood and willow trees for shelter. If it proved to be a horrible cold night, at least the wind wouldn't get at us so bad. We ate bread and cheese again, being afraid to draw attention with a campfire so close to town.

All day long I'd been thinking admiring thoughts about the heroes in my dime novels, about the real men who rode like this day in and day out. No one ever wrote about how sore their heroes' butts were, or how their feet swelled after hanging at the side of a horse for hours. Jumping down from the buggy pony sent sharp pains shooting up my legs.

I tethered the horses to a branch, but Maude wouldn't rest until she'd cut another tether rope from the clothesline and tied Flora to her ankle. She insisted I do the same with Goldie.

"I don't know that I want this pony tied to my ankle. If she decides to run, she could drag me for miles," I pointed out.

"You just told me they weren't going to get loose," Maude said to me.

"They aren't, but you want them tied to our ankles in case they do. So I'm just saying what would happen if they do. What mine would do. I grant you, that old plow horse isn't going anywhere."

Maude got a stubborn look. "I can't rest till I know we aren't going to lose these horses. If we don't hang on to them, we'll die out here."

I wasn't sure this was true. Not till we got further from civilization anyway. But in the interest of peace and quiet, I tied Goldie to my ankle. I gave her a long lead so she could graze over some distance without bothering me.

I dug those letters out from the bottom of the sack. "There are only five, but they're all addressed to Aunt Ruthie," I said.

"Let me see," Maude said, so I handed her one after I looked to see if it had a return address. It did not, and neither did the next letter. I opened it anyway and looked to see who it was from.

"Signed 'A.' No return address in here anywhere," Maude said as I was finding the same thing. She went on reading while I went through the letters.

"Here it is," I said, unable to hide my excitement. "This one has the earliest date, and it's from Uncle Arlen. I think this postmark says 'Independence.'"

"Give it to me," Maude said, but I threw her the rest of the packet. This was *my* find. "He says, '*Hope this letter finds you and the girls well. Have finally found someone I can work for and may not get shot up in the course of the day. You were right, as you often are, no one gets rich here without working.*'"

There was more, but I skipped to the bottom where it was signed, "*Your brother, Arlen.*"

"Doesn't that sound like he wanted Aunt Ruthie to come along with him?"

"I wonder if he wanted her to bring us along," Maude said.

"He asked after us."

"Yes, and here, this one says he has enclosed money to help pay down the house." Maude glanced at me. "He sounds like a nice enough fellow to me."

We hurried through the remaining letters because it was getting too dark to make them out easily. In one, we found bad news. Maude read, "'*I cannot say exactly where I shall end up, but will write to you once it is decided. I would write more often if I thought you welcomed my letters. Do not worry about me, for I am more of a man than you remember.*' He sounds sad, doesn't he?" Maude said.

To my ears, he sounded like a man about to move on, and I didn't like the sound of that at all. I slumped into a position best suited for staring into the darkness, when it came on full.

Opening the last letter, Maude said, "Here he says he got shot full of arrows."

I sat up straight. "Let me see that." Sure enough, he wrote: "*The Indians have been rough around here. Last week I took six arrows in the back and would've died but for the fact that an army patrol rode over the hill in time to run off my attackers.*"

"Not much to go on," Maude said as I skimmed through the rest of the letter. There was not so much as a hint of where this happened.

"It has the same postmark," I said, inspecting the envelope. I could just barely make it out.

"But then at the bottom of the letter he says someone is going to mail it for him, as he isn't moving around much just yet. They could have carried a letter back to Independence to be mailed, couldn't they?"

"I'm too tired to wonder," I told Maude.

I found rocks in my mattress when I stretched out, so I knew it was going to be a poor night's sleep. I wondered why the likes of Joe Harden never complained about bruises. But then, that's what made them heroes, I figured.

"Sallie," Maude said. She lay beside me, and the horses munched steadily, making a soothing sound. "We'll be fine, even if we don't find Uncle Arlen. But somehow I think we will."

"You don't have to treat me like a child," I said.

"I'm not. I'm telling you I have faith in what we're doing. That we'll be okay, no matter what."

"All right, then." I wished I felt some of the same faith, but mainly I felt cold and uncomfortable.

"You're really good at this," Maude said, somewhat reluctantly. "I want you to know I see that."

Before I could think of the right thing to say back, something humble but in full agreement all the same, she said, "We have to find Uncle Arlen. We have to."

"We will," I said, realizing she felt miserable too.

"You think so?"

"Yes," I said very surely. Maude didn't say anything right back, and she didn't say anything for a while and neither did I, waiting to hear what it would be if she did.

She began to snore.

I wished I could sleep so easily. In sleep I wouldn't still notice how hard and full of small stones this soft-looking grazing land had turned out to be. But I lay awake for a time. It was a lucky thing I did because that buggy pony did act up. Instead of lulling us to sleep with the sound of steady chewing, both horses acted some bothered, and started blowing through their noses, and brought Maude and me quickly to sitting up.

I was struggling to get the rope off my ankle, and telling her to do the same, when an old dog wandered into view. I stood and quieted the horses as the dog made one trip all around us. "It's afraid we'll throw rocks or something," I said to Maude.

"Maybe it's wild," she said. "Maybe it's wondering if it ought to attack."

"If that were so, it would snarl," I said, making a guess. Aunt Ruthie had never allowed us to have a dog, so the truth of the matter was, we were neither one real sure of how a dog would act. "Give me a piece of cheese."

Maude rummaged in the bag, cut a piece, and tossed it to me. The dog watched this with interest but didn't come any closer. I held out the cheese, and still he wouldn't come.

I walked out nearly to him and set it on the ground. When I walked away, he took it. "Give me another piece," I said.

"That cheese is to fill our bellies," Maude said. "Let him go home and eat."

She had the right of it, so I didn't bother her for more. But the dog slept in that spot where I laid down the cheese. The horses had calmed down enough that we could tie them to our ankles again.

This time when I laid my head down, I slept.

Maude woke at first light.

Those horses were better than roosters for waking a body up, yanking me this way and that. I'd been awake on and off for better than an hour but reluctant to leave the blankets. In between the awake moments, I'd had bad dreams.

"Get up, lazybones."

"I'm awake," I said, still not making a move to get up. The morning was chill. Heavy dew had dripped off the leaves of the trees and wetted down the blankets. My stomach felt like it hung in my middle like an empty sack. I was in no mood for roughing it. I wanted the smell of biscuits to be on the air and the sweet taste of bacon in my mouth, and I didn't want to rustle up a fire to get it.

Maude gave me a smart kick to my rump.

I put one arm out to test the weather and found it every bit as unpleasant as I expected. "Here," Maude said, putting a fork in my hand. "I thought we might as well finish off this cheese today. But then I found pie. You crazy girl, you brought pie?"

"Doesn't seem so crazy at just this minute." I sat up, still rolled in my blanket.

"It's broken up some, but the forks don't care," she said.

"Eat up." We ate mostly pie, saving the rest of the cheese and one pie for later.

But we felt rich enough to give the dog another piece of cheese, and he followed us for about half an hour. Maybe by then we were taking him too far from home, for I looked back once to see he'd gone. I was sorry to see him go.

I felt the lack of company, although Maude rode alongside me. Even days spent in only Aunt Ruthie's company had been more filled with the doings of the world around us. Out here, it was hard to be sure that somewhere else people were working together, sitting down together, someone was probably getting a tooth pulled. I decided I was lucky not to be that one. For her part, Maude could tolerate going for hours without saying a word.

At first I worried that she was let down by the letters, which we'd read through once more before starting out. We had no idea where Uncle Arlen might be found; we had only the strongest feeling that he'd already moved further west when he wrote the last letter. We had agreed not to worry about it till we got to Independence. "One worry at a time," Maude said, echoing Aunt Ruthie's advice on meeting trouble.

We rode all day at the same good clip we'd done the day before. We moved north of any wagon tracks we came across. I didn't want to ride north. It made no sense to me, but Maude was of the firm opinion this was the same thing as moving to higher ground. Anyone could see the land was flat, but logic was not a partner to Maude's opinions.

I agreed to move a mile north, not because I believed we could see around us any better but I figured the further from the wagon trail we got, the fewer people we'd meet. Then we traveled due west for a while. I turned us south again as soon as I could manage to do it gradual.

"We can't go around dressed like this and calling each other Maude and Sallie," Maude said.

She had been quiet for so long, we both had, that her voice came as a surprise. "Why not?" I said, slowing up a little to make it easier to talk. "That's our names."

"We might come up on some other people, and we do want them to believe we're boys," she reminded me. "We ought to get used to calling each other something else."

"What do you want to be called?" I asked.

"Something that starts with an *M.* Monty?"

"Monty?" I didn't much care for the sound of it. "I think I'd get confused and call you Maude in a heated moment."

"A heated moment?"

"Like if we were under attack or something."

"I doubt it will matter if we're under attack," she said in a tone that reminded me of Aunt Ruthie. A moment later, she asked, "What name do you suggest?"

"How about Pete?"

"Only if I get to call you Repeat," she said.

"I like Johnnie. How does that hit you?" I said, thinking I would take that name.

"I'll be Johnnie, you be Pete," she said.

I didn't want to be Pete, but I only frowned and said, "Let's think about it."

I kept an eye on the sun, but I could only make the sorriest guess which direction we were going. Every so often I had to ride ahead a little to steal a look at the compass. "Why do you keep doing that?" Maude complained after one of these forays. "It makes me nervous."

"I'm learning to ride faster on bareback," I said. It wasn't an out-and-out lie. "If we got chased by something, I'm not sure I could stay on. Why does it make you nervous? You can see me the whole time."

"I don't know; it just does."

"Well, get over it."

We didn't stay mad at each other the way we once would have. We couldn't. We only had each other, and we knew it.

THIRTEEN

B Y LATE IN THE DAY I HAD GROWN USED TO THE LONELY feeling it gave me to never see another soul. We had been moving at a trot for some time. I didn't like bouncing around so much in a saddle, but it was some worse riding bareback.

I spotted a stand of trees maybe a mile or so away. "Let's head for those trees and set up camp."

"I'm not so bone tired today as I was yesterday," Maude said.

"I'm bone *sore*," I said, and scootched around a little on the horse. We'd only recently nibbled at the last of the cheese as we rode. Now I wished I was hungry. When my belly was full and feeling good, I noticed my every other complaint all the more.

"We sound like Mrs. Golightly in the middle of winter," Maude said to me, "nursing her achy bones."

I reached into my pocket and brought out a peppermint candy. "Want one?"

"Oh," Maude said in a little-girl voice. Tears stood on her eyelashes, but she didn't say anything about Aunt Ruthie's fondness for peppermints.

"We don't have many," I said, reluctant to use them up too quickly. "Maybe we ought to save them for special occasions or something."

"I will always buy peppermints," Maude said fiercely. "No matter what. I would steal them, if need be." I couldn't imagine Maude stealing anything but food and horses, and I had to bully her to get her to do that. But I decided to let the remark pass.

"I want to fry up those chickens," Maude told me as we settled on a place to camp for the night. "Before they spoil."

While the chicken sweetened the air, she got me to help her collect greens to boil up. They were not the sort of thing to grow on a person, even with the right gravy of bacon fat and onion, which Maude said she wouldn't waste on them even if she had the onion. She boiled some of the eggs over the same fire that fried the chicken.

"You'd make a decent range rider," I told her.

"Don't look now," she said, "but I *am* a range rider. And so are you."

We ate those eggs while we rode the next couple of days, and eked the chicken out over the sit-down meals. We had agreed not to worry, but we read through Uncle Arlen's letters again and again, trying to make out the kind of man he was.

It was a mark in his favor that he made it to Independence in the first place, but less of one that he might have left it not long after. We were, needless to say, hopeful of him being a man who stayed in one spot.

"Do you think the Peasleys miss us?" I asked as we put the letters away.

Maude burst out laughing, and although I had not meant it to be a funny question, I very soon found it made me laugh too. Maude got the hiccups and began to say things between each one—"Ungrateful girls, hic...Didn't even make their beds, hic...before they left, hic...hic..."—till I worried I would get hiccups too.

For a farm horse, Flora was a strong swimmer. Maude quit wearing her boots with the pointy toes after taking them off to ford a river. She'd held them over her head as she let Flora make her way across the river, but then made room for them in one of Flora's bags. "They make my feet go numb," she complained.

"Then maybe they don't fit after all," I said, growing hopeful that they might fit me.

"They do," she said. "But my own toes make as good a horse prod as the boot tips. If I wear those things very long, I'm going to walk like a real cowboy. I'll never find a husband that way."

"I didn't know you were so goldanged interested in finding a husband," I said. My seat wouldn't have been so sore if she hadn't been so picky about the two husbands she'd already turned down.

Maude sighed. "I'm not looking for him today. But I have to think ahead. And don't swear, Sallie, it's not becoming."

Of all the unbecoming things we had done, swearing appeared to me to be the least. "Maude, do you think we're going to find Uncle Arlen?" I asked her as we rode on.

"Yes, I do," she answered.

"It doesn't seem likely, though, does it?" I said. "Even if

he was the type to live through getting there, he could be anywhere."

"Shut up, Sallie."

We'd been making our way mainly west, by my best reckoning, and I made up my mind to work us further south, and not only because Independence lay to the south. We could feel the cold at night and rode away from it by day.

By what I figured to be Wednesday, I had seen enough of grass and sky. To make matters worse, a chill wind blew in. It was cold work, sitting a horse in the wind. Maude layered socks on her feet. We pulled those pieces of dishtowel up to cover our noses and wore folded blankets like shawls.

Riding face into the wind was hard on the horses too. They were willing to run, but then tired quickly. So we let them strike their own pace. When the wind blew up their noses, it was a trot, jouncing us around too much, so it wasn't long before we slowed them to a walk. I began to doubt we'd cover ten miles the whole livelong day.

I was ready to set camp by the middle of the afternoon. "This seems like a waste," I told Maude once. "We might just as well see what we have left to eat."

"A little further," she said, and so we went on.

"I'm just sick of it," I said a few miles later. "I wish Uncle Arlen had gone back east. Then we could go by train. We could have sold off all the furniture to make our fare, if we'd had more than one night to do it. I wish we were on our way to Philadelphia."

"Be careful what you wish for," Maude told me.

"What was the last thing you wished for?" I asked her.

"To be my own boss," she said sadly.

I didn't ask her when that was.

We had been lucky so far, finding water every day. Sometimes it was green and scummy, but we could let the horses fill up. When we came to clear water, we drank till we sloshed when we walked. After we'd made some room in the potato sacks, by virtue of eating much of what they held, we were able to put an assortment of the household items in them. Once the bucket was emptied of these things, we were able to carry some water.

"Look at that," Maude said.

I pushed my hat up. "Look at what?"

"The grass there." Maude pointed. "See how it's been stomped down?"

There was, in fact, a trampled path. Looking more closely, I couldn't decide what it might have been. The ground was too dry to take a print. Too narrow for a buckboard, I decided. Even a one-seat buggy left wheel marks on the grass. But there weren't any wheel marks.

"I think it's a single horse and rider," Maude said. "That's the same kind of trail we leave behind us."

"When did you look at the kind of trail we leave behind us?" I asked, immediately looking behind to see we'd made two battened-down paths. I smarted a little to think Maude was going to turn out to be a better range rider than I was. I had a dozen dimes, or at least I once had, that went into some detail on the subject of trailing, and I considered myself well-informed. I didn't like making a poor showing of it right when we'd found our first trail to follow.

"I think we should follow this trail," I said.

"I don't know, Sallie. Maybe it would be smarter just to ride a mile north and stay away from this fellow."

"I don't want to catch up to him," I said. "I just want to know where he is."

"It's getting late. We'd have to go without a fire."

This was a point.

"And we're short on water," Maude said. "What if he plunks himself down right on the only water? What if he sees us before we see him?"

She was right, but I didn't care to admit it. I said, "If we have to ride north a mile every time we're likely to run into someone, we're going to end up in the Canadian territories."

Then I headed us south. There was not a word of protest from Maude. It made me smile to know that I was not the only one who needed a compass.

FOURTEEN

W E NEEDN'T HAVE WORRIED ABOUT THE WATER. WE had more than we could use. We didn't have to worry about a fire either; it rained too hard to get one going. The clouds rolled in fast, coming from the northwest.

We had seen them in the distance all day, but they never seemed to be coming our way. Their arrival felt a mite sudden. Because one minute we were remarking that it looked like rain on the way, and the next minute the world was a darker place. Rain started to fall in big, fat drops. We were very soon soaked through.

A mile and a half further on, we huddled under a dripping hemlock. We had to count ourselves lucky at that. It stood alone in the middle of nowhere, with long branches that swooped to the ground.

Behind those branches that had green needles, we found a rabbit warren of bare branches that had to be broken off to make a circular room. This was easy, they were awful dried out. We had the makings, but it didn't look like a good idea to try to start a fire there. We were in for a cold night.

We rubbed the horses down and tied their ropes to the

flexible branches of the tree instead of to us. The horses wandered in and out of our makeshift house to nibble at the wet vegetation. Now and then one of us had to unravel the tangle of rope in the branches, but for the most part, things were fine.

We changed into dry clothes. Maude praised me for thinking of the extra set I had packed—at least we were able to warm ourselves. She tried to make the best of things, crediting me even for the pine-scented air. I used one of the branches to sweep the ground free of twigs and pine cones so we could lay our bed down on a smooth floor. We ate one of the chickens entirely.

We were going through our food faster than I thought we would, and it worried me. We had walked our share of miles today, but the fact still remained it hadn't been many miles. The wind had slowed us up, and the rain had stopped us altogether. To start foraging for food meant it would likely take us into winter before we made Independence.

"Let's go to sleep," Maude said, although we had probably another hour to go before full darkness. "Maybe things will look brighter in the morning."

Neither of us could sleep. We wrapped ourselves snugly in our blankets and rested our backs against our carpetbags. We talked a little, trying to stay away from worrisome subjects.

"You're going to think I'm crazy, but I brought a piece of stitchery with me," Maude said.

"Aw, I don't think you're crazy." I did wish, if she was thinking up things to bring along, that she'd have thought of something more practical than her handiwork.

She said, "I just loved that pillow cover with the violets that Mrs. Peasley set me to work on. Do you know the one?"

"I do. It was right nice." Which was more than I could say for the project Mrs. Peasley handed me. But I wasn't all that much of a hand with a needle; I couldn't blame her for giving me something that was ugly from the get-go.

"It was too dark to see what I picked up," Maude said. "I didn't take the one I was after. Look." She pulled the embroidery out of her carpetbag and handed it to me.

It was my clumsy stitching and the dark outline of a horse, which I had not even begun to fill in. I had worked on the letters, which read, TROUBLE RIDES A FAST HORSE.

"So much for good intentions," Maude said.

I dug through my bag and found the dress remnants. "Oh," Maude cried, much the way she had over the peppermint. The fabric brought on such a rush of tears, she had those dress pieces completely wet down before she was able to stop. She was sweet, though, and tried to offer the soggy patches back to me.

"You keep them," I said. "I'll ask for them if I want to see them."

She folded them up like a stack of hankies and put them into her pants pocket. After a moment she took out the gingham, to tell me all her stories of it. "Momma and I walked to town that day, leaving you at home with Poppa..." She always started there and went on to tell how they chose the pattern from a book and ate licorice on the way home, making their teeth look black.

I wished there was something else she could have thought to talk about. These stories had never made me miss Momma, although I sometimes wished I remembered her better, but this time they made me ache for Aunt Ruthie. I wanted to talk to her just one last time, to tell her how I had begun to see her differently, to tell her I knew how good she was to us.

My eyes started to burn with tears, but Maude looked happy and I let her go on, while I recalled page for page the last Joe Harden dimer I read. This was not too hard, since I had read it till the cover was coming apart.

Joe had been hot on the trail of a wolf hunter who had murdered a rancher.

I had gotten to the part where Joe hears the crunch of small stones right before he is ambushed, and he shoots the hunter left-handed with a rifle, while holding the reins of his rearing horse with his right hand, and wings him. The picture showed very clearly the spurt of blood and the pain on the hunter's face.

That picture was bright on the backs of my eyelids when we heard someone call, "halloo," as he stepped in out of the rain, holding his hands in the air. Maude shoved the remnant into her pocket.

"Sorry to surprise you fellers," the man said, keeping his hands up, "but if I stand out there waiting for an invitation I'll drown or freeze, one." His hat was so completely wetted down the brim hung over his face.

"Where's your horse?" Maude asked him. "Are you by yourself?"

This was a good question, one I wished I'd thought of myself. I would have liked to be able to say I heard him coming, the way Dagnabit Darby always did. I was sure everyone knew the line, "Dagnabit, Darby, you got the drop on me again," that could be found in every Dagnabit Darby story. As it was, Maude and I were wrapped so tight against the cold, we were caught in our blankets.

"It's just me and my horse, that's right," he said. "I see you have room for one more, if you wouldn't mind it." For a moment there, something about him looked familiar to me, but I shook that notion off. "I'd appreciate it if you wouldn't keep your gun trained on me," he said. "I mean no harm."

"Bring in your horse," Maude said, using her most no-nonsense tone. I glanced at her and saw that she had raised herself up on one elbow; she looked half set to leap up from the ground, blanket or no blanket. In the dim light, with one hand still in her pocket, it did look like maybe she held a six-shooter hidden in the folds.

I reached out and poked at her elbow. "Put down your gun," I whispered.

We sat up to free ourselves of the blankets, standing up just as he came back in. "I'm Johnnie," Maude said, "and this here is Pete."

I might have resented this, but the idea was wiped out when the man said, "Joe Harden, son. I'm right sorry to have startled you, but that weather is bearing down hard."

This brought me up short. It was him. I remembered him, although I had even less light to make him out than last time. I was excited, of course, but I was upset that I hadn't known him right off. Well, I had known, he seemed familiar, but I hadn't listened to my gut. This was not the kind of mistake a frontier fighter ought to make, so I was some disappointed in myself.

"How'd you come to find us," Maude asked him.

"I started back for the only shelter I could be sure of. There's a farm another couple of miles east and north."

"That's right," Maude said, like she knew anything about it. She could be cool under pressure, I'd say that for her, so long as a man wasn't looking to marry her.

"I backtracked, looking for shelter, and saw you veered this way," Joe said. "I figured you must know something I don't. Turns out you did. You boys live around here?"

"We used to," Maude said. "Not anymore."

"I don't mean to be any trouble," Joe said. "I'll just rag down my horse and make my bed over here, if that's all right with you."

"That's fine," Maude told him. "Have you eaten yet?"

I poked her. She wasn't supposed to act like a hostess. We were range riders. Didn't she know that?

"I'd appreciate anything you could share," Joe said. "Otherwise, I'm gonna sleep hungry. I hadn't yet settled when the rain started. Can't very well start a fire under this umbrella, now can we?"

Maude gave him the last two boiled eggs. She avoided looking at me.

"Why do you keep your horses tied to these long ropes here?" Joe asked. "Don't they get tangled up?"

"They don't wander away," Maude said, as if we didn't have to sort out those horses every morning.

"Let me show you a little Indian trick," he said. "It's a way of tying their feet together so they can't take but itty-bitty steps. Called a hobble. Takes a whole lot less rope, and they get better graze."

FIFTEEN

———

WHEN WE TURNED IN, THERE WAS NO TALK BETWEEN Maude and me, except with our eyes. Our eyes said, no sleep until Joe Harden snores. As it was, he snored for some long hours before I was able to shut my eyes again. Maude tossed and turned, so I knew she wasn't sleeping easy either. It felt strange to have another human being so close to us.

I listened to the rain hit the ground all around us. Under our so-called umbrella, the slower drip of water trickled from branch to branch. It was getting colder every minute, too, and I was glad we'd brought enough blankets. Or, that Maude had.

I kept thinking about how many mistakes I had made. I might have walked right into Joe's tracks without noticing them if Maude hadn't spoken up. I never gave a moment's thought to trying to cover up ours. Not that we could cover up wet, trampled-down grass.

It bothered me most that I hadn't known he was there until he came in under the tree, even though our horses had shuffled around some, huffing and blowing. I just figured they were settling down for the night.

I was turning out to be a real disappointment in the hero category.

And then there were the questions that still churned in the back of my brain. If he was Joe Harden, how could he be so different from the way he came across in those stories? How could he shoot Aunt Ruthie? If I wondered more, I don't remember. I slept a black sleep till Joe Harden woke me with the smell of frying bacon.

Maude was already up and ducking under the branches on the far side of the tree for a minute of privacy.

I followed my nose to the campfire. Joe had gathered enough dry pine needles under the tree and had broken up a few of the dry branches to start a fire a little ways off. The rain was still coming down, although not as hard as the evening before.

"How'd you get a fire going?" I asked him as I stood in the rain. He gave me a kind of quick, startled look, then went back to studying his cooking. After a moment he said, "I hold my hat over it till it gets going good. Now the frying pan is doing most of that work."

I noticed, too, that he had a metal grate that stood on its own, so no need to go around looking for stones to set it on. "Get your beds rolled up and come on out here for some eats," he said. "You boys supplied supper, and I've made breakfast."

"Thank you kindly," Maude said, coming out from under the tree. I ducked under there and out the other side for a minute of privacy. When I got back, they were talking about riding on together for a time.

"I don't know about that," I said. "Mau—my brother and me figured to travel alone."

"Hard to travel in winter," he said, "'specially when you have far to go."

"We'll get to Independence before the snow falls," I said.

"I didn't tell Joe all that much about our plans, Pete," Maude said. "I just said we could ride west together for a time. Don't see that it makes no never mind."

I stared at Maude. Her grammar was atrocious. I gathered she thought it would make her sound more like a boy. I knew she thought I told Joe too much, and she was right about that. But she acted like she didn't even know it was Joe who killed Aunt Ruthie.

"I don't see why we have to ride out at all," I said, hoping to look like a boy turning stubborn. "We can just sit here and stay dry today."

"You don't want to get caught on the plains in a blizzard," Joe argued in a mild way.

"I don't want to die of pneumonia either," I said.

"Why, you're no boy!" Joe said suddenly. "You're that girl that came asking if I was going to hang."

"What?" Maude said, the blood draining from her face.

"I am not," I said. There was no going back, though; I'd tipped him off somehow. "How'd you get out of jail anyway?"

"Sallie," Maude said, "what are you talking about? What is he talking about?"

"You're not supposed to call me Sallie."

"It's one of those heated moments you mentioned," Maude said, going pink with embarrassment.

"I thought you said you had a sister," he said, giving Maude a measuring look. "You're no boy either. Is that it?"

"How did you know me?" I asked him. "Did I do something girlish?"

"It's your voice I knew," he said. "I have a memory for voices, that's all. Why're the two of you dressed up this way?"

"So we can travel," I told him. "We're on our own now. You made orphans of us, once and for all."

"He's the one who shot Aunt Ruthie?" Maude asked, her eyes going wide.

"He is," I said. "And it's a sad state for a man like you to arrive at, Mr. Harden. I've read about your exploits and you never conducted yourself so poorly—"

"Sallie, hush!"

"I told your little sister, here," Joe said. "I'm right sorry."

"Then you did shoot our aunt?"

"I wasn't shooting at any relatives of yours," Joe said. "I wasn't shooting at anyone."

"Joe Harden never misses," I told Maude, and she clapped a hand over my face the way she used to do when we were younger, clapped a hand over and squeezed so that her thumb and a finger bit painfully into the hinge of my jaw. It always shut me up when I was little, and it shut me up now.

"What were you shooting at?" Maude asked in a polite fashion, as if she weren't squeezing the life out of my face.

"Bottles," Joe said. "First I was winning at cards, but then I could see the worst loser was getting up the juice to shoot me. So I bet him I could hit more empty bottles in a minute than he could. He's known to be a handy enough shot, and my intention was to lose a few dollars back to him."

"What if he was too drunk to shoot his best?" Maude asked him.

"That was the tricky part, all right," Joe said. "We checked that our pistols was fully loaded, and borrowed as many guns as we could from the other men in the room. This was more armament than you might expect. Cedar Rapids isn't the kind of town a man expects to get shot up in."

If this was a bid for sympathy, it was lost on Maude, who said, "Go on. Tell us what happened." For that matter, it was lost on me. It was a bitter disappointment to me to hear of Joe Harden taking part in such poor sport to save his sorry skin. To find that Maude was only too right; he was not much of a man at all.

"Since I was to shoot first, I figured I had to miss altogether to ensure that I lost," Joe said. "So I pretended I was just drunk enough to be clumsy as we stood a long line of bottles at the end of the alley."

He paused, as if the picture he drew bothered him too much to go on. Maude went on waiting for the rest of the story, her eyes boring into him like coals through a blanket. I waited too, because she never let go of her grip on my face.

"One of the loser's buddies knew my reputation and kicked my foot out from under me as I took aim—I got a bad ankle on this side. The shot went wild as I fell, hitting a stone bench, and the bullet ricocheted. It's purely bad luck that I didn't hit one of them fellers instead of your aunt." Joe thought for a moment and added, "It's a rough crowd those saloons draw, miss."

"So you're sure it was your bullet that hit Aunt Ruthie?" Maude asked. She relaxed the hold she had on my jaw.

"Of course, he's sure," I said. "He's Joe Harden."

"Oh, will you stop nattering about those dime novels, Sallie? He's no more Joe Harden than I am."

"You're wrong—"

"Your sister is right, my name ain't Joe Harden."

"It ain't?" Maude said, but then shook her head as if to clear it. "Well, of course, it isn't. You're a real flesh-and-blood man, not a walking piece of a story."

"We're all walking pieces of a story, miss," he said. "My name is Marion Hardly. I wouldn't last long out here with a name like that, though."

"But you are the man who killed our Aunt Ruthie," Maude said, never one to let a thing go.

Marion said, "They were going to hang me. They don't take an accident lightly when it appears you were careless of another's life." He nodded. "That's as it should be, I agree, but I wasn't drunk, and I wasn't careless, I swear to you."

"It doesn't matter to me, one way or the other," Maude said.

Marion couldn't be satisfied with this. "It took nearly every penny I had to make good on that bench I damaged, but that's the kind of man I really am."

"It just seems like such a no-account reason to die," Maude said sadly. "Getting shot while doing a little household shopping."

"I don't personally know anyone who died of a good reason," Marion said.

SIXTEEN

WE RODE DESPITE THE RAIN AND COLD, ACCOMPANIED BY Marion Hardly. He told us it was the wisest thing to do, if we were on the run. He said the rain might hold up the ones who were chasing us for a day. That would put us a day ahead.

We had not told him we were on the run, but the man made good guesses. *He* was on the run, of course. "So how did you get out of that jail?" I asked him.

"I just waited till the middle of the night when everyone was sleeping. There's only one lawman around most times anyway, so once I figured the whole town was asleep, I just jimmied the lock and left."

"You were there for a long time," I said. "Why didn't you leave before?"

"I didn't want to go till I was sure they wanted to hang me. There's no reason to add being a hunted man to my bug bites unless it's the only way to stay alive."

"You thought they would find you innocent?" Maude asked him, but not as if she found this ridiculous.

"No, Miss Maude, but I thought they might see the accidental side of it."

She nodded and asked him no more about it. I hadn't figured out how she managed to be so forgiving. Not that I expected her to shoot him to get revenge, but she did seem to swing far and wide to the other side.

Myself, I thought he deserved hanging for shooting Aunt Ruthie. Not that I wanted it to happen. I had the strongest notion that hangings were nowhere nearly so entertaining as dime novels would lead a body to think.

I had come close to seeing a hanged man only once. A number of those people who were tall enough to watch the whole business vomited in the street directly after, and that's the main thing I remember about it, that smell.

I decided to let the matter drop, for the time being. There would be plenty of opportunities to question the finer points of Maude's thinking on forgiveness, I figured, and better times to do it.

"What were you doing in Cedar Rapids?" I asked Marion.

"Just passing through," he said. "I was running short of funds, and I thought a card game would put a little change in my pocket. But as I said, things went wrong. It didn't look like such a temperamental little town as it turned out to be."

Maude gave him a hard look.

"I mean the card players," Marion said. "About your aunt Ruthie, well, the sheriff was doing his job, of course."

I found I didn't want to hear any more about Aunt Ruthie's misfortune. It made me feel a little low. So I was just as happy when Marion turned the conversation in another direction. "If you don't mind me asking, what made you girls settle on Independence? It's a long, rough ride through Missouri."

85

"You have a better suggestion?" Maude asked him.

She sounded rude to me, but Marion took it in stride. "You might have gone back east."

"We don't have any people back east," I told him. "We might be able to find our uncle Arlen in Independence."

"Well, now, there's some good news," Marion said, almost heartily. If he was taking comfort from the notion that we weren't orphans after all, Maude wasn't about to let him have it for long.

"We don't know if he's dead or alive," she said. "Even if he is alive, we don't have any idea where to look for him once we get there. We have a letter that stated he was leaving for parts unknown. If we find him, we don't know that he'll want to take us in. If we make it that far ourselves, which we might not."

She settled his hash.

We rode without another word said for nearly half an hour before Marion came up with a less touchy subject. He instructed us on the wisdom of pacing horses in the rain. Warm them up by starting out with a longish walk, shift to a brisk trot, offer them a little gallop to get their blood running, but then let them slow down again.

"Prairie dog burrows cave in and become hidden mud holes," Marion said. "You don't want a running horse to step down in one of those holes. Less'n you want to fly to Independence."

Maude didn't have anything to say to this, but I sensed he'd softened her up a little. I didn't know what more there was to say about horses, so after we had our little gallop, I asked him again if he was the Joe Harden in the book, even if he was really Marion Hardly.

"What book would that be?" he asked me.

"*Joe Harden, Frontier Fighter.* Those books."

"I imagine it's purely coincidence," Marion said. "I can't believe anyone is writing about me."

I told him the one Joe Harden story I could just about recite word for word. And I gave him the gist of the other stories I'd read. I finished by saying, "I'm sorry to say I haven't been able to get even half of them."

"Who wrote these stories?" Marion asked.

I had to think for a minute. "J. H. somebody," I said. "I always thought it was you, because of the initials. I thought maybe the last name was just for show, so you could tell the stories without embarrassment."

Marion gave me an odd look. "You mean you thought it made it easier for me to brag?" He sounded half mad.

"I don't think it's bragging to tell how things were," I said. "You'll see. You can have a look at one of them later."

Marion made grateful noises, to be polite, I guess, but I gathered he didn't have a good opinion of dime novels. "I read one once," he said, "and I had to put it down. The hero made such poor decisions, I just knew it for a story written by someone who had never come as far west as the Mississippi. But I allow John Henry might have learned a few things since then."

"John Henry?" Maude said. "You know who wrote them?"

"No, no," Marion said, pulling himself up straighter in the saddle. "It's just the name I give to those initials your sister told me."

This conversation only carried us into strong daylight, not that strong daylight was so easy to find under a sky the color of pewter. By late morning the three of us were soaked to the skin and wishing for another pine tree. We hadn't bothered with conversation for two hours at least.

The wind picked up and pushed darker clouds across the sky. "Looks like we're in for some weather," Marion said. "I hope that's a cabin up ahead."

"Where?" Maude said, and stood in her stirrups to see. "I don't see anything but that wagon."

"Your eyes aren't adjusted to distances," Marion said kindly. "Mine are adjusted, but don't get your hopes up; it might not be a cabin. It's just a bump in the flat as yet, even for my eyes. I reckon we're an hour's ride from it."

I kept shut. I couldn't even see the wagon.

We picked up speed a little, but it seemed like the longest hour of my life. By the time we reached the bump, my teeth were chattering and so were Maude's. The bump in the flat was not a cabin. It was an abandoned wagon.

"I guess you were right," Marion said to Maude.

A rocking chair sat next to it like an invitation. Or a cruel joke. The disappointment was severe. Maude choked back a sob. I understood. She thought he must have seen something beyond the wagon.

"I told you not to get your hopes up," Marion reminded her. "We could tip the wagon for a windbreak and get a little fire going. But that don't shelter the horses. I say we keep going."

"How far?" Maude asked him, shivering.

"We can make Skunk Hollow by nightfall," he said. "But I hesitate to take you gals in there, even looking like boys. It's a rough place. We'd best push for Des Moines."

Maude's teeth clacked, which I took for a kind of giving in. Marion was made of hardier stuff; his teeth kept quiet. His fingers were no less blue than ours, I noticed, so he understood that Maude was nearing the end of her rope. "It's not much further."

"Des Moines is not rough?" Maude asked.

"Every place is rough, just some places are rougher than others."

"We're too cold," I said, thinking warm thoughts about that fire he mentioned.

"Get down and walk. If we walk fast, we'll warm up, you'll see. We'll warm up and then give the horses a little run to return the favor."

SEVENTEEN

MARION WAS RIGHT ABOUT WALKING. HE WALKED US fast, and inside an hour we did warm up as good as sitting by the fire. I never would have thought of it myself, but then the cold numbs your brain, that's one thing I learned as well.

We had another river to ford, but Marion was familiar with the territory and walked us alongside the rushing water in fading daylight. After an hour or more of watching the water boil and of me wishing we didn't have to face it, Marion brought us to a point where a ridge of land could be walked across it.

I was filled with admiration for the man.

"Wrap the reins around your hand a time or two. If you end up in the water," he said to us before we started across, "don't let go of your horse. Stay on it, if you can."

The horses were underwater up to their bellies in fast-rushing water, however shallow it was at that point. It took some coaxing to get them to walk it in the dark. They kept wanting to give in to the flow of water around their legs and swim. But Maude and I were more able to bully them than we once were, and we riders got no wetter for this crossing than any others.

We rode till I had lost all hope of finding a place to sleep. When we saw lights in the distance, I thought it was a trick of my eyes. "How late is it?" I asked, instead of asking, was it real?

"Past midnight, I reckon," Marion said. "Not all cities sleep." So I knew, it was real. I had been near the point of asking to walk again, but I decided then to bear the cold and get there quicker.

Des Moines was a more sizable place than I expected. It wasn't all shut down, the way most towns would have been by that hour. There were voices raised to sing "Rock of Ages" as we passed the church, coming into town. A little old place stood open to feed people; it didn't have any other purpose that I could see.

The streets weren't dark either, even if many houses looked shut tight for the night. Torches had been stuck in barrels of dirt every so many wagon-lengths and gave off enough light to get by.

As we got deeper into the city, piano music lit the air around one of the saloons and a bathhouse stood open right next door. A sign offered shaves and haircuts and tooth pulling, and a man stood ready in the doorway to do all three. We rode through town for a longer time than would have been my plan. It was not my plan we were following. We crossed another river, but this one could be crossed by bridge, hallelujah.

We passed two likely-looking hotels before Marion

stopped at a bootmaker's shop and knocked on the door. It was shut tighter than a hatbox and dark inside, so I waited to see what good this would do. He knocked two or three times more before a window above the store opened.

"Who's that out there?" a man asked.

"Joe Harden," Marion answered. "I'm looking for a place to stay."

"Who's that with you?"

"I'm traveling with my younger brothers."

The window shut with nothing more said. Maude and I glanced at each other, waiting to see what happened next. A lamp was lit upstairs. After what seemed like a long time, the door in front of Marion opened.

I gathered from their conversation that Marion had stayed here before and slept on the floor for twenty-five cents. Now the man wanted twenty-five cents for each one of us. "For that kind of money, I might just as well take a room at the hotel and have a bath," Marion said. "We ain't taking up nothing but floor space."

Maude put in, "The night is more than half gone, besides." For my part, I kept my teeth from chattering, which might have been considered an argument to bolster the bootmaker's side.

After considerable haggling, a deal was struck: forty cents. The money was handed over, and the door shut in Marion's face without a friendlier word being spoken. But Marion looked pleased with himself as he turned to us and said, "Let's take the horses around back."

It wasn't more than a lean-to hanging off the back of the building, but there was grass about hip-high back there. We picked it, broke the thin stems down to make handfuls of it, and wisped the horses until they were dry. They began to eat the grass tops around them as we worked.

The back door had been unlocked for us, and Maude went inside to break out the frying pan and start something to eat. I was glad I wasn't expected to act like a girl, even if I was going to stand cold a little longer.

"How'd you come to use the name Joe Harden?" I asked Marion. "I mean, how'd you choose it over any other?"

"Joe is a friendly enough name," Marion said. "There ain't too many killers named Joe. And I just fixed my other name to sound stronger. Hardly to Harden, you see? But I did notice that it opened more doors than any other alias I'd tried. I didn't know why."

"No one ever asked you about your adventures?" I asked him.

"Well, now, if they did, I just told them what I'd been up to lately. Maybe since there was nothing much to tell, they let it go at that."

I could see that. Even heroes had days when nothing untoward happened, and they had nothing of interest to talk about. "They probably figured you just hit a dry spell, adventure-wise," I said.

This struck Marion funny, and he kept chuckling to himself as we tied blankets over the horses. We took everything else inside. Marion locked the door behind us.

EIGHTEEN

HE PLACE WASN'T ENTIRELY DARK, I SAW ONCE I GOT inside. Light from the street came through the big shop window at the front. It smelled of leather and boot blacking and something else I couldn't make out. "Glue," Marion answered when I asked about it.

We took off our boots to keep the quiet and made our way over to the woodstove, which was bucking out heat. We unrolled our wet clothes from the day before and stretched them out to dry.

Maude had set a fry pan on the woodstove and started some bacon. Marion laid his wet blankets all around the room, and I did likewise for Maude and me. We were quiet as we could be, but we were industrious.

There was a water pump at the back door, and Maude put some up to boil the salted ham. Then she laid the bacon on slabs of bread and handed it to us. The bread was awful dry, but it seemed like we ought to be glad something was, so I didn't complain. We ate well, and until we were full, there was no talk, just chewing.

Maude offered Marion fifteen cents for our space on the

floor. "Now what if I was to say we ought to split it more even like?" he asked her.

"I gathered it costs you twenty-five cents to sleep here alone," Maude said without flinching. "The extra fifteen cents was our cost."

Marion grinned. "I love the way a woman thinks."

Maude ignored this, but I couldn't. "How's that?"

"I should've set Miss Maude on the feller in the first place," Marion said. "She'd have struck a deal for the two of us to sleep for the usual twenty-five cents, I don't doubt. And got your space for nothing, arguing that you don't take up all that much room."

"Fair's fair," Maude said.

"See there?" Marion said as if everything was now made clear.

It was probably another good hour before we settled down with any notion of rest. But we were once more fed and warm, and everything we owned was stick-dry too. I couldn't account for how cheerful I felt. All I knew was, it had become the center of contentment to have warm toes and a full belly.

Leaving the door on the woodstove hanging open gave us enough light to read by. "Want me to get out a few of those dimers?" I asked Marion, hoping to stretch the evening a little. It was just wonderful to feel too good to go to sleep.

Marion said, "Maybe we can find me another good name in there."

"Why do you need another one?" I asked him.

He answered, "Joe Harden is a wanted man now."

I hadn't thought of that. But once he'd pointed it out, I

started looking for a name in earnest. Marion found a newspaper and gave that to Maude, since she didn't care for dime novels worse than he did.

"It's recent," he said, as if that would matter to Maude. She tended to go through a paper back to front, first looking through the lists of what people wanted to hire or buy or sell. Maude's idea of a really good newspaper would be one that was entirely made up of such things.

She took the paper as if she intended to do some justice to it. "It came all the way from Cedar Rapids," she said in surprise. "Home."

"Somebody probably had it wrapped around his boots," Marion said. "Somebody riding the stage," he added, accounting for the fact that the newspaper beat us there.

Maude was propped against her carpetbag and spread the paper over her knees. Her carpetbag had been turned to and fro in front of the woodstove, smelling like a dead cat, till it could be felt to be dry inside and out. I had not followed her lead until she had made a success of it. So it was my carpetbag that now smelled like dead cat.

"Not all of these fellas have so many finer points as Joe Harden," I said to Marion. "Some are loyal. Some are honest to a fault. Some are good shots."

"Don't give me the name of a good shot," Marion said. "I have had my fill of that."

Maude gasped and sat straight up. "Look at this," she cried, forgetting to be as quiet as she could. "Would you just look at this? I am ruined!"

I looked. A pretty fair drawing of Maude looked back at me from the page. I pushed the newspaper down so I could read the print. "Read that out loud, would you?" Marion said, sitting back again.

AN UNLIKELY HORSE THIEF

A Story of Tragedy

On Friday night of last week, policeman Billock received the intelligence that one Maude March, a girl of but fifteen years of age, stole two horses and food supplies from the good Reverend John Peasley of Cedar Rapids. As the reverend told the story, Maude March has of recently been a matter of some concern, having gone quite mad with grief after the death of her only relative. He states that he does not care to see her punished, but returned to his care until she is seen to be of sound mind once more. Maude March has light brown hair, brown eyes, is small and thin for her age, and therefore, easily recognizable. No reward is offered for reports of her whereabouts, but a small recompense is promised for the return of a black buggy pony.

"Taking the horses was my idea," I said.

Since I was riding the pretty one, why didn't they even put my picture in the paper? I looked to see if my name showed up in the small print.

But no.

Maude March and Maude March and Maude March was

97

the only name I saw. To hear it from this paper, I didn't even exist. Marion said, "They don't want to hang you. They think you went mad with grief."

"My picture has been shown all over," Maude cried. "I'm a known horse thief, grief-stricken or not. I can't show my face anywhere ever again."

"Naw," Marion said. "This is the *Cedar Rapids Times.* Even if the Philadelphia or New York papers get a copy of this, they ain't likely to run a picture of you. They don't care much what happens out here—unless four or five people got killed as you stole those horses. You'd probably need to steal more horses too."

I could see Marion was trying hard to make her feel better.

"Are you sure?" Maude asked.

"I am," he said. "Besides which, you don't hardly look like yourself anymore, Miss Maude. Your hair is short and your face is rough and—"

Maude all but hit him with the newspaper, she shoved it back at him so fast. She flopped down and flipped the blanket over her shoulder, leaving us to look at her back.

"Maude," I said.

"Burn that paper," she said. "I don't want to see it again."

"Maude—"

"Don't speak to me."

Marion and I sat like we'd been turned to stone. For all her upset, Maude had no trouble falling asleep. Inside five minutes, Marion and I were able to whisper back and forth. He whispered, "I'm sorry," and I whispered back, "She's just touchy lately."

Maude's upset did change our mood somewhat. With as

little rustling of the paper as we could manage, Marion pointed out his own picture on the front page. Maude had missed that entirely, since her story was on page two.

"The light's too dim for my eyes. Could you read me that?" Marion asked.

BROKE JAIL

The Famous Joe Harden Escapes Hanging

About midnight of Friday night, three masked men broke into the Cedar Rapids City Jail and overcame policeman Billock. The unknown men freed the famous Joe Harden, whose exploits are widely known and read, although the publisher's claim is that they are known to be fictional.

The paper went on to give an account of the way the once much-admired Joe Harden went wild and shot up the town, killing one Miss Ruth Ann Waters, schoolteacher, who left no family.

"They make it sound like I was the only one did all that shooting," Marion said.

"Maybe they figured it was the last shot that counted," I said in cool tones.

"There was a whole bunch of fellows shot off their guns after I fell down," Marion said. "They were pretty juiced up. They're the ones who shot up the town."

That made sense. Aunt Ruthie dropped when the first shot was fired.

But something about the other story didn't hang right. I couldn't quite put my finger on it. I turned the page and read all about Maude again. I asked Marion, "Don't you think it's funny they don't mention me?"

"Don't look a gift horse in the mouth," he said.

"Aren't you worried about the fellow upstairs?" I asked Marion. "What if he'd seen this paper?"

"You're right," Marion said. "But he knows me by this name. It was too late to change it."

"Yeah, but—"

"We needed a place to stay the night," Marion said. "Joe Harden's name was likelier to be known in the hotels by now, and not for being good for two bits. We ain't all that far from Cedar Rapids."

"Should we take turns sitting up, to make sure he doesn't go for the sheriff?"

"Nah. People don't question killing so much as they question thieving, it seems to me. Most of them don't expect to get killed, but they do expect to get stole from. Some of them think if somebody got killed, he probably deserved it."

He started, like he got the meaning of what he said at the same time I did. "I'm not saying a thing against your aunt Ruthie," he said. "It's just that most killings aren't so accidental, like."

I figured he was right. I suddenly felt tired. More tired than I thought I ever could be, which was saying something, considering the way things had been going. "I'm turning in," I told him.

But once I was down, I got to thinking. I looked at Marion. "Are you a good shot? Could you hit all them bottles?"

"Yep."

"Even if you were drinking?"

"I don't drink a drop," Marion said. "Can't take the stuff too well. But in the end, it gives me some advantage."

"Don't the others notice? The ones you play cards with?"

"Nah. I set my glass down near someone else's and take their glass when it's near empty. No one ever mentions it."

Just before I fell asleep, I heard Marion chuckling. "What's funny?" I asked him.

"Joe Harden," he answered, and laughed out loud. "He sure is a wild one."

NINETEEN

IN THE CHILL DARKNESS OF EARLY MORNING, MAUDE acted like she was mad at me and Marion, both. He did just as she told us and burned the paper, for what that was worth, to get the fire going fast. I figured it wasn't the only paper left in the territory, but I didn't say so.

Marion stoked the stove till it shed a welcome warmth on the room. Then he set to trimming his beard. I went about folding up blankets and all else we had spread out to dry.

Maude mixed up flapjacks with jerky movements that spilled flour and water on the floor. I cleaned the mess up. She did not say a thank-you or even smile. Maude was not made up of forgive-and-forget clay.

At first I thought Marion might not have noticed Maude's manner. But when we sat down to eat and talk about how to go on from there, I realized Marion had spruced himself up to some advantage. He did not look much like he slept on boot-shop floors.

I hadn't had a chance to talk to Maude in private, but even before getting to Des Moines, I figured we'd do well to travel a few more days with Marion. The newspaper did change things some.

It seemed they weren't looking for two girls, but for one. No one on the lookout for Maude March, Horse Thief, would know to look for me at all. If we all traveled together, we were a man with two younger brothers in tow; no one would be on the lookout for us.

Needless to say, Marion was heavily in favor of this plan. He told me, "You can choose a name for me while we ride the trail."

Maude made a rude snorting sound.

"If you don't mind me asking, Miss Maude, how old are you?"

"I'll be sixteen in another month or so," Maude said. "How old are you?"

"Twenty-seven," Marion said.

"I thought you must be a lot older," Maude said. It was not very flattering of her to say so, but Marion did not look embarrassed.

"It's that I'm going bald," he said. "My daddy was bald to nothing but a fringe by the time he was my age. It's the way of it in my family."

"Where is your family?" Maude asked rather pointedly.

At that moment, we heard the bootmaker coming downstairs, and Maude ducked her head over her plate of flapjacks and bacon.

"I hope you can spare a platter for me," he said.

"Help yourself," Marion said, although it was Maude who'd done the cooking.

I had a bite more myself. Although my belly was full at the moment, there had been talk the day before of popping a few prairie hens, and my mouth could still water at the thought.

I mentioned this, and Maude ignored me. Marion said, "They'll be all over the place, after a day of laying low and keeping their feathers dry."

"I could eat three of them my own self," I said.

"It's best to pop only as many as you really can eat," Marion warned. "Don't ride with anything that smells too good. You're likely to attract bears."

Maude and I glanced at each other, and even though I suspected she hadn't meant to step that far out of her sulk, our glances meant the same thing. Bears? We hadn't for a moment worried about bears.

But now that Marion had mentioned them, I could think of all kinds of animal dangers we might have run into. Wolves and cats and maybe even bears. We were lucky nothing worse than bugs was attracted by the smell of those chickens we had fried up.

"Best to remember to carry your gun with you everywhere. Every time you step away from your horse, you take your gun. You step behind a bush, you take your gun."

"You never know where a nice plump meal will turn up," I said, cheerfully pushing away thoughts of disaster.

"That, too," Marion said.

"Tell me something else," I said when it looked likely he was going to leave off talking. What he told us was useful, but I wanted to take up any spaces where Maude might get in a lick or two.

"Be sure to collect dry matter the night before to start the morning's fire," he said. "Cover it up so it don't get wet with dew."

When breakfast was over and done with, the bootmaker said, "You never mentioned you traveled with no brothers, Joe."

"Now that's because people don't trust brothers," Marion said. "Not since those James and Younger boys have made a name for themselves."

"You're right about that," the bootmaker said. "I only let you in with them since I knew you from before. But it did give me a turn to see you brought company."

"That's quite a pair of boots you have there," Marion said to the man. He got up, most likely in hopes of turning the conversation. "Don't know that I've even seen any quite like them."

"Elephant skin," the bootmaker told him. "Belongs to some English feller who owns a big stretch of land north of here. Seems his brother shot an elephant over there in Africa and sent him a piece of the skin."

"You don't say," Marion said. He made a show of wiping his hands on his hankie, but in the end he only touched the boots with the inside of his wrist. "Soft, ain't it?"

"Wrinkles something awful," the bootmaker said. "They ain't the easiest pair of boots I ever made. I hope he ain't going to refuse to pay for them, ugly as they are."

"Elephant skin, you say," Marion said, ignoring the bootmaker's complaint. "Big animal. Got any scraps of the stuff left?"

"Not enough to make a wallet," the bootmaker grumbled.

"Those English fellers got a reputation for being good hunters," Marion said.

"Not this one. Money's his game, not elephants," the bootmaker said. He picked up a boot and took up stitching where I guessed he'd left off the day before. "Owns the bank. He's got plenty more land than anyone else around here, and he's looking to buy more. Bought out the mill too. Likely he figures to buy out the town."

"Never saw myself a rich man," Marion said. "Not land and money rich, both. What's he like?"

"Like a little king, that's how he is." There was more talk of the kingly banker and payrolls and land deals while Maude and I picked up after ourselves.

"Men's gossip," I heard Maude mutter to herself. I poked her with an elbow. We were going to be men ourselves. That was my message. But by the time we had picked up all our clothing, Marion had bought a pair of resoled boots for Maude. They were a near match for mine.

The bootmaker said, "I believe these'll fit, 'specially if you double up on the socks."

Maude ducked her head, as close as she was going to come to saying thank you. Which was maybe just as well if we were to convince the man we were all brothers. Men seemed to approve of a certain lack of good manners.

Marion came over and tried to tell her how to pack up so the makings for bread could be got to all at once, the way a chuck-wagon cook would do it. Maude just sulked all the while he showed her and then went ahead and did it her old way.

He saw this and went out to tend to the horses while we

finished packing up. That was no doubt the reason he told us, as soon as we were ready to go, "I've rethought it, and I think this is where we ought to part ways."

We all stood in a little back room, near the door, and had reasonable privacy if we kept our voices down. "I thought you were headed our way," I said. I had begun to like traveling with Marion, and I thought Maude liked him too, when she wasn't in a mood. I wasn't ready to leave Marion yet or for him to leave us.

"I may be," he said, "or I may not. A man of my ilk is prone to sudden turns of mind."

I didn't know what his ilk might be, and I wasn't sure it was proper to ask. I hoped Maude would say something to change his mind again, if it was all that easy to turn, but she stood by the back door, sullen and silent.

She had always been one for sulking, and she had clearly made up her mind to sulk over the ugly surprise of finding her likeness in the newspaper. Or maybe it wasn't the likeness so much as the accusation. But it wasn't likely I would know for sure what she was sulking about till she came out of it and talked to me.

"We could wait till you make up your mind one way or the other," I said to him, feeling a little desperate. If Marion came along, at least I would have someone to talk to. Maude didn't look like she would be talking for a week at least. "It's not even half light yet."

"It's been nice having you girls for company," Marion said kindly, "but I think it's best if we all go our separate ways."

Which I figured meant, no, I won't travel with you. But I needed to make sure. "You won't change your mind?"

"There's nothing to change," Marion said, noticing the bootmaker had come to stand nearby. He'd been so quiet we more or less forgot about him. "What?" Marion wanted to know.

"Nuthin'," the bootmaker said, and went back to his stitching.

TWENTY

"IT'S YOUR FAULT WE'RE TRAVELING ALONE AGAIN," I SAID, feeling mean. "You treated Marion badly."

"He killed our aunt."

"You didn't mind that so much yesterday," I pointed out. "You're only mad because of the newspaper. If you hadn't seen your picture in the newspaper, we would still have Marion here to help us along."

"We don't need his help."

"You don't know that for sure," I said. "You're the one who said 'if we make it.' "

"We'll make it."

"If we don't, if we're attacked by Indians or get drowned in some swollen river or"—I thought fast, pulling out sad, bad ends that heroes meet in dimers—"or hung for horse thieves, it will be because you drove off someone who might have protected us."

This didn't move Maude, so I took another tack.

"The Toleridge boy wasn't sweet, I understood that," I said. "Mr. Wilburn was old. I'm not sure that's really so bad, but I helped you get away. There ain't nothing wrong with

Marion. He's sweet enough and he ain't too awful old and he ain't asking you for nothing either, but still you treated him poorly."

Maude sped up on Flora and stayed a distance in front of me for another mile or so. But then she turned and headed back to me. Passed me without a word, and I knew she was headed back to Des Moines.

Maude can be bullied. She just likes to be bullied gently.

My heart lifted as I turned Goldie, unlucky as I was to ride back through a nearly visible cloud that she'd dispatched only moments before.

The saloons were not open for business at this time of day, but many of the shop doors stood open. There had been hardly anyone on the boards when we left an hour or so before, and even fewer horses on the street. Now it looked like someone had started handing out free eats, there were so many people milling about.

We didn't have to ride as far as the bootmaker's before we saw Marion's horse in front of the bank. Right off I could see Marion could do with a couple of riding partners. Why, he hadn't even hitched his horse to the post. Just left the reins laying over it, like.

Maude tied Flora and stepped away, but I called her back with a short whistle. I raised my rifle, reminding her that she was forgetting hers. I wanted to show Marion that we took his advice to heart. It might sway him if he was still of a mind to ride alone. Maude took the hint and untied her rifle. I was right behind her as she opened the door and went into the bank.

I saw everything at once.

A teller stood with his hands in the air. A second teller had stopped midway in filling a lumpy canvas sack with money. Marion stood near the tellers, his gun in one hand and another such sack in the other.

A man lay on the floor, money spilled all around him. Another man—his shirt struck me as such a bright white in the overall dim of the room—lay nearer the door.

"Marion," Maude said, shock making her voice squeak.

"Miss Maude, what are you doing here?" Marion said, looking equally surprised, but he didn't squeak.

The man nearest us made a quick motion I saw out of the corner of my eye. He reached for his gun, and just as quick, without thinking, I stomped that hand with the butt of my rifle. He yelled and dropped his pistol, so that it skittered across the floor a little.

Maude bent to pick it up, hooking it with her pinkie finger. She moved awkwardly, crossing her rifle in front of her, so that the man took a notion. He moved fast, very fast, and snatched at the barrel of Maude's rifle.

She held on with both hands, even though the pistol still dangled, and would not give up her grip on the rifle. I didn't know what to do. I looked at Marion just as he shot once and the man screamed, falling away from Maude.

I saw blood on the white shirt.

"Run, Miss Maude," Marion shouted. "Sallie! Run!"

We ran.

TWENTY-ONE

I LED AND MAUDE FOLLOWED. WE RAN OUT OF THE BANK and down the boardwalk, ran past the bank and then a dress shop, still closed. I ducked into the first narrow alley I saw, and by then Maude was pushing me from behind. I could feel the butt of the six-gun against my back, still hanging from her finger.

Behind us a volley of gunshots broke out. There were four, six, seven shots, maybe. I couldn't count them.

We broke into the open behind the buildings, where there was a scattering of small houses and other sheds. We headed for the edge of town, still running away from the bank, but there was no safe place to go. No one had yet followed us here, but it was only a matter of time.

I ran to the far side of a small barn, stopping to catch my breath. "Maude!" I said, finding two saddled horses hitched to a post. I loosed one and climbed on.

Maude didn't hesitate but was hampered by managing both the rifle and the six-gun with one hand. She passed me the gun and swung up on the other horse, kicked the animal into a lunging gallop and bent low in the saddle.

We rode straight out into the grasslands. My hat was lost in the foot running, Maude's was lost during the ride. We rode without sparing the horses, for three or four miles. At first it was exciting; I felt like we were living in the pages of a dime novel.

But then it got so the ride was just pounding, pounding, pounding, and after a while I knew I couldn't take it for much longer. We stopped at the top of a hill to look back and didn't see any sign that we were being followed.

"We better slow up some," I told Maude. "It won't do us any good to ride these horses into the ground for nothing. Let's save a little of their strength in case we need it later on."

It was only when we stopped to water the horses that I realized I'd somehow thought we would come back to having our own horses to ride, that these were only for the moment. But that wasn't true, of course.

It struck me that at only one other time in my life had the future been so uncertain, and then help was offered to us in the form of Aunt Ruthie. We didn't question this turn of events but trailed after her like goslings, setting our feet in her footsteps. These horses had looked to me like the same kind of gift. Without them, we were lost. But now we were genuine criminals. I felt bad. Guilty of wrongdoing—not at all the same feeling I'd had after making a fair trade, as when we left with the Peasleys' horses.

"We're in a fine mess," Maude said, now that we'd caught our breath enough to talk. "We don't have thing one to eat, or a pot to cook a chicken in if I shoot one. We don't even have a hat."

I had nothing to add to this. I watched the horses drink.

"And now we're horse thieves, for certain," she went on, starting to pace back and forth. She was working herself up into a fine lather. "Whoever owned these horses didn't owe us a thing. Nothing. They may not have wanted to hang me before, but they're going to want to hang me now."

"They'll hang us both," I said.

Maude stopped pacing. "Is that supposed to make me feel better?"

"Yes."

"Maybe you should turn back," Maude said in a voice I didn't know.

"Turn back?"

"I mean, go home. Before we get into any worse trouble. Just go home and pretend this morning never happened. Tell them the last you saw of me, I was riding north."

"You're talking crazy," I said, and started to cry. I didn't mean to cry, but once begun, I couldn't stop it either.

"We could both go back, maybe," she said, mopping me up with the tail of her shirt. "I'll let them think I'm crazy as a bedbug, at least for another week or two. It'll be grief, like the paper said. Mr. Wilburn might still have me once I come to my senses."

I decided to ignore this manner of talk. It made me feel lost in a way I hadn't been before. Even if the horses were forgiven, even if things worked out so that people believed Maude had for a few days gone mad, it would be a long time before anyone trusted her again. I wouldn't want to go back to that either.

It seemed like a very long time ago that I thought life was simple. Not easy, but simple, in the way that it went from day to day, and we were safe. At least we felt safe. I had not done away with the idea that life could be that way again, but I was certain that I could never go back to it, or even find it elsewhere, without Maude.

"We aren't going back, either one of us," I said as if Maude was the one who'd been doing the crying. "Mrs. Peasley will put chains around our ankles, and not a soul will speak up for us."

"If Mrs. Peasley doesn't, the law will," Maude agreed. She looked a little lost herself. "It's too late for us, Sallie; there is no one to save us but each other."

"Is that supposed to make me feel better?" I asked her.

She rolled her eyes in answer.

"We'd better watch for a chicken," Maude said, boarding her horse. "Or maybe that bear Marion warned us about. If I shoot us a bear, we'll have a blanket."

"Only if I consent to do the skinning," I said, "and I might not. Skinning a bear is a lot to ask of a ten-year-old."

"You're eleven," Maude said as we started off again, our horses somewhat refreshed. "At least that's what I was given to believe. But I'd guess you were twenty if you were a day. Are you watching for chickens?"

She was right about everything, of course. We weren't hungry now, but we would be soon. And we would be cold. These horses didn't carry a blanket roll. I didn't care to point out just yet that they didn't carry any cooking utensils either. Whoever was going to ride them wasn't planning to go far. It was doubtful they were range riders. More likely, ranchers.

My thoughts turned back to range riders, and colored the morning's episode with a rosy glow. It wasn't much fun while it was happening, but it was a good memory to embroider. It made me ride tall in the saddle.

"We did that old plow horse a kindness," I said after a time, "leaving it behind. It could never have taken such a rough ride. It would've keeled over dead, and we'd have been nabbed for sure."

Maude didn't reply to this. She was deep in her own thoughts.

"Do you think Marion meant for us to run to our horses?" I asked.

"I'm pretty sure he never meant for us to run past them," she said.

I guess the whole business had begun to get to us because we looked at each other and laughed. We had a good, long laugh, and I don't think either of us knew what was funny.

"What do you think happened to him?" I asked Maude after a time.

"I don't know," she said wearily. "All those gunshots... Did you have any idea he was going to rob a bank?"

"No." Now that the question stood in the air, I asked, "Do you think he really is Joe Harden?"

"Sallie!" Maude shouted. "What is the matter with you?" she wailed.

"Nothing," I said.

"Marion is not as nice as we believed him to be," Maude said in a sharp tone. "Even though we knew he killed Aunt Ruthie, we trusted him." She broke off to sob loudly and sob long; the cords in her throat were drawn taut as wire. Finally she said, "He shot that man right before our very eyes. Did you see that? He's dangerous, Sallie, and even if he's famous, we still do not admire him. Do you understand?"

"I don't admire him," I said. "I just like him. I can't help it."

"It's not right to like him," Maude said. She blew her nose into the cuff of her man-sized shirt and then rolled the cuff up again. "We have to hate him. He killed Aunt Ruthie."

"It's not right to hate him either," I said. "Aunt Ruthie believed it was wrong to hate, even though she didn't much like anybody."

"Let's not talk about it anymore," Maude said. "Do you have any idea where we are?"

"We rode west," I said, thinking on it. "Mostly west."

"Are we still headed mostly west?" Maude asked, looking around her like there would be a printed sign.

I looked at the sun and decided it must be coming on noon. But it would be another hour or two at least before I knew for sure what direction we were headed in. I had to get a look at my compass.

"Just keep going," I told her.

TWENTY-TWO

ALONG ABOUT MIDAFTERNOON, WE TOPPED A RISE AND found a small town laid out before us. Behind it ran a river, a river we would have to cross sooner or later. From here, we could see a horseman being ferried across on a wooden raft.

The raft was pulled across on rope traces, but we could see the race of the river put a little strain on the whole works. Before I could get my hopes up, Maude said, "Let's ride north."

"I'm hungry and so are you," I said. "Let's go on in and get the supplies we need. Then we'll take the ferry."

"What if they recognize me?" Maude said. "Even if they don't have a newspaper, the sheriff could have my description. I've already been in one shoot-out today. I don't think I can tolerate another."

"We have to have something to eat. It's too late in the year to hope for corn or berries to be picked."

"You go," Maude said.

"Do I look passable?"

"You look a mess. But you don't look like a red Indian anymore. You just look like you've been living on the land."

Maude waited for me to say I'd go, and when I said nothing, she tried acting bossy. "Get us each a hat. Thank goodness I kept the money in my pocket, or we'd be in really big trouble."

"I don't know," I said, but I did know. I didn't want to go in there alone. I had a bad feeling about it.

"I don't see any way around it," Maude said, softening a little. "I'll wait for you east of town."

"No, wait for me here," I said, seeing the flaw in her planning. "I should ride out the way I came in. That way no one will know for sure which way we were heading."

"All right." She gave me part of Aunt Ruthie's nest egg.

I watched her count out five dollars and change. I said, "That's all?"

"We have to hold on to as much as we can. So don't spend any on foolishness. Except peppermints. Have we lost them too?"

"No," I said, "I have the last few here in my pocket." We'd come to depend on the peppermints, and we ate one or two of them daily. Marion liked them too, and considered we were awful stingy with them.

"Better get some more," Maude said. "No dimers. We can both eat peppermints, but I'm not buying dimers."

I hesitated, thinking longingly of a time when I would have argued that was unfair. Maude must have thought I was working out my argument because she said, "You can read the one you have until our fortunes change."

As it happened, I hadn't stuffed one into my shirt that morning, not knowing we were going to lose all our belongings, but I didn't say so. I started out, making a list in my head of the bare necessaries, when an ugly thought popped in. I rode back to Maude and said, "You won't disappear on me, will you? It won't be a kindness."

"I'm not brave enough for that," she said.

Still, I kept looking back over my shoulder. I needed to see her there, sitting that horse. My nerve was shot.

The town was smaller than it looked from a distance. The one general store was sizable enough. It carried everything from saddles and horse liniment to farm machinery, ready-made clothing, dry goods, household items, and finally, food-stuffs. Sausages and cheese hung from the rafters, filling the air with a smell that made my mouth water.

Two men and a woman in aprons helped customers in the aisles. They only barely looked up as I tried on hats. The woman helped me hunt up matches and a can opener. They didn't bother me or worry about what was I up to. The secret of this is only touch what you plan to buy.

A girl about Maude's age worked the counter where I did my food shopping, and she wasn't much given to curiosity. I chose what we could eat on the run if need be. I was so taken with the smell of fresh-baked cookies in a box on the counter that I paid a dear price for as many as could be put in a small sack.

The girl wanted to put everything in two boxes but was willing enough to put it all in feed sacks when I told her I was on horseback. I remembered the peppermints at the last minute and added some licorice whips and toffees to the candy order.

I climbed into the saddle to tie one of the feed sacks to the pommel, and then got off again to get the other sack off the ground. That's when I heard a man say, "You're mighty young to be a hand at the Fieldings' ranch."

I looked up and saw a lawman looking down at me. His glance moved to the brand on the horse's rump. "My pa works there," I said, going weak all over.

"You're awful far from home, aren't you?" he asked, taking the weight of the feed sack so I could climb on. I needed the help.

"We're going to look at a horse," I said. "Another two days' ride."

"Bob Fielding riding with you?" he said, looking up and down the short street.

"Nope," I said, hoping this would be the right answer. The last thing I needed was a lawman's company. "It's just my pa and me for this trip," I said, tying up the feed sack.

"You tell your pa's boss I said hello," he said. "Landers is the name."

"I will," I said. "Thanks for the hand."

I rode slow as I moved away from him, deciding to ride toward the smithy at the end of town. Landers might get the impression my pa was there, getting a horse shod or something. Whatever he thought, I hoped he'd lose interest in me.

I didn't dare look back over my shoulder. What I did was ride to the smithy, got down slow and easy, and went inside. From the darkness of the interior, I made sure I was no longer being watched.

"Help ya?" someone said from behind me.

"I need oats, five pounds," I said. This was true enough. We needed to be able to hobble these horses too. "I need a length of rope. Two lengths would be better."

He added them to the bill, pretty much finishing off my little wad of cash. "Fill your canteen?" he asked, pointing. One hung next to the saddlebags, half hidden by the saddle blanket.

I hefted the canteen, trying to look like I was familiar with it. Filled up, it had to be. "Thanks anyway," I said. I looked down the street again and couldn't see the lawman anywhere. I rode out of town, moving at a leisurely pace.

I didn't tell Maude about the lawman. I figured it was enough one of us was as nervous and jerky as a turkey two days before Thanksgiving. "Let's get moving," I said as I rode up to her. I passed her the hat I'd gotten for her.

"What did you get us to eat?"

"Sausage, cheese, corn bread, and crackers. Tinned things, but no fish." Maude and I were not fond of tinned fish. "I bought a knife. I was supposed to look like I was picking up odds and ends. I couldn't very well start buying pots and pans and platters. We'll pick up the other things piecemeal."

"Give me some of that corn bread, will you?"

"I wish we could have taken the ferry," I said, because the river looked cold. It looked fast too, although the surface was smooth enough. But that only meant it was deep enough to drown in.

I was thinking I wished we'd taken the ferry before I ran into that lawman. But when Maude looked back, I added, "This way is best; no one will have any stories to tell the newspaper about Maude March paying to use the ferry."

TWENTY-THREE

WE FOLLOWED THE RIVER FOR A MILE, THEN MADE OUR preparations to cross it. I wanted to go on a little ways, following the river, but Maude was determined to cross sooner than later. We cinched up the saddles and took off our heavy pants, to be hung around our necks with our boots stuffed in them.

Remembering a lesson learned from reading *Lamar Lafayette, River Rat,* I divvied up the matches, and we put them in our shirt pockets. If one of us fell into the water, we might still save some.

Maybe we were lucky to hit the river where we did because I had been right; it ran fast as well as cold. We were lucky not to be riding old Flora or that buggy pony too. Mr. Fielding's horses were strong swimmers, and still the river carried us more than a mile before we got to the other side.

I couldn't feel it when my feet came out of the water. We let the horses walk in wide circles till the water stopped running off them, and we took this opportunity to unburden ourselves, dropping boots and sacks to the ground. I barely felt my feet touch the ground when I got off the horse.

"Sallie," Maude said when she came over to me a minute later, "are you all right?"

"Just like you," I said, because her teeth were chattering as hard as mine. She had put her pants and boots back on, though.

"Why are you sitting here?"

"My feet," I said. They were real white. Maude rubbed them dry with the horse's rag till tears poured from my eyes. The warmer my feet got, the more they hurt. They were at their worst when she made me put my socks and boots back on. "Now walk," she said, "real easy."

"Should have been going barefoot like you were there for a while," I said, blubbering. "I'd've toughened up some."

"You don't need to be tough," she said. "You're only a little girl."

"I remember I used to be."

While I walked in circles, she wiped her horse dry. The pain in my feet subsided after a few minutes, leaving only the dark echo of an ache as I rubbed down my horse. Maude put a wet feed sack on the ground and gave the horses some oats.

I'd hoped to hang on to that feed sack for a while, but when the horses had finished with it, it was too full of horse slobber even to fold it up, let alone fill it up again. Maude picked it up by one corner and threw it into the river.

We had to walk for a time to warm ourselves through and through, the way we'd learned from Marion. We were lucky Maude thought to put the corn bread and crackers in her shirt and had told me to do the same with anything else that would be killed by the wet. As it was, the labels came off the cans when they got wet, so we couldn't tell the peaches from the beans.

I dug out the sack with the oatmeal cookies. Maude's eyes lit up. They were some broken up, being mashed under my shirt, but the crumbs tasted just as good to us as a whole cookie.

We rode past sundown and forded another river. This one was not fast, but it was mighty cold. Because the night was chill, we weren't going to dry out so well either. I missed the change of clothes we didn't have anymore.

Maude complained about the mean pace, but I didn't let up. I was worried that lawman would get wind of Mr. Fielding's stolen horses and come looking for us. We needed to put in more miles than anyone would believe we could.

Maude didn't complain so much once we were over the second river. Of course, she was cold, and that took some of the bite out of her. We walked fast for some time.

Twice we rode past homesteads where dogs barked. Where light shone from the windows. The smell of wood smoke brought self-pitying tears to our eyes. We had no blankets; I'd been afraid to buy them.

"We must've made thirty miles today," I said. I hoped.

"I'd feel a lot warmer all over about that if we did it headed in the right direction," Maude said.

"This *is* the right direction," I said, stung to the marrow. "I'm not lost."

"Never mind," Maude said. "I'm just feeling moody."

"Speaking of warm," I said, "let's find some place and build a fire."

"No fire."

"Maude."

"No fire. Too many farms around here. We don't want people coming out to see who's camped on their land."

I slid off my horse to warm myself again, walking. But I was tired, and warmth was something that took a lot of energy. Maude was shortly walking beside me and set a pace that did, in a while, warm us.

"I'm sorry, Sallie," she said.

"For what?" I said, already knowing what the answer would be.

"For getting you into this."

"You didn't—"

"I should have just married Mr. Wilburn and thought myself lucky."

"You should have married him so *I* could feel lucky," I said. "Think how many dimers he would have brought me between now and the wedding." Maude reached over and swatted me, then laughed. The moment passed, and things were all right again.

When finally we did pick a place to spend the night, we thought of turning one of the saddlebags into a trough for the horses. We still needed that last feed sack. Maude hobbled both horses.

Emptying the saddlebags from my horse, I found a currycomb, and a rough cloth, some carrots. Mr. Fielding, whoever he was, took good care of his horse. Further down, I found a tin spoon, a real pottery cup, and a few other items that would come in real handy. Fish hooks and a reel of line. A saw-toothed knife to gut the fish. Some cartridges for a gun we didn't have. Just as well, since the cartridges got wet.

"It feels strange to be going through somebody's belongings," Maude said, refusing for the time being to look through the bags on her horse.

"Someone's going through ours," I said, like it didn't bother me. But it did. It felt wrong. I told myself this kind of wrong was just being practical. I told myself we couldn't afford to worry about right and wrong just this minute, but I knew that wasn't true either. This was the time to abide by right and wrong, when we were being tested.

Then I found something else in the bottom of the bag. A dimer! I lit a match to get a look at the damp cover. I figured, with my luck, it would be something I'd already read. But in fact it was something I'd never seen before: *Gallop Garrity, the Gritty Cowpoke.*

Maude had pulled the scraps of dress fabric out of her pocket. She spread them over her leg and smoothed out the wrinkles. She looked almost happy.

I blew out the match with a lighter heart than I'd had moments before.

We ate potted meat from the tins—it went well enough with the last of the corn bread—and peaches. We were glad to have the spoon. We were glad to have the saddle blankets too. We slept on one and covered ourselves with the other, lying back to back.

"Sallie? There's something been bothering me all day."

"What's that?"

"Marion's horse. It wasn't tied to the hitching post. Do you remember?"

I knew she didn't want to admit she was worried about Marion. "I remember. I pointed it out to you before we went into the bank."

Maude said, "The gunshots didn't scare it away, did they? It was used to gunshots."

"I didn't see any horses on the way out," I said, and we laughed again. It was that terrible laughter that, I knew now, came from surviving something that could've killed you.

TWENTY-FOUR

WE STARTED OUT BEFORE LIGHT THE NEXT MORNING. We couldn't have started a fire even if we thought it was a good idea; the ground was wet with a heavy dew. We woke up cold and miserable.

We walked, passing a tin of beans and the spoon back and forth to each other. I had hoped for peaches, but when the can was opened, it was beans. "You should have put the beans in one sack and the peaches in the other," Maude complained. "You knew we had to cross that river." She had the sniffles.

"Don't go getting sick now," I said.

"Why not?" she said in her most sullen tone. She wasn't awful fond of beans, and we hadn't saved one crumb of the corn bread or the cookies for the morning. She didn't want the crackers either; it would have ruined her mad if something suited her.

"It'll be a terrible embarrassment if we can't ride the range for a few weeks without catching our death," I said. "Wild Woolly has been lost in the Yukon for longer than that, and he didn't even get sniffles."

"Guess you better ride with him next time," she muttered.

The sun finally came up high enough to warm us. But it didn't do enough to keep Maude from working up to a cough, a hard, choking cough that made her face turn dark before it would let up.

We stopped talking, since that could bring it on. The peppermints staved it off, so Maude took one peppermint after another all the livelong day. I was glad we had a plentiful supply.

That night we slept in an abandoned log cabin. It was breezy; a lot of the mud chinking in the walls had dried up and crumbled away. But the chimney was in good working order.

The furniture had been broken up some. There was nothing about the place that looked like anyone had even come there to get out of the rain lately. There were no footprints, and a thick layer of dust had settled over everything. We burned the square bench seats, the table legs, and the smaller pieces of the bed frame.

We had the warmth of the fire, that was something, but we didn't have it to ourselves for long. Maude insisted that we bring the horses indoors too. "I don't want to be cleaning up horse plop in the middle of the night," I said.

"I'm willing to take my chances with horse plop," Maude said. "I just don't care to let my horse out of my sight."

The horses proved well behaved, and we slept without disturbance. Even Maude's cough seemed to leave her alone. We woke to broad daylight and an unfamiliar sound. "Maa-aa-aa, maa-aa-aa."

Maude sat up, shivering. "What's that?"

"A baby?"

"Maa-aa-aa."

"Sheep," she said, her voice filled with dread. Sheep meant people. Sheep most likely meant somebody did live here after all.

I looked out the cutout that served as a window, squinting into the bright sunlight. Even once my eyes were used to it, I didn't see anyone on horseback; I didn't see anyone at all.

"Maa-aa-aa."

I went to the door and pulled it open. There was a goat right outside and a snake nearer yet.

I stood stock-still. The snake was coiled and had turned my way. The rattle alerted Maude.

"Don't move," she said, reaching for her rifle. "The important thing is, don't move. They don't like it if you move."

I didn't move.

"Maa-aa-aa." The snake swerved back to threaten the goat.

Maude moved gingerly in her bare feet, but still that snake took notice. The rattle sounded again, and one of the horses blew air out of its nostrils. The snake's tongue flickered, tasting the air, as its rattle kept up a steady beat.

One shot rang out, and the snake's head disappeared entirely.

The goat took off, lickety-split. The snake's body darted out in little searching motions, then settled back into a coil, the rattles still going. That made the hair on my arms dance. I did a little hop-step to shake off the willies. This excited the snake into making a strike.

"Maude!"

She had turned away to sit down. "I feel sore all over," she said, resting her head against her hand.

When Maude's rifle butt knocked on the floor, that snake body struck at the door with a thump. I saw it. I heard it, even though my ears still rang from the gunshot. I thought it must be a trick of my mind. I stared at the hole in the floorboards, that was real enough, and so was the spatter of blood. The snake's head was gone; any fool could see that.

The horses had startled at the rifle shot but were much more disturbed at the rattle of the snake's tail. They shuffled around, ears laid back tight, which was not a good sign. We had not bothered to hobble them since they were indoors, but we did put rope loops around their necks once we removed their headgear. I reached for the nearest horse, but it shied away from me, eyes wild.

I was afraid one or both of them would bolt, making this cabin a new back doorway. I got a bed slat that was propped against the wall and went back to move the snake's body out of the doorway. I'd no sooner touched it than it struck at the stick.

I yelped and jumped back.

"What?" Maude said, looking up.

I touched the snake and again it struck, not once, but three times, in a maddened way. This so unnerved me that I dropped the stick.

Maude made a sound like a cat mewing.

The headless body threw itself at the only victim it could find—the stick. In all its writhing, the snake fell across the doorsill and coiled for another strike. The horses showed cracked yellow teeth as they clomped around.

"Shoot it again," I cried. I did get hold of both horses and wrapped one dangling lead rope a few times around a hook on the wall, knowing that wouldn't hold the horse long. I led the other horse to the opposite side of the room and hoped for the best.

"I think I'm going to be sick to my stomach," Maude said.

The snake had begun to make little jabbing motions into the air, like it was searching for us. The rattle never stopped. "I don't think I can hit it again," Maude said. "But if I do, what will we do if that doesn't kill it?"

"I don't know," I said. "Just shoot it before we lose these horses."

She took up my rifle with shaking hands, and the snake did indeed turn toward her and make several more frenzied strikes, driving Maude to the other side of the room. "Shoot, Maude!"

She did, with both eyes closed, it looked like to me. So it was largely a matter of good luck that she hit that thing and cut it in three pieces, all of which wriggled wildly on the floor, the rattle making a constant racket.

Maude dropped a saddle blanket over the whole mess and shoved it outside. The place went amazingly dark and quiet when she shut the door. She sighed and set to picking up our stuff, and packing everything she possibly could into the saddlebags.

One of the horses had knocked the sack of oats on its side, spilling them across the floor. I got a splinter scraping them up. "If this isn't a fine start to the day," I said.

"It's the start we've got," Maude said, sounding an awful lot like Aunt Ruthie. "Let's make the most of it."

She went out for the other saddle blanket and brought it back, saying, "It knows it's dead now." She slapped the saddle blankets over the horses' backs, and we saddled them up. That was Maude's way, and Aunt Ruthie's too. They could neither one of them be called a whiner.

Once we were outside on the horses, things settled into the pace we had grown used to. Almost familiar enough to call it home, although not that comfortable. I began to think about how well Maude handled herself, considering she didn't like snakes worse than me. "That was fine shooting," I said, thanking her for saving my life.

"I should never have neglected your shooting lessons," she said. "If it was the other way around, I'd be dying now, and you'd be alone in the world."

"It's never too late to start."

"We'll buy ammunition today," she said, "should we come across a town. We'll get blankets for ourselves too. We may not always be lucky enough to have a fire."

"I don't know that I can learn to shoot the head off a snake," I said. But Maude didn't want to talk about it.

TWENTY-FIVE

WE CAME ACROSS THE GOAT AFTER ABOUT HALF AN hour's ride. She was crying again, and the reason was easy to see. She needed milking. She acted like she remembered us as I put a tether rope around her neck. She let me fill our pottery cup over and over. After Maude and I drank our fill, I stripped the rest of her milk into the dirt.

"Who do you figure she belongs to?" I asked.

"Nobody, judging from the filthy state she's in," Maude said. She seemed to consider the animal's other state, that of sheer misery. "Maybe she had a kid and something carried it off. A bobcat or something."

"I'm taking her with us," I said.

"How are we going to travel with a nanny goat tagging along?"

"Since we aren't moving so fast as it is, she's not going to hold us up all that much," I argued. "We're bound to pass a farm soon. We'll set her loose near enough that someone will find her."

"Someone will find her anyway. We did."

135

"She was nearly bit by that rattler. I know exactly how she feels," I said. "She looks like an orphan to me."

"All we have in common with that goat is our dirty faces."

"We drank her milk," I said, "and now I just don't feel right about leaving her to fend for herself."

I'd begun to regret this decision an hour later. We'd eaten our breakfast in the saddle, cheese and crackers, then goat's milk, then more cheese and crackers. We were ready to put some miles on the day, but we were still moving along at the nanny goat's pace.

It halted Maude and me in our tracks when we heard laughter. The goat trotted on ahead till it ran out of line and then looked like it was leading the horse.

After a moment we heard it again. High, girlish laughter.

It came from behind some blueberry bushes off to one side of us.

We rode over and found two little girls in the middle of a tea party. One of them wasn't so little, she was nearly my age, but she seemed awful young to me. They stopped their play and looked up at us, a little afraid.

"You are just the two we've been looking for," I said in a friendly way.

"We are?" the older one said.

"We found this goat here, wandering around all by her lonesome and looking for a home." I got off the horse so I wouldn't look so tall.

"Does it butt?" It was just that girl and me doing the

talking. The little one and Maude sat like they'd been struck dumb.

"Not that I've seen," I said, and joined her in looking the goat over for any sign of bad habits. "Her milk tastes good."

"My ma wants a goat," the girl said. "I'll take her, if she isn't mean."

"I don't believe this one's mean." I led the goat around so the girl would see. That animal acted like she thought she was the star of a parade. It made me glad I took the trouble to find her a home, seeing her show off like that with her rumpled coat and dirty face. "She needs a little cleaning up," I said.

This girl was not put off by a few smudges. "We'll take her."

"Shall I tie her to this bush till you're ready to take her home?"

"I'll take her now," the girl said. "We can come back here later."

"Where do you live?" I asked her.

"That way."

I nodded. "We're traveling a different way. Can you manage on your own?"

The girl took the rope and started off; that was all the answer I got. Her little sister sat for another few seconds, then got up to follow. Maude and I waited till they moved out of sight behind some more bushes. "Now that looks like a happy ending," I said as we started out again.

"You never know," she said, turning down the offer of a peppermint.

"What do you mean?" It wasn't too late to snatch that goat back if I had to. But Maude wasn't thinking about the goat.

"Those girls. They could have been us the day our folks died. They were about the same age we were then. And we played tea party that day. I remember. We played tea party to stay out from underfoot."

TWENTY-SIX

MAUDE AND I RODE QUIET AS WE PICKED UP SOME MILES. When we stopped again, as we came across a railroad track aimed in a southwesterly direction, she was feeling very low. "If we follow these rails, they might take us straight into Missouri," she said. "The riding would be a lot easier."

"I don't think we should risk it," I said, thinking a posse might guess two green girls would follow laid track when they could.

"I don't think anyone would go on looking for us this long. They're looking for Marion, mostly."

"Let's don't do it," I said. I didn't want to say so, but everything I'd read in those dimers made me think it didn't matter who the posse caught, so long as they caught somebody they could hang.

"All right, then," she said. "Give me a piece of that licorice you're harboring."

"You don't like licorice."

"That's why I want some. I don't want to ruin peppermints for myself by eating them when I don't feel well."

As the day wore on, she didn't eat much other than

licorice and began to complain of a sore throat. I got worried. I had no idea what we would do if she got sick out here.

"What's that up ahead?" Maude asked me some time later.

I couldn't see a thing. I'd finally had to accept it; Maude's eyes were better suited to range riding than were mine. She didn't see all that well up close. She complained the tiny print in the Bible looked fuzzy, and it gave her a turn to thread a needle, but she could see a crow out of sight. I wondered if that wasn't what made her such a good shot.

We rode on a bit and she said, fast and low, "It's a rider. He's going the same way we are."

"What'll we do?" I said.

"Stay behind him."

"What if he finds out we're here?" I said. This was her question the other day, and I thought it was a good one.

"We'll know it if he does. He'll turn off one way or the other. Or he'll ride back to find out who we are."

"You've toughened up, Maude," I said admiringly. "You're real good at range riding too."

"Now that's high praise, coming from you," Maude said with a grin.

We followed the man for two hours before he dropped out of sight. Maude's hair liked to stand on end. "I knew it. We should have ridden north," she said, her toughness fading fast.

I would have replied smartly to her remark about riding north, but she added, "I hope you know what to do now."

I thought quickly; many of the stories I'd read had situations such as this. "Keep your rifle cocked," I said. "Get down and walk. Stay between the horses. And then we'll move up on him real slow."

We walked for some time before we got a whiff of wood smoke on the air. "He's made camp," I said. "There must be a hollow up ahead."

"Now what?"

"Wait here," I whispered, and gave her the reins to my horse.

Maude didn't wait but followed, staying only a few steps behind me. This was annoying, but I couldn't argue about it. I moved through the grass as quietly as I could and found I was right; he had set up camp in a hollow.

The closer we got, the sweeter the air smelled. My stomach started to growl. Before it could give me away, I stepped up on a ridge of land that dropped off sharply.

"We've got the drop on you, so just sit real still," I said.

"I've been waiting for you," Marion said without turning around. "I threw on some fatback and sliced you some real fine bread. I didn't think it would take you so long to get the drop on me, so I'm afraid the meal's grown cold."

A brief bewilderment crossed Maude's face. Then she set about making herself at home. She led our horses down the rise and hobbled them the way Marion had shown us. Once I saw we were to stay, I slid down the rise on my butt and headed over to take the saddle off my horse. We worked over the horses in silence.

I noticed Marion had shaved his grizzled beard off. I kept sneaking glances; it was like looking at a new man. A strangely young man. He was looking back, one time I glanced, and I wished he'd turn his back to us, so I could talk to the Marion I knew best.

It was not until we had finished that he came up with something to say. "I'm glad to see you had the good sense to steal yourselves some better horses."

"All our worldly goods were tied to that plow horse, including my momma's Bible," Maude complained as she sat down by the fire.

I had already beat her to it and stretched my fingers toward the warmth. The one thing I missed about town living was warmth.

"We don't have a blanket," she said, "or a change of dry clothing, and if I didn't have some money in my pocket, we wouldn't have had a bite to eat this whole livelong time."

I didn't even try to point out it wasn't Marion's fault we hadn't run for our horses. Neither did he.

Maude had another bone to pick with Marion. "You've gotten us into a heap of trouble," she said. "If there was one thing we didn't need more of, it was trouble."

I had finally figured out what really bothered me about the beard. He now looked a whole lot more like the Joe Harden on the dimer covers; if Marion had a little more hair in front, he'd have looked exactly like him. Maude didn't seem to notice his new face. She didn't say one word about it. But then neither had I.

"I'm sorry," Marion said. "It's the life I lead. You can go along for years with people looking at you like you're some kind of hero. Then, one bad break, and you're a hunted man. Once you're a hunted man, it's a lot easier to act like one."

"I believe it was Aunt Ruthie who got the bad break," Maude said.

Marion's face flushed dark and for a minute he didn't say anything. When he did, he had decided to ignore the remark about Aunt Ruthie. "I'm talking about the bank now. I can't help that you were seen with me," he said. "You wouldn't let me out of your sight."

"I suppose you're right," Maude said. "But that wouldn't have been the case if you'd told us you planned to rob the bank."

"I didn't plan," Marion said. "I just watch for opportunities and seize them when they come along. I never had the opportunity to rob a bank before."

"You mean you would have robbed a bank if you'd had the chance?" I asked. I would never have needed to ask the old Joe Harden that question, but now that we had turned this corner where Joe wasn't even Joe anymore, I couldn't be sure of anything.

"No, no," Marion said. "It was an act of desperation. I've never been threatened with hanging either, before I accidentally killed your aunt Ruthie. I thought if I had enough money to get to the Oregon territories, I could start over. Go straight again."

I was heartened by this whole conversation, in some way. I had not given much thought to the matter from Marion's side of things, but it made sense to me that he didn't regard himself as a murderer any more than we regarded ourselves as horse thieves.

"So the bootmaker told you about the payroll, and

it seemed like as good a time as any," Maude said, her temper rising.

"That's about it," Marion said as if we were all reaching an understanding. His problem was, he didn't understand Maude.

"Why, oh, why did you do it?" she cried, throwing the last piece of her bread at him. He startled, but otherwise took this treatment in stride.

"I've been down on my luck for a while now," he said. "I thought I might turn it around."

Maude yelled, "By robbing a bank?"

I'd hoped Maude might be more forgiving once Marion said he had never done this before. But I could see that idea was dead in the water. "You owe us some of that money," I said.

"Sallie!" Maude swatted me hard enough to bowl me over.

"It's true," I said. "We were his partners in that robbery, whether we meant to be or not. We deserve a cut."

"We were not his partners," Maude said. "Don't ever say that again."

"We helped," I said.

Marion said, "If you ask me, you were mostly in the way."

"Oh, yes, you had things well in hand before we got there," Maude said bitingly.

"There's no need to get into a fight over this," Marion said.

Seeing her attention was entirely taken up with Marion, I folded bacon into a slice of bread and took a bite. Maude had only begun to get the need to swat someone out of her system.

"Did you kill that man in the bank?" she wanted to know,

thwacking him on the shoulder with the flat of her hand. He reared back a little, but otherwise sat still for it. "Is he dead? I want to know. Did you murder that man?"

"How did you get away?" I asked him as I enjoyed the taste of bacon in my mouth. "The town was full awake. We heard shots too." Luckily for Marion, this was something that interested Maude enough to stop her in midswing to wait for the answer.

"I know this Indian trick for riding at the side of my horse. If the shooters don't hit the horse, they probably won't get the rider either." After a moment he added, "Of course, the horse has to be willing to go along with it."

"Where'd you learn all these Indian tricks, anyway?" I asked.

"Aw, a man picks these things up if he lives from place to place, the way I do," Marion said bashfully.

"He learns how to rob banks too, I guess," Maude said.

"Now I hope you aren't going to go on holding that against me," Marion said.

"That bacon goes down real well, Maude." I hoped to distract her from picking more of a fight with Marion. We could do with his company. He knew a lot of things we needed to learn.

She sighed and turned her attention to the food. I could see Marion was burning to explain himself. However, he understood Maude well enough to let her put that first bite into her mouth.

"If you and your sister had a chance to make out all right in that town, I never would have robbed the bank," Marion said finally. "I wouldn't have sent you off on your own either."

"It's not just the bank," Maude said. "We weren't really horse thieves before."

"I know you thought that way," Marion said, "but the law thought different. When you take a man's horse, even if it's an old plow horse, you're a thief. It don't matter even if the horse's owner did you worse. It's your own actions that count against you."

"They might hang us too," Maude pointed out. He'd gotten her all worked up again with his remarks about the horses. "They might hang us by the neck until dead," she said when Marion didn't seem to hear the mention of hanging.

I wished Marion would come up with an answer that would settle Maude, so I could relax. If it was me she was talking to, she would hit me right on the head, and I figured any minute Marion would get his. It didn't matter he was pouring coffee; Maude hated it when somebody didn't listen.

But Marion just handed her the cup of coffee, and she took a swallow. "It's sweet," she said in surprise.

"I try to carry a little sugar for hard days," he said.

"Do you figure we're safe here?" Maude asked him. "Are you sure nobody followed you but us?"

"They followed me, but I doubled back on a branch of the river and let them pass me by. That's an Indian trick too. Needs a fast horse, but I've got that."

Maude said, "Nothing worse than a man bragging about how fine he is."

"I passed you too," Marion said, grinning. "Spotted you and passed you by before I slowed up to let you catch me."

Maude gave a snort that would have done a hog proud. Despite this, Marion gave us one of his blankets. It made me feel like he was taking care of us, but Maude only scolded him for the loss of her quilt. It looked to me like she was running out of steam.

"She's somewhat crabby," I told him. "She's got a sore throat."

"For how long?"

"It started yesterday, with a cough."

"Let's get some sleep," Maude said in a tone that made me think of Aunt Ruthie.

But Marion threw a few of the morning's twigs under his fry pan. He started a new fire to melt the grease. "You got a clean rag?"

I had only the toweling for the horse. But I went through Maude's saddlebags, as yet unplumbed, and found a white shirt. Marion tore the back out of the shirt and had me put the remains back into the saddlebag. "You may need it for something later on," he said. "Or if you put a new back on it, you still have a shirt."

He took a little can of turpentine out of his saddlebags and doused the rag, then folded it and poured a little grease on it. "Here," he said to Maude, "wrap this around your throat. Get under the blanket and breathe in the stink."

I expected Maude to voice a loud complaint, but she must have been feeling worse than I thought. She settled down quickly to making a warm space, the saddle blankets beneath and Marion's blanket atop. Maude and I slept as warm as the night before, even without a fire.

Marion was right about one thing. The turpentine did stink.

TWENTY-SEVEN

"DID YOU THINK UP ANOTHER NAME?" I ASKED MARION AS we saddled up the next morning.

"I'm thinking Dusty," he said. "I don't know the second part yet."

"Dusty Har de Har Har," Maude said in a mean tone as she came out from behind a bush. Her cough was gone and so was the sniffle. She claimed not to have a trace of sore throat left, but she had not thanked Marion for his trouble.

She'd been sharp with him once or twice already, and the sun hadn't yet burned all the pink off the horizon. I worried he would leave us flat, the way he did after the boot shop. I planned to speak with her about it as soon as we got a minute alone. But Marion decided to have it out with her right then.

"I have explained myself more than I had to, Miss Maude. I won't explain myself anymore. If you don't care to ride with me, you and Sallie here can pick your direction, and I'll ride in another."

Maude shot him one of those narrow-eyed looks that should've sent him packing right then, but range riders are made of stern stuff. We all got on our horses and rode off in the general direction of Missouri, which is to say, mostly south but some west too. I had not had a chance to check my compass.

After a time, even Maude's kinks worked themselves out, more or less. She didn't talk much, but she wasn't mean either. Marion and I talked a good deal. "How come you're sleeping on shop floors if you have all that money from robbing banks?" I asked him, which was a mistake.

"For the first thing, I never robbed a bank before," Marion said as if I'd hurt his feelings some. "I said that, didn't I?"

"Sorry."

"The other thing," Marion said, "you can get yourself shot up in them hotels easier than you think. It happens all the time. A little brawl starts up in the bar and next thing you know, a bullet comes up through the floor. That's all she wrote."

Talking to Marion was an education.

We rode without coming across a sign of another human being until late in the day, when we stopped in a pasture to milk a cow. We drank most of what we got, but Marion caught more in a pot and carefully held it before him as we rode the horses at a walk.

"What do you plan to do with that?" Maude asked him after a time. Slow riding did breed talk.

"I feel like having a real dinner," Marion said. "It'll take some doing. When we make camp, I'll go off and do some hunting."

"Maude can shoot real well," I said. "Maybe she can pop a rabbit or two before we even find a place to camp."

"That so?" Marion said, and turned a curious eye on Maude. She turned red up to her hairline. She busied herself with readying her rifle, and by the time she finished, had recovered her businesslike manner.

We came upon a rabbit not a hundred yards further on. Maude snapped her rifle up, stood in her saddle, and aimed. Some rabbits will sit still as a stone. Not this one. It zigzagged across the field and leaped over a bush. When the bullet hit, the rabbit dropped out of the air. Dropped straight down.

Some horses will tolerate gunshot, and some will not. Maude's did well enough, especially considering Maude was doing the shooting. Mine startled and ran with me to a point long past the rabbit before I could settle him down.

Having impressed Marion with her rabbit-popping skills, Maude shot one more, and got a prairie chicken as well. We made camp by another river. Iowa was full of rivers. Marion skinned the dinner and had me walk the fur and feathers out of sight and then some. Meanwhile, he cooked the pieces slow, cooked them in the chicken's own fat, cooked them fit to feed a king. I followed my nose back to camp.

Maude had done her part, tending to the horses. While I gathered more kindling for the next morning's fire, Marion made milk gravy to pour over the meat. Maude smiled the first smile I'd seen in some time as we sat down to eat.

"I still have that man's six-shooter," she said when we had begun to fill our bellies.

"You don't say," Marion said, showing some interest. "You let me have a look at it later, and I'll see if we can't find some cartridges for it."

"Out here?" Maude said.

"You have to know where to look," Marion said.

We didn't talk much more than that. Marion was a restful kind of man to be with. Not at all what the dime novels would lead a person to believe a frontier fighter would be. Especially a frontier fighter turned bank robber.

After supper, he looked through the saddlebags from Maude's horse and found a box of cartridges, about half full. He held them up like he'd found a pouch of gold nuggets. Maude made a face at him, but she looked willing enough to give the six-shooter a try.

I spread the horse blankets in the spot I figured would do for a bed. The food made me sleepy. So did the air. The cooler it got, the more the air made me want to sleep. But I watched the shooting lesson for a time, resting my head on the saddlebags.

"It's some different than shooting a rifle," Marion said. He stood behind Maude and helped her set up for a shot. "You can sight along your arm, if that's the only way you feel sure. But you might try just looking at what you want to shoot and expecting your bullet to go there. It works just as well, if not better, for someone who can shoot like you do."

"What should I try to hit?" Maude asked him as he stepped away from her. For a fact, there wasn't much to look at but grass and more grass.

"Don't try to hit anything," Marion said, coming back to the fire. Shooting lessons had come to an end without anyone firing a shot. "Don't waste what cartridges you've got. When you have cause to shoot, try it."

"I hope I don't have cause," Maude said, and threw our blanket over me.

As I drifted between the sweetness of wanting to sleep and the good taste hot gravy left in my mouth, I heard Maude say to Marion, "Tell me the truth about how you got your name."

"I told you. I made it up."

"You expect me to believe you have nothing to do with those dimers?"

Marion said, "I swear on my grave, I don't."

"You can't swear on your grave," Maude said. "You don't have one."

"Men who ride rough don't always get graves," Marion said.

Maude said, "I'm not in the mood to feel sorry for you."

There was a silence that left me thinking Marion had lost patience with her entirely. "I know it's hard to believe," he said with an air of starting over. "But the first one I saw was in your sister's hand."

"Then how could this happen?"

"What I know is this. I ran into a newspaper fellow some years back. He was heading east. This was just after I started using the name Joe Harden. I think maybe he's been writing those stories."

"How come?"

"I was riding shotgun on a stagecoach then, and when some fellers tried to hold us up, well, the newspaper fellow was pretty impressed with my shooting. The way he hung around after we got to the end of the run, always scribbling in that little notebook he had, made me curious at the time. I wondered why he didn't just get on eastward if that was where he was going."

"I don't know that that's enough proof for me," Maude said.

"Me either," Marion said. "But one of those stories Sally recited came too close for comfort. Some things we really said were in that story. So now I'm just putting two and two together, and I believe it's coming up four."

"I don't want you to tell Sallie," Maude said. "She sets too much store by dimers as it is."

"All right."

Maude said, "We can't go on riding with you."

"Why not?"

"Because of the bank. I can't be sure what else you'll do."

Marion said, "We all do things we regret. I didn't think it out. I'm sorrier than you may believe."

"Even if I believe it, I have Sallie to think of. She has no one to look up to. She can't remember our folks, and now Aunt Ruthie's gone."

"She could look up to you," Marion suggested.

Maude said, "She looks up to you, sad to say, and you forget she's only a little girl. You ride too rough for a little girl. I can't let her ride so rough. She's young yet, and she'll forget how things ought to be."

"I don't intend to rob another bank."

"I can't change my mind, Marion. The next time we come to a town, you will go your way, and we will go anywhere else that looks likely."

TWENTY-EIGHT

WE DIDN'T COME ACROSS ANOTHER TOWN IN THE NEXT eight days. We did cross three more rivers. One of them we crossed by ferry, which is a grand word to describe a water-logged raft. A rope lay in the water, pulled into a narrow letter *C* as the current dragged at it. We got on the raft in a gingerly fashion. Water washed across our feet. Maude and I looked at each other doubtfully. Even Marion seemed to have his doubts.

We stood silent as two boys Maude's age pulled on a tighter second rope to take us across. The current did most of the work, it looked like. On the other side, where our feet touched dirt again, we became very cheerful. It was a mood that lasted for some time.

Later in the same day, we met up with an oxen train carrying some fellows who were headed out to work on the railroad in Kansas or Nebraska. Marion paid out some of the bank money to buy the necessaries we'd otherwise be doing without once we went our own way. Not that Maude or Marion, either one, made mention of this fact as he tied a sack full of flour and lard and such to the pommel of her horse.

He hung the fry pan and the Dutch oven from my horse. He couldn't get the right supplies for Maude's rifle, but he got pellets for my shotgun. While Marion did his trading, the railroad workers stood around the wagons, joshing the cook about bugs in his flour and such. It was easy to see they didn't mean anything by it. Then one fairly high-spirited sort said, "That older boy is almost pretty enough to be a girl."

"*Almost* makes all the difference," Marion said in a voice to dampen spirits. "He'll grow out of it."

"No offense," the man said.

"None taken," Marion said back. But he finished his business in a crisp way that settled everyone down.

I knew how Maude felt, that Marion wasn't a man to look up to, that he wasn't Joe Harden's kind of man anymore. I agreed with her, it wasn't right to rob banks or to go around shooting people. But it wasn't right to steal horses either, and sometimes people did what they knew wasn't right.

Reading those dime novels, I had always figured there was something different in people who did wrong. That they had changed somehow, along the way, and it didn't hurt them to do wrong. Now I saw it did hurt them. But it didn't change something deep inside them, necessarily.

The best part of Marion had not been changed; he was still a man to look up to. I only wished Maude could see that too. I wished she could see that before we went our separate ways.

I knew Marion was figuring on leaving us pretty soon. All

day he kept telling us the things he thought we might need to know. He told us we'd gone west far enough, so what we needed to do was head south.

A river ran along our left side, and he said we ought to follow that for a while. "But when it takes on an easterly direction," he said, "you keep going south. If the land continues dry, don't go looking for water, just keep moving south. Either you'll find it, or the rain will come."

This could have been taken for thinking out loud, for planning ahead. Then his thoughts moved in another direction, and he told us what to do if we got caught in a blizzard.

"It's early for a blizzard," Maude said.

"Stranger things have happened in these parts. Dry weather like this, and then a flood. Early snows. Late snows. Ice storms. You have to know how to manage, that's all. The almanac predicts a big snow."

"You a big reader of the almanac?" Maude asked him with a faint challenge in her voice.

"People pass that kind of information along," he said easily enough, but I could see they were going to get into it again. They were getting as testy as the Peasley children.

But then Maude's mood changed. "So tell us about snow," she said.

"Find shelter and build a fire, of course," Marion said. "But if that isn't possible, let yourselves be covered with snow. Keep pushing it away to make a little air space, and shove an arm through to the outside every so often to make a kind of chimney so fresh air can come in. Don't go to sleep."

"I read *Wild Woolly*," I told him, hoping to interest him in

156

something besides our education. "That's the very thing he has to do."

He gave me an impatient look and said, "Here's what to do if you meet up with Indians. Look them in the eye, and go about your business. Don't be bullied into trading. In the old days they didn't know any better, but now they know the white man trades with money."

I mentioned another dimer, one that told of renegade Cheyennes that were a present danger on the Kansas frontier. But neither Marion nor Maude understood the value of a good book.

Marion said, "Most Indians that you might run into these days just want to know that you don't mean harm either. The ones you had to worry about have been sent to Oklahoma or further west or north." It seemed to me Marion worried about us a lot. But he was still going to send us on our way. I was sorely tempted to point this contradiction out, but chose silence as the wisest course.

It was still daylight when we settled down to camp. Maude had popped some prairie chickens, and Marion had it in mind to fry them up. He was laying wood for a fire when he told us to stop moving around. He put his ear to the ground.

"What are you doing?" Maude asked.

"Shh," he told her.

Maude looked the question at me: what is he doing?

"It's an Indian trick," I whispered. "He's listening."

"Listening to what?"

"Riders," Marion said. "Several riders. I want you girls to

get on your horses and keep riding south. Due south, you hear, till you reach Independence. Go on now," he said as Maude and I stared at him.

He gave Maude a little kick at the side of her boot, and sure enough, we both got moving. I picked up the chickens. I'd nearly plucked them clean. No sense in wasting them.

"Where are you going to be?" I asked him.

"Leading them in another direction. Then I'll lose them."

"Don't do that," Maude said, surprising me and Marion, both.

"Go. There isn't time for talk," he said. "I won't try to catch up to you, so don't look for me. Remember all the things I told you."

"We were going to ride together till Missouri," Maude said.

"No, we weren't," Marion told her, eying the dust cloud we could see just rising in the distance. "But if we were, our time is up. You're standing in Missouri. Now ride. Ride!"

"Good-bye, Marion," I shouted as he slapped my horse's rump.

I looked over my shoulder and saw Marion riding straight toward the dust cloud. At first this confused me. After I thought about it for a while longer, it saddened me.

TWENTY-NINE

—————•◆•—————

WE RODE. WE RODE FAST. DUE SOUTH.

We rode that way for nearly an hour before we let the horses slow down. Our horses weren't so fast as Marion's, but it wouldn't do to run them into the ground.

"What do you think?" Maude asked me, now that we'd slowed enough to talk.

I told her the truth. "I think Marion was afraid a posse was catching up to us, and he didn't even lead them a chase. I think he gave himself up." I thought it ought to sadden her a little too.

"He's been too smart for them before," she said. "Too smart and too fast."

"He never had anybody else to worry about before," I said.

There was a question that had been knocking around in my head for days, that I hadn't dared ask her. If there was ever going to be the right moment, this was it. "What if Uncle Arlen isn't the kind of man you think he is?" I asked her.

"What do you mean?"

"It might be like you said to Marion. Maybe he won't want us."

"We're his blood kin," Maude said.

"So was Aunt Ruthie, and this is nothing against her, but she was much different from our momma, right?"

"Well, she turned out to be good enough," Maude said.

"What if Uncle Arlen turns out to be a lot like Marion, unpredictable-like? Are we going to stay with him? Or do we keep on going?"

"When did you turn into such a question box?" she said to me. "I don't remember you ever asking so many questions."

"I never had so many questions staring me in the face."

"I don't know why they would still be looking for him after all this time," she said.

"Looking for Uncle Arlen?"

"Marion. I don't think a posse would follow him all the way into Missouri."

"Not all posses are made up of lawmen," I said.

"Who, then?"

"Men whose money he took." I was sorry as soon as I said it. Maude would never have thought of that. I could see right away she was unhappy to think it could really be a posse of angry men that was chasing Marion.

"We should go back," she said without turning her horse.

"No, we shouldn't," I told her. It was too late to do anything for Marion. For once, I kept my big mouth shut.

The night came on cold, making me think about the fact that it could get colder yet. Riding at a trot got our blood moving. We headed due south until the moon disappeared behind a bank of clouds.

* * *

We'd hit a wide piece of pastureland, from the looks of it, which made us feel like we could see for miles. So it was just as well we didn't feel up to cooking the chickens by the time we stopped for the night. I set the saddles over them, hoping they might not get carried off in the night by a fox. We shared a can of beans.

We no longer had Uncle Arlen's letters, which Maude felt pretty bad about. "I wish we had them so we could give them to him, that's all. It would show him Aunt Ruthie cared enough about him to keep them."

"If he's there, we'll find him," I said, hoping she would tell me that she still felt confident of finding Uncle Arlen. She didn't. We didn't mention Marion to each other, either, although we slept under his blanket, huddled together for warmth.

In the morning, we saw what Marion would have called a bump on the flat. It was much nearer than the wagon Marion had pointed out, though, and we could see it was a house.

"We'll just ride in and ask if we can't buy another blanket. How's that?" I said, thinking of how cold we had been during the night. I kept waking up to wish we had one of Aunt Ruthie's quilts to throw over the blanket.

Our tattered gloves and scratchy scarves were going to be missed, unless we bought some others. It seemed to me a woman might be willing enough to sell an unused item if she could add some coins to her sugar bowl.

"Fine with me," Maude said in a tone that meant it wasn't. She went along with me, though. We rode in, slowing our pace as we got nearer.

"Something's funny there," I said.

"What do you mean?"

"Just let me figure it out," I said, pulling my horse to a stop.

The house was real nice, painted white, and kept up the way Aunt Ruthie wanted to keep ours, but never could. Lacy curtains in all the windows. Porch on the near side. Big barn out back. Chickens scratching around in the yard. "Is there anything that doesn't look right to you?" I asked finally.

"Wood smoke," Maude said after a moment. I had to hand it to her. Maude was quick. "There isn't any. It's cold out here and there's an awful lot of wood stacked right there on the porch."

"You think nobody's home?" I started forward again.

"Sallie—"

"Right back."

I meant it when I said it. That was before I heard cattle lowing in the barn. And there was something else, something heard so low I couldn't know what it was, but it raised the hair on my arms.

THIRTY

HE CLOSER I GOT TO THAT HOUSE, THE MORE I DIDN'T
see any sign of things happening the way they should—
no one came out to meet me. I knocked on the door and
went in.

Behind me, Maude yowled. I heard the hoofbeats that
meant she was coming after me. Which was fine by me all
over. Maybe I should have headed back to Maude instead of
going into the house. That would have been the smart thing
to do. The kind of feeling I had always made a range rider
take warning. But I figured if I wasn't going to be the kind
of range rider who was smart, I'd have to be the one who
was brave.

The kitchen was real cold. No one had made a fire in
here for a day or more. It wasn't so tidy as I expected it to be
either. It looked like people had been eating here but not
cleaning up after themselves. The sour smell in the room
didn't have anything to do with dirty dishes.

A small sound shivered the hair on my arms. I
stopped cold.

When it came again, "Help," I realized it was a woman's voice, weak and low.

"It's just me," I said, feeling a sight better than the moment before. "Don't be afraid. I'm looking for you."

"Here, in the parlor."

The smell was worse there, much worse, so bad my stomach turned over. A woman lay stretched out on a davenport, covered with several blankets. Her white hair stood around her head like a messy bird's nest. "Don't come too near, child," she said. "I'm ill. Influenza, I think."

Maude came into the kitchen then, shouting, "Where are you?"

"Here," I called back.

"It's my animals I'm worried about," the woman said as Maude came in and started opening windows. "I haven't been able to tend to them for two days."

"Cows and chickens?" I asked her.

"And three sows out behind the barn. A mule. Could be anywhere. The ox out in the pasture should be fine."

"Stay deep under your blankets now," Maude said. "We have to air this room."

"Don't bother looking for the mule. He'll come as soon as he hears a bucket rattle. You shouldn't be in here. You're likely to get sick yourselves."

"We can't leave you like this," Maude said as I took away the smelly slop bucket. Maude brought in a load of firewood, and I pumped some water.

"We'll need to see to your cows first," I said when we got the fire going good.

"Now if you girls are going to act like farmhands," she

164

said, making Maude and me shoot looks at each other, "there are some heavier gloves in that boot box under the window. See if there isn't something that works for you."

"I'll get started in the barn," I said.

We milked the cows, tossed hay for them and the mule. We set our horses out to pasture with them. We fed corn mush to the pigs, made with most of the milk, saving only enough for gravy. We spread gravel for the chickens.

We got the fires going and put our chickens and some potatoes on the boil. We tidied the kitchen, sweeping the floor and wiping down the wood-block table. When the house was warm enough, we sponged down half the woman's bedding and hung it on the line to dry.

In that time, we learned her name was Cleomie Dow, and we told her ours. We didn't bother with aliases. She was already on to us. "How did you know we were girls right away?" I asked her when we had ease enough to talk.

"It takes one to know one, I guess," Cleomie said with a little shrug. She was sitting with her back to the wall, sipping at the chicken broth.

I tried not to show it, but I was some bothered. Twice our disguises hadn't worked. If Marion hadn't stood up for us with the railroad men, it might've been three times. I didn't know how two skinny girls were supposed to pass for boys if no one even noticed that's what they were trying to do.

"You're smart to travel that way," Cleomie said. "You're all the safer for it. It's not but a thin line between Missouri and the wilderness."

"No, ma'am," Maude said, looking none too happy at a mention of the wilderness.

"Hair grows back," Cleomie said stoutly.

"Yes, ma'am."

It took most of a day's effort to set the place to rights, and then it was time to start all over again with bringing in the cows. When we finished, we ate the last of the chicken and potatoes.

"What now?" I asked.

"We'll sleep in the hayloft once we've settled her," Maude said.

I groaned.

"I'm sorry, but she's right; we shouldn't take chances. People have died of the influenza."

"I bet they died of the work," I said, thinking of Aunt Ruthie. I had a better idea of why Aunt Ruthie worked us so hard. She could never have done it all alone. She taught school too.

"Sallie."

"She didn't die, and she's old," I said, coming back to the subject of Cleomie. "Maybe she's wrong about what made her sick."

"We'll ask her if she has a blanket to spare," Maude said in her that's-final voice.

Cleomie said, "I won't hear of it. Sleep upstairs in the back bedroom. I haven't been in there for two weeks at least, long before I took sick." For someone so weak, she put forth a surprisingly strong protest. "You can't sleep in the barn. You'll freeze."

"We haven't frozen yet," Maude said, getting stubborn. This time, I knew it only meant she truly wanted to sleep in a real bed.

Cleomie said, "Are you girls going far? Are you expected to be there anytime soon? Because I could surely use your help till I get on my feet again."

"We're in no hurry," Maude said.

I didn't want to be the one to tell Maude otherwise. I waited till we were upstairs, sharing the bed Cleomie said we were to sleep in, to ask, "Don't you think the law must be looking for us? For those horses?"

"Likely they are," Maude said. "But they don't seem to be looking here."

"So we're hiding out."

"This is not a dime novel, Sallie," Maude said angrily. "This is our sorry lives."

THIRTY-ONE

WE DIDN'T RIGHT AWAY TELL CLEOMIE ANYTHING about how we came to ride up this way. For one thing, we were too busy getting her place in order. For the second, she had a little business of making cheese, and it had to be made every day and stored in a springhouse till she took it to market.

But we were also too comfortable while staying there. And so was Cleomie. So we went on not telling her. "I think she's going to ask us to stay," I told Maude on our fourth night of sleeping in a bed again.

"We can't stay." Maude smiled a sad smile. "All we have to do is tell her our story. That will put her off."

"I know it." I did know it. But my heart fought the knowing. "We'll go while she's asleep. It will be easier that way."

"No, it won't," Maude said, looking like she might get tearful. "I can't believe how good it is to live this way again. The sad truth is, my resolve is worn thin. I don't know if I can make it to Independence."

"You can do it," I said. "It's just this has reminded us of how it was before Aunt Ruthie died."

So the next morning we told Cleomie our story, including the part we had taken in the bank robbery. She was not put off. "I don't care if you two girls are the Younger Brothers' little sisters. I was sick to death, and you took care of me when I needed you."

"You'd have been fine," Maude said.

Cleomie shook her head. "I'd been off my feed the whole day before I took sick. I tended the cows and just managed to pour all that milk into the pig trough. From that point until you found me, I couldn't get myself a drink of water or put wood in the stove. If you gals hadn't found me when you did, I'd have died for sure. By the time anybody got out here to look in on me, they would have found me stone cold."

"Don't talk like that," I said.

"It's the simple truth," Cleomie said. "Just moving around seemed to start the whole thing up again. Somebody had to take care of my animals. I'd've died of sheer wore out."

"How are you now?" Maude said. "That's what we need to know."

Cleomie tried, but she wasn't able to stay on her feet for long. She sat breathless in the kitchen after showing us how to make her cheese. "It's just knocked me for a loop," she said.

Maude insisted that Cleomie remain in bed for the rest of the day. We agreed to put off leaving for another week, time enough for her to get her full strength back. We hoped. Every night it had been colder than the night before. Each morning frost lay on the ground. The longer we stayed with her, the less chance we had of making it to Independence before snow fell.

Three days later, we were in the barn loft, tossing hay

down to the cleaned-out stalls, when a lone rider came up the road. Maude saw him before I did and pointed him out. Pointed out, too, that we had left the horses out in the front pasture with the mule.

As he got closer, the rider reminded me of Reverend Peasley somehow. The way he had of riding in like he was sure to be welcome. He was dressed like Reverend Peasley too. Cleomie stepped out on her porch in a housedress and a shawl. She had improved to the point of being able to wrap the cheese after we made it, and she was dressed to greet a surprise visitor.

"Good," Maude said. "So far, anyway. We'd best leave off what we're doing and sit tight till he goes."

Cleomie sat down on the porch rocker to wait.

"Miss Cleomie," the rider shouted out a few minutes later. "I came to find out why we didn't see you in church this week. Are you feeling poorly?"

"Just a little setdown," Cleomie answered back. "Nothing serious. I thought it best to rest it out."

"You have company?" the preacher asked her.

"Why, no, what makes you ask?"

"The horses," he said. "You don't have horses."

"Oh," Cleomie said, looking puzzled. "The horses."

"Miss Cleomie?"

"They came into the yard yesterday," Cleomie said, and gave him a brilliant smile. "I put them up for the night. Won't you come in for a bite? But I'm going to let you get it for both of us. I've about worn myself out with making cheese."

The reverend got down from his horse. There was more conversation, but we could only hear their voices; we couldn't make out the words. The reverend went into the house to put together the bite of lunch Cleomie had mentioned. Maude and I sat down in a corner of the loft and, because we were truly worn out, were soon dozing.

We snapped awake to hear the reverend in the barn below us. He brought the horses in and saddled them up. Maude and I looked the same questions at each other, but we didn't make a sound.

We listened to the reverend take the horses and watched him down the road. When we felt certain he wouldn't turn back, we lit into the house to get the full story.

"He was too interested in those horses," Cleomie told us as we set about finishing the job of wrapping the freshly made cheese in layers of a thin, see-through cloth for storage. "He said he was going to see if he knew the brand, so I asked him to take the horses with him to save me the bother of returning them."

"You did right," Maude said. "His only other choice would have been to send the sheriff out here."

"Well, that's good and bad, isn't it?" Cleomie said. "The sheriff might come out here anyway."

"What's worse, I think we ought to go soon," Maude said to me. "I didn't like that he came into the barn. We had just tossed the hay. How long will it be before he wonders if Cleomie could have done that work herself?"

"You're right. But we don't have a horse to ride," I said.

"You can't walk to Independence," Cleomie said. "I don't

have that mule for nothing. If you are certain of the need to go, saddle him up and be gone. By midday tomorrow, you'll reach a place where you can buy a horse."

"We ought to pay you for the mule," I told her.

Cleomie folded her arms around me and held me to her for a long moment. This was surprising at first; Aunt Ruthie had not hugged us often, but Cleomie's hug was welcome. It felt good to know someone loved me just a little. Someone besides Maude, of course.

When she let me go, she said, "I'm sending you to the trader who sold me this mule. He'll sell you a good horse, cheap. All you'll have to do is tell Ben I want him to get the animal back to me."

She laughed and said, "You don't even have to tell him. This mule used to run away from me and go back home to Ben about once a month. Then Ben would bring him back again."

"Why did he run off?" I asked.

Cleomie said, "Ben told me I probably worked him too hard. Maybe that was true."

Maude said, "What about you, Cleomie? You aren't up to doing all this work yet."

"The reverend insisted on sending someone out to give me a hand. I figured I'd have to hide you girls in the attic. I see it's going to work out in the end, though. You don't need to worry about me. Now let's get you ready to go."

THIRTY-TWO

I T WAS GOOD THE REVEREND HADN'T TAKEN THE SADDLE-bags, which we'd left in the barn. We loaded them with things needed for the trip. We took a healthy portion of cheese wrapped in more cheesecloth and then in layers of newspaper the reverend had handily brought along. We packed biscuits spread with butter and jelly, sliced ham, boiled eggs, and corn bread. Cleomie wouldn't have it any other way.

We rolled blankets and an old quilt, and tied them down. As we outfitted the mule, Cleomie put a few more things in the saddlebags, like matches and gloves and scarves. She was sure we couldn't do without these. She found knitted caps that she said had belonged to her boys, and they were a fine fit under our hats.

Cleomie's mule was a good animal, nearly as good as a horse in every way. It was even able to carry one of us. Cleomie said one of us should walk while the other rode, so we could make as much distance as possible.

"I want to hear from you when you get where you're go-ing," Cleomie said to us as we moved off. If our preparations were hurried, our good-byes were even more so. We started out less than an hour after the reverend left.

The hard part was the starting out, when the urge to look back and wave led to wanting to turn around and go back. At first we didn't talk about this, and then we did. Finally Maude said, "Don't look back anymore." It was easier that way.

We didn't expect to make many miles on the mule. But where we were headed, we had just enough money left to buy another horse. The good thing about trading off on who rode the mule was that Maude and me, both, managed to stay fairly warm.

The day had started out sunny and nearly warm, but by late afternoon, as we started out, clouds hung low and heavy with the promise of weather to come. I could hardly regret the time spent helping put Cleomie back on her feet. I did wish it hadn't set us back so many days.

"Do you think the law will come out to see if Cleomie is hiding us when he finds out where those horses came from?" I asked Maude. We'd left fast, on the strength of the possibility, and we hadn't really talked this through.

"I think the law will come out to be sure Cleomie is fine," Maude said. "To make sure we aren't hiding around her farm. If he doesn't see any sign of us, he won't come looking for us out here. I don't think."

"I wish we still had those horses," I said, even though Maude had already said twice that she felt better knowing we weren't riding stolen horses.

We found the first marker that Cleomie told us to watch for. She was not a person to ever need a compass. She had the world around her mapped out by heart. Here was the tree with a hole in the bole, the bee tree. From there we watched for a stand of three tall pines, and aimed right at them when they showed up.

The wind picked up as darkness fell, chilling us when we sat the mule, so we both walked to keep warm. There was a new, bitter feeling in the air, dampness, that meant snow might be on the way. I said nothing about this, nor did Maude.

We talked to take our minds off the cold. For a while we talked about the horse we would buy because it made us miss Cleomie less. We talked, too, about arriving in Independence. That made us feel hopeful. By silent agreement, we talked as if we knew right where to find Uncle Arlen. We talked as if he was waiting for us as hard as we were heading for him.

Sometime past nightfall we could hear the river in the distance, and followed its sound further into Missouri. We stopped to eat in a little stand of woods with prairie grass blowing all around it and a creek running through it.

While I secured the mule with a tether—Cleomie had warned us he didn't take to being hobbled—I decided we'd eat some of Cleomie's cheese. Maude took her rifle and tramped around some in the woods, to see if we could sleep there. Marion had mentioned bears, and Maude took particular care since we were camping so near the trees.

Maude and I couldn't bear tinned fish, but we were very fond of fried. Thinking we might have fried fish for the next morning's breakfast, I kindled a small blaze. While I waited for it to become a cooking fire, I put chunks of cheese on each of the fishing hooks, tied the line around and around a bush, and threw the baited trotline out into the water.

Cleomie's cheese was wrapped in cheesecloth, then

wrapped in newspaper. It was while I was putting the cheese away that I realized Maude's face stared up at me from the newspaper.

These drawings of Maude showed her with long hair, and one with her hair cut short. Goose bumps ran up my arms and down my legs, the likeness was that good. It didn't escape my notice that she had made the front page this time.

I listened to know for sure that Maude wasn't coming, then moved the cheese and read.

"MAD" WOMAN IN DISGUISE

As She Goes from Bad to Worse

The notorious Maude March held up the Des Moines Savings & Trust on Friday morning. Eyewitness reports told authorities that she passed for a man, and shot like an outlaw "without hardly taking aim." She was identified by a man who called her by name in the heat of the moment when the robbery went bad. The bank guard, Mr. A. J. Todd, reports that Mad Maude shot him and ran from the bank without a backward glance, leaving one gang member behind to hold off the chase. The gang got away with seven hundred dollars. Adding insult to injury, gang members stole the horses of the robbery victims.

I heard Maude coming. I yanked that page out from under the cheese and balled it up. I believed my hair could easily be standing on end. The paper was turning to ash as Maude came noisily tramping out of the woods.

"What's the matter?" she said at once. "You look like you've seen a ghost."

"You scared me, coming on with so much noise," I said. "I thought you must be a bear."

"Nope," she said with no little satisfaction. "Nothing in here but us chickens. And Cleomie's mule. Did you brush him down?"

"I didn't get to him yet."

"I'll do it."

"No, let me," I said. I bundled the cheese up with badly shaking hands.

"Sallie," Maude said, seeing this. "I didn't mean to scare you."

"Just see if you can find the biscuits, will you? And keep an eye on the fishing lines. My hands got cold is all."

I brushed that mule to within an inch of his life. He didn't seem to mind. I just kept thinking over the words I'd read. They thought Maude shot that man. They thought robbing that bank was her idea. They thought she was heading up a gang.

The thoughts swirled till I couldn't think them anymore. Behind me, Maude had been talking and talking, I didn't even know about what. She'd cut the biscuits in half and put a slice of cheese on each one so it looked like a ladies' tea.

"That mule looks good enough to lead a parade," she said. "Come on over here and have some cheese and biscuits."

I threw a woolen blanket over the mule and tied it at his neck. Cleomie called this his baby blanket. Then I sat. In fact,

177

I fell back against the saddlebags, suddenly too tired to eat. I did not know how I could go on. Every move we made threw Maude into deeper and deeper trouble. I had begun to wish it wasn't too late for her to go back to Cedar Rapids and marry Mr. Wilburn, where she would be safe even if she was not happy.

"Just cover me over and wake me in the morning," I said.

"Oh, no, you don't," Maude said. "Eat. And if we catch a fish, we're frying it up. I don't know that I can eat enough cheese and biscuits to hold me."

By the second bite my strength was returning. But the few moments I felt otherwise got me to thinking. "You're getting skinnier, Maude," I told her. It was true. Now I thought about it, the likeness in the paper was all off. Maude's chin looked pointy, and her cheeks had hollowed out.

"It isn't just me that's thinned out. We're both going to need fattening up once we get to Independence."

"No one from Cedar Rapids would know you if they came across you."

"I wish that was true," she said.

I watched the trotline as we ate and warmed ourselves by the fire. I just stared and gave my brain a rest from thinking. It was better that way.

"I thought we'd get further than this," Maude said after a while.

"We'll get where we're going tomorrow anyway," I said.

One of the fishing lines jigged, and I ran over to pull it in. I got a big catfish. Before I finished bragging about that one, I'd caught another. I cleaned them up, and Maude fried them.

We ate our fill of sweet meat and still had plenty left for breakfast. We could wrap that in a sheet of the newspaper.

It was terrible dark; not the stars or even the moon could be seen in the sky above. We were cold, so we built up the fire and set a small store of broken branches to use during the night.

I tried to figure out how much longer it would take us to reach Independence once we were riding a horse again. My best guess was twelve or fourteen days, but it made me want to build a little shanty right where I sat. I built in my mind a very large fireplace. I was not much in the mood to be a range rider at just that moment.

When she'd done with wrapping the fish, Maude woke me and rolled me into a blanket. She curled up behind me, herself wrapped in a worn quilt Cleomie had made some years before, and threw an arm over me. In this way, she let me sleep closest to the warmth of the fire.

THIRTY-THREE

WE WOKE TO AN UNUSUAL SILENCE. THE SNOW WAS coming down fast and steadily, and where it had fallen on our faces, it was melting and dripping like tears. A silvery gray light made it early morning to my eyes, but I felt we had slept late into the day. There was not a bird sound to be heard.

The ground was blanketed, but tufts of tall dried grasses poked holes in the look of a clean sheet. "Oh, no," Maude said, sitting up and letting cold air sneak under the blankets. My first thought was to tuck in, but then I thought better to get it over with. I threw off the blankets.

"Let's just get moving," I said as a wave of shivers went through me. "We'll eat on foot." Maude buttoned her jacket up to her chin and pulled the sleeves down over her fists. "Pull out those gloves," I said to her. "Scarves too."

It was while we were shuffling through the powdery snow, hurrying to put our necessaries back on the mule, that I noticed the tracks. First the mule's tracks in the snow told me he'd been pacing back and forth behind Maude while we slept. This looked strange to me.

Near the creek there were cat tracks, paw prints with no claws. Good-sized tracks, belonging to probably the biggest bobcat I had ever seen. The fish heads and the innards I'd left on the bank the night before were gone.

I didn't say a word to Maude.

We walked fast to warm ourselves, each of us wearing one glove so we could eat fried fish out of the fold of newspaper with our fingers. We had to hold it in our mouths for a minute to make it warm enough to chew. But the taste was good, and our bellies welcomed the weight of it.

The wind was cold and bit right through our clothing. It was easier to bear when we were moving. Gusts of snow blew like gauzy curtains, first one way, then another. After a time, still eating, we began to suck on our fingers to warm them.

We had started on the hardest part of the trail. We would be watching for certain trees till we came to a stone wall that led right to the ranch. We were nearly all the sound we could hear; there was the wind, the creak of a branch, and the crunch and squeak of our boots in the snow. Sometimes we could hear the river off at a distance.

The light, the ghostly light of early morning, remained the same. If the sun was up there somewhere, it was behind a cloud bank as thick as a feather mattress. I thought sad thoughts for Wild Woolly, and hoped he had by now found his way home.

"If the snow gets any heavier, we won't see the stone wall," Maude said when she pointed to the lightning-struck tree that we were still watching for up ahead. We were passing right by it, having veered a little east.

I began worrying that we might get lost. Finished with little-girl games, I pulled out my compass and checked that we were still headed due south.

"Where'd you get that?" Maude asked.

"It was Daddy's," I said. "Aunt Ruthie showed it to me once, when I asked her how explorers kept from getting lost."

"Is that how you've kept us headed aright?" she asked.

"It is."

"Good girl," she said. "Tell me now, are we headed south to Independence?"

"We are," I said, which was near enough the truth. It might be a little to the east or west, but it was south of us, sure enough. "But I don't know that the horse trader Cleomie told us about was such a straight line from her place. We have to watch for the landmarks or we might miss him."

"Let's keep our eyes open," Maude said.

Walking gave me a chance to think about things. It seemed to me that I'd been too hasty in burning up that piece of the newspaper. I had not thought to look through it to see if there was any mention made of Marion's capture.

On the other hand, it no longer seemed likely that it was Marion that posse was hunting. The thought gave me a chill that had nothing to do with the snow falling down the neck of my jacket.

The other thing I thought about was how alone we were out there. Only the day before, we had passed herds of grazing deer. We had seen a fox, three raccoons, any number of turkeys and prairie dogs, and birds had flown overhead. Now we saw nothing.

The snow piled up fast. Pretty soon the tops of grasses

were only freckles on the white. Falling snow had been catching around the tops of our boots, where it melted down our legs. Both of us had socks wet around the ankles. Maude stopped and stuffed the last of the newspaper in the tops of our boots.

"I'm glad I've got these," she said of her boots. "I'd've had frostbite by now if I was wearing those ones with the narrow toes."

It was on the tip of my tongue to remind her Marion had bought them for her. But then I doubted she needed me to remind her. I shook my head and said, "I wonder how it is that cowboys do so well with those boots."

"They probably shot off all their toes practicing those fast draws," Maude said with some irritation, maybe because she'd reminded herself to worry about Marion. "They need those long, hard boot toes to keep them from falling on their faces."

For some reason this struck me funny. Laughter escaped me in bursts until even Maude was affected. That laughter carried us another mile or more.

We kept on the move, but we were slowed down as the snow got deeper. We tried to get the mule to take his turn at beating a path, but he would have nothing to do with it. He liked having us clear a path for him. "It's only fair," Maude said when our efforts to push him ahead were twice failed. "He's carrying everything but us."

We had walked on for some time in this manner before Maude said, "Maybe we ought to just hunker down somewhere. It's getting so I can't see very far ahead of us."

"How far does that mean?" I asked her.

"To that tree," she said, and pointed.

"That's as far as I can see," I said, "and it's good enough for me. Let's keep on going." It wasn't that I wanted to keep on going. It was awful tiring. But I wanted to step inside a house and be offered cake with thick frosting. I wanted to sit so close to a warm fire that I felt the need of a mug of cold milk.

But I wasn't going to get that. I wasn't even going to get close. The snow had covered any fire makings we might have used. What I wanted least was to sit huddled under some makeshift cover, chilled to the bone and hoping the snow would stop soon.

So we walked. Always panting with the work of driving a path through the snow, we walked.

I was hot enough to open my coat if I was the one breaking snow. And when it was Maude's turn, I got so cold my teeth chattered. The snow came down more heavily all the time, and the wind got stronger, but I didn't like to mention this to Maude.

"There's probably a place far enough south that it never snows," I said. "Do you think Independence is that far south?"

"I hope not."

"Why?"

Maude said, "I keep telling myself it's only a day further. If I have to think of walking past where it can snow, I might sit right down here and cry."

We went on, hardly speaking. We ate fish or boiled eggs when our stomachs growled. We ate because we had not filled up at the start of the day, but we neither one of us mentioned stopping to have a real meal. When I judged it to be late in the morning, perhaps early afternoon, I said, "I'd just like to think Independence is going to be really good."

"Do you want the last piece of fish?" Maude asked me. I figured we were eating something every hour or so, not because we were hungry that often, but because we felt better when we ate. We didn't think that much about the cold when we had the fullness of egg or the sweet taste of catfish in our mouths.

"Half of it," I said.

We were just finishing it off when Maude said, "What was that?"

"I didn't hear anything."

"You were chewing," Maude said.

The wind howled all around us, so I thought it might be that Maude only heard the wind. "What did it sound like?"

She pulled her rifle off the mule and cocked it, then moved around to the other side of him. I got my shotgun and pulled back one hammer.

Then I heard a yowl.

"Holy Maloney," Maude said.

"A cat," I said with a certainty that surprised even me. I had never heard the like before. I had only read a description of such a sound in one of my dimers, as something to raise the hair on the back of the neck. It seemed a close enough match to me.

The mule bolted.

The reins were pulled through my hand so fast they left me with a burn.

Practically everything we needed was tied to that mule.

Our food, our blankets, the matches, that six-gun. Even our spare ammunition. We couldn't get by with the loads we carried in our guns. That mule meant life or death to us.

It helped a little that he ran straight ahead, because when Maude and I both ran after him, he'd done a fine job of beating a path through the snow. We ran, carefully because we carried guns ready to shoot, but with a purpose. Maude had a different purpose in mind than I had.

"When I find that mule, I'm going to kill him deader than a door," Maude shouted at me. For once she was not careful of her grammar.

THIRTY-FOUR

I SAVED MY BREATH FOR THE RUNNING. WE HAD TO GO on and on; it felt like we'd run at least a mile when Maude came to a sudden stop. "Look at this, Sallie," she said as I caught up to her.

I saw the mule's path crossed another; it was the imprint of a boot, fast filling with snow. "That fool animal has run himself in a circle," Maude said, recognizing the boot track for our own. "He might even be headed right straight at that cat."

The mule screamed.

It didn't sound all that far away, but it did sound like it was all around us. It went on braying as Maude took off running again, following the path of broken snow. I will say this for Maude. She could run.

She got some distance on me again before she stopped. But this time she put her gun to her shoulder. I pulled even with her just as she took a bead on the cat. I saw that the mule bucked like a bronco, making a tight circle, and the cat rode him like a buster.

It was not a clear shot, with the mule rearing up at one

moment, then kicking up hind legs in the next. It was not a shot I could have made. Maude's gun barrel drew little figures in the air, then stilled, and she fired.

The mule and the cat both fell to the ground.

"Oh, no," Maude cried, and started to run again.

"Maude, wait," I yelled after her. She kept on running.

If the mule was hit, then the cat was not; that was my thought. I raised my shotgun and aimed, hoping that I would get a clear shot if the cat went for Maude. But I didn't have high hopes. Not only was I not a good shot, but shotgun pellets don't make a clean hit. Maude was sure to take a few pellets.

I saw the mule lift his head. He looked fairly calm, all things considered. I lowered the shotgun and watched the mule come to realize he was not done for.

Maude had killed the cat with an incredible shot through its eye. She claimed that was only a bit of luck; she was aiming to hit it anywhere at all. But she might just as easily have said that about shooting the head off that rattler if she had been willing to talk about it.

We stood over it, catching our breath, my throat burning from the cold air I had let come rushing in so fast.

"Did you know you hit it?" I asked her.

"I thought so," Maude said. "But when the mule fell, I wanted to beat that cat to a pulp for making me kill the mule."

It wasn't even a bobcat. It was a mountain lion. Called a painter, a panther, in the dimers. I never expected to see one. Smallish, but long-legged, the cat had that young look that older kittens have. Soft around the edges in some way.

"You would make Wild Woolly proud," I told Maude, staying away from a mention of Joe Harden. It occurred to me that I might have been wrong; Maude might make the better range rider after all. Before I could say so, my thoughts were turned back to the mule.

It had a bite on its neck that bled hard until Maude packed it with snow. Together we dragged the cat away, and the mule worked its way back up to a stand. We checked the pack and found we had lost nothing.

It was probably the fact of being so fully loaded with bags that protected the mule from the cat's claws. There was not a scratch on him, save the teeth marks.

"Can you set us back on course?" Maude asked me. "This animal has completely lost us our direction."

I brought out the compass and held it as we walked, keeping us headed due south, even when the mule's tracks, and ours, veered eastward from where we heard the cat scream.

"You sure you don't want to take the cat?" I asked Maude. It seemed quite a trophy to leave in the snow. "I could skin it if you want."

"I doubt the mule will consent to carry it," Maude said. The mule had moved right on past its old tracks and was breaking snow, which made the going somewhat easier for us. It seemed wise not to remind the animal of the old rules.

"The cat was awful young, did you see that?" Maude said. "It hadn't even learned how to make a big kill yet, I don't think."

"It ate the fish heads last night."

"Sallie, you have to tell me when you see something like

that," Maude said, sounding more tired than mad. "It probably followed us all day, eating crumbs that we dropped in the snow."

"What would you have done different?" I asked her.

"I wouldn't have been surprised, that's the important thing," she said.

"You're tougher than I knew," I told her.

"I know it," she said.

For those several minutes we were distracted from the storm. But the weather was only getting worse. Sometimes the snow drove right at our faces, and we stumbled ahead blindly. Other times it pushed past us from behind, and still we were as good as blind.

Only now and again we could see some distance before us. Never a great distance, about the length of a horse and wagon, but we saw there was plenty more of the same ahead of us.

Very shortly we came to a point where the mule would not break snow again. Maude took the lead, muttering something to the mule that I couldn't hear. We had to nearly shout to make ourselves understood over the wind now. But the mule laid his ears back as if he'd had no trouble hearing what I guessed were threats of sending him straight to the glue pots.

"We'll have to find a place soon," Maude said after a time. The snow was well up to my hips, so that for me, breaking snow was more or less a matter of falling through it.

"We're getting too tired," Maude said breathlessly. "We have to have enough strength left to get through the night."

"I keep hoping we'll get to the horse trader's." My toes

hurt with the cold, and I wanted to spend the night where it was warm. I wanted to get there soon.

"We won't make it that far," Maude said, lunging ahead again. "The snow slows us down too much."

"We need a pine tree, a big pine tree," I said. "Maybe we can even build a fire under there."

"Under a pine?" Maude said. We had once caused a chimney fire by throwing some pine branches into our fireplace, thinking to make the house smell like Christmas. She said, "We're likely to burn the whole tree right to the ground."

"Sounds good to me," I told her. "A nice size fire like that ought to keep us warm for a while."

Maude laughed. I admired that laugh. There wasn't much that seemed funny to me right then. And I wasn't even the one breaking the most snow.

"Are we headed south?" Maude called back to me.

I looked at the compass and yelled, "Bear right."

"What happened to the river?" Maude asked me.

"It's there. Let's don't walk right into it."

"We'd hear it, right?" she asked.

"I hope so."

"I don't see any trees, Sallie." We were stopped now. "Shouldn't there be trees near the river?"

I looked at my compass and turned it in my palm. It struck me that the needle didn't turn so freely as it did once. "Maybe this thing gets frozen," I said.

"Put it under your arm," Maude said. "Then we'll look at it again later."

"But how can we be sure of our direction now?"

"We can't stand here and talk about it, Sallie," Maude said, her teeth chattering slightly. "Let's just go. Keep watching for trees."

We went on this way for another hundred steps. Maude breaking snow, me leading the mule. And then suddenly Maude picked up speed. Not a great deal of speed, not enough that it was alarming, but it did raise my curiosity. A moment later, I found I was walking more easily too.

The snow was not less deep here, because on either side of me, it stood as high as my waist. But it had been tamped down some right where we walked now. Although fresh snow had fallen on that, it was not such hard going.

"What is it?" I shouted to Maude.

"Something went through here," she said, turning back to speak to me. "Animals, I guess. I'm going to follow this path."

I followed Maude, trying to think if this was something Wild Woolly would have done. It seemed unlikely. I tried to think of what kind of animals we might be talking about. Wolves? Or even one large bear, heading for a cave?

THIRTY-FIVE

WE HAD NO IDEA WHETHER WE WALKED SOUTH OR EVEN north. But we walked nearly as easily as when we had started out that morning. We didn't even think of trying to break snow so long as that path lay before us.

It seemed we were on that path for some time, maybe half of an hour. All at once something loomed ahead of us, and it was a moment before I saw that it was trees. Snow-covered trees.

Maude stooped down on the path and brushed the loose snow away from the packed snow underneath. "What are you looking for?" I asked her.

"I hoped we were following cows back to the barn," Maude said. "Now I'm trying to figure out just what it is that we're following."

"Deer," I suddenly realized.

"Do you see a track?"

"Everything else has a burrow or a cave," I said. I had read that in *Wild Woolly.*

"Are you sure?"

I shrugged. Reminded of the compass in my armpit, I dug

it out and found the needle was looking a little more lively. But we had seen no sign of the stone wall Cleomie told us to look for. The stand of trees was all that lay ahead if we went on moving south.

"We have to try it," I said, shoving the compass into my pocket for safekeeping. "There isn't any other place for us that I can see. I think it's getting dark." In fact, I knew it was getting dark; I just hadn't realized it until we saw how shadowed the trees looked.

"All right, then," Maude said. "Move slowly. Let's don't talk unless we have to. Just till we know how things stand."

Maude carried my shotgun because she'd never reloaded her rifle. She moved slowly, looking for a place to part the branches so that I could lead the mule through. He was so eager he all but trampled me getting in first. It was probably for the best that his big horsey face took the lead.

There were deer beneath that stand of trees, huddled in groups for warmth. While the mule made a startling appearance, it seemed that his presence made us less scary than if we had gone in alone. At least that was how it seemed. Because while there were wide, watchful eyes upon us, and some shuffling of hooved feet, not one of them skittered off to another spot.

"Don't look at them," Maude said, leaning in close to whisper. It was much quieter under the trees, and the scent of the needles sharp and sweet in my nostrils.

"Real slow," I whispered back as I took the rein off my hand and tied it to a branch.

Slow and quiet. That was how we did everything. Unburdened the mule and wiped him down. Laid his blanket over him.

Maude took out biscuits for us, and oats for the mule. The deer watched all of this with a kind of interest. Maude filled her hat and walked around at a very slow pace, spilling oats on the ground. The grain dust hung in the air like a small cloud. The mule followed her, eating, but it wasn't long before most of the deer had a mouthful too. And a few very bold ones followed her for more.

The excited light in her eyes as she walked back to me made me smile. Maude had always been fond of deer. "Don't grin," she said in a low voice. "Deer don't like to see teeth." I clamped my mouth shut.

We had been aware of the cold all day, and always fighting the wind. Our feet were never anything but cold. But we couldn't easily freeze to death while we were on the move. Sitting so still, we were getting chilled, and there was no chance of a fire.

But we had the sweet, fruity jelly in the middle of our biscuits, enough biscuits to satisfy us, and there was little I felt I wanted to complain about. Delicious as they were, I didn't rush through my share of the biscuits but ate them slowly.

"I think we have to try Marion's way," Maude said as I licked the last bit of jelly from my fingers.

My mind was a blank. "What way is that?"

"We have to bury ourselves under the snow."

"That sounds very cold to me," I said.

It *was* very cold.

We talked all around the doing of it in low voices that

didn't seem to bother the deer. We thought up different ways it might best be done, now that all that snow lay out there. Never did it seem very likely to be an idea that worked.

In the end, we just wrapped our blankets around ourselves and picked a spot only a couple of steps from the tree line. I sat down, leaning against Maude, back to front, to share our warmth.

Maude took the trouble to pull snow down in front of us. "It seems to me the idea is to heat a small space with our own bodies. It won't do to have a big open window."

I didn't reply to this. We were as good as sitting in an open window. That morning the snow had fallen in wet, soft flakes. Now it had turned dry and fell in sharp bits that stung my face.

Maude pulled the top of her blanket over our hats and wrapped her arms around me. We had only to wait for the snow to cover us over. Maude began to talk in a low voice about walking to town in the snow the winter before, going for Aunt Ruthie's medicine, and how long and hard a walk that seemed to her then. Maude said that walk hardly seemed real to her anymore. She thought that once we reached Independence, none of this would seem real to us.

I thought it would seem real. I thought about my feet, which ached with cold. I wondered if I wouldn't do better to take off my boots and put on some dry socks. But while I thought about it, a strong lazy feeling crept over me. I felt lazy and warm.

So warm.

"This was a good idea," I said to Maude.

"What did you say, Sallie? You're mumbling."

I sank into a warm, sleepy place. If I never had to leave that place, it would be too soon for me. I tried to tell that to Maude.

"Good night, Sallie," I heard her say, and then I was dreaming. I knew it for a dream, because grass had never been so green, the sky so blue, the flowers so many. Aunt Ruthie dangled her feet in the water of a sparkling brook and said to me, "There now, that wasn't so hard, was it?"

"Aunt Ruthie," I said, "I've been meaning to tell you some thank-yous."

Sitting on Aunt Ruthie's other side, her hair grown long again, Maude laughed.

THIRTY-SIX

I WASN'T SO WARM AS I HAD BEEN BEFORE; THAT WAS THE first thing I knew. I reached for that warmth again and again, falling into it with open arms, like falling into a feather bed. But still there came a time when I could not bring it back to me.

I sat in the chill darkness for some minutes without moving. Taking stock, more or less. Maude slept on, and I had the warmth of her breath in my ear. I wished bitterly that I could sleep some more, but it would not come.

The snow was a cold weight all around us, and yet the air seemed only brisk, not frigid. I realized that we had not made the air chimney Marion had talked about, but we didn't seem to have needed it. We hadn't frozen to death either, even though we'd fallen asleep. This was all good news.

My stomach growled every so often, so I figured it was hunger that woke me. We should have eaten more than biscuits, but we had been too tired to care. I let my mind drift from one thought to another, but after a time, I got so hungry I felt sick. Just when I had begun to think about waking her, Maude said, "Me too."

"What?"

"I'm answering your stomach. I'm hungry too."

"I think it's still dark," I said.

"It doesn't matter," Maude said. "We'll follow our path back to the tree."

But when I pushed my foot straight out in front of me and broke through the snow that Maude had pulled down to shut us in, I saw light. Bright at first, making me blink, but as my eyes grew used to it, fading to no more than a pearly gray dawn.

I could see the branches of the tree right in front of us. The snow had quit. This cheered me enough to make me want to crawl out into the open, anyway. When I looked back, I saw that much of our snow cover had not even fallen down as we left. It looked like a cave.

We moved slowly, stiff with cold. Deer still stood huddled under the tree, and some of them now stood around the mule. They had pawed through to the grass, where the branches reached to the ground and the snow left off. In some spots they had eaten right down to the roots. The mule had done this, judging from the dirt on his nose.

Maude and I crawled over to the tree trunk where our bags rested, wrapped our blankets around us again, and ate. We opened paper-wrapped parcels of ham and corn bread. Although my belly was filled, my mood was not helped at all.

The wind still blew hard enough to make a whistling sound as it slid through the branches. When Maude said, "Let's get a start," I didn't really feel like going on to break snow another day. There was so much more of it than when we started out the day before. I was colder and tired now in a way I hadn't been then.

I said, "Everything has gone wrong for us, Maude."

"There is nothing in it for us to stay here," she said. "Our food will soon run out."

I said, "The snow will melt if it warms up."

"Cleomie thought we would make it to the trader's by midday yesterday," Maude argued. "He may not be that far away. We could make it by midday today."

"We can't be sure of Cleomie's signs anymore," I said. "The stone wall is covered with snow."

"His chimney smoke will be rising."

Although the thought of a fire raised my hopes a little, I said, "We may be too far off to see it. We walked south, as south as we could, but Cleomie's direction struck a winding path, and for all we know, it would have taken us east or west of there. We could miss him by a mile."

But I knew too that Maude was right. This was the beginning of winter, not the end, and we couldn't stay under the trees. I wanted only one more day. I wanted to sleep and dream of being warm. I wanted to dream of Aunt Ruthie smiling at me. The odd thing was, my feet were by now warm, even in the socks wet since the day before.

"Are your feet warm?" I asked.

"My feet are numb," Maude said, "and so, very likely, are yours."

"Don't let's think about it," I said.

Maude grimaced at my grammar, but she said, "Don't let's."

She filled her hat with oats and sprinkled the ground, the way she had the night before. She did this twice, letting the deer eat along with the mule. She was spare with the mule because he would find no grazing to aid his digestion while we walked. She fed him, because till we found him a bale of hay, he would be walking hungry.

I got my compass out. It had a little fog inside it but otherwise seemed lively enough. I moved from tree to tree, staying in their shelter as much as possible, until I came to the southernmost fringe of branches.

I looked out, expecting to see nothing but snow and more snow. That was exactly what I saw. The day was cloudy, but the look of the sky did not promise more snow. That did not lower my spirits but did not raise them either. I looked for smoke. I saw none. My spirits fell impossibly lower. I went back to help Maude load up the mule.

"See anything?" she asked me.

I shook my head.

"I keep thinking I smell bacon," she said.

Now that she said it, I imagined it too. Not only bacon, but wood smoke. It ought to have been a pleasant thing, but the cruelty of it brought tears to my eyes.

"Buck up," Maude said, sounding like Aunt Ruthie.

When we were ready, we made our way through the trees again, to strike out from that southernmost point. "We'll find the trader's place today," she said to me. "Let's just both say it."

So I said it, and I did feel a little better.

I kept saying it to myself because it was hard going. We made twenty feet in maybe ten minutes, or so it seemed. "My turn," I said, because Maude was already tiring. She turned to say something to me, but her gaze was caught by something else.

I looked behind me and saw a log cabin at not very great a distance, maybe half a mile. It lay low, looking all the lower for being half buried in snow. Smoke rose in lazy spirals from the chimney, quickly blending with the cloudiness of the day.

We had passed the cabin by the evening before, so intent were we on following the path the deer had broken. Maybe we could never have seen it anyway, the snow falling so heavily as it was at that time.

"Didn't I tell you?" Maude said to me, grinning, and because my mood was suddenly greatly improved, I said to her, "Don't show your teeth."

We went back under the trees, only stopping long enough to spill some more oats on the ground for the deer. Maude said we owed them that much for leading us to the trees. Then we were out again, and planning.

Maude said, "We'll use the deer path to get as close to that cabin as we can before we start plowing again."

We took turns often. Having that cabin right there before our eyes helped us along. Still, it seemed to take forever to get close enough as made any difference. My heart pumped furiously, sweat spilled off our foreheads, sweat soaked our clothes from the inside out.

"This is going to take all day," I complained.

For the first time, I realized that we never would have made it to anywhere before we fell exhausted in the snow. The only thing that made Maude right about leaving shelter was that we finally saw how close we had come to saving ourselves.

We were lucky to find another path of some kind. We came to the edge of it and had to step up a ways. Although the fresh snow on top was deep, the snow below had been tamped firm. When we walked there, the looser stuff came up only to our knees and we walked more easily.

"Maybe a wagon went through here before the snow got really deep," Maude said when she got her breath back. "The wagon bed may have ironed out a path right to the barn."

Even with this stroke of good luck, the second path, it took us easily more than an hour to get from the trees to a gate. It was some relief to us when the door up at the house was flung open and someone called out, "Bet you thought you would never make it. Keep on coming. You can be sure of hot coffee when you get here."

He stepped out, buttoning himself into a heavy sheepskin coat.

THIRTY-SEVEN

BEN CHAPLIN BROKE SNOW OUT TO MEET US.

"I'd know that mule anywhere," he said.

"Cleomie sent us," Maude said. "We need to buy a horse from you. And then Cleomie wants you to send this mule back to her."

"Ran into some bad luck, did you?" he asked.

"Some," Maude said. She introduced us as Johnnie and Pete. I felt a spark at hearing this, but I didn't have it in me to burst into even a small flame. It only went through my mind, if I was ever to have a name a range rider was more deserving of, I was going to have to speak fast and first. I resolved to do that. Next time.

"You boys follow me out to the barn," he said. "I couldn't believe my eyes when I saw you out here. Where'd you overnight?"

This talk took us out to the barn. Ben Chaplin broke some snow going around the cabin, huffing and puffing as he told us he dreaded a winter that snowed him in as early as December. "I don't mind being snowed in," he said, "but there's January and February still ahead of us. By then I start to talk to myself."

"My aunt Ruthie used to talk to herself all the time," I said. "So long as she thought no one was around to hear."

"What did she talk about?" Ben Chaplin asked.

"The shortcomings of other people, mostly," I said. It surprised me that he found this funny.

A path had already been cleared from his barn to his back door. A buckboard, loaded with household furnishings and covered with a waterproof, had been pulled inside the barn. "See here?" he said, as if the buckboard were a piece of evidence. "No one expected this snow."

"I believe the almanac mentions it," I said.

"Whose wagon is it?" Maude asked.

"Belongs to the Newcombs," Ben Chaplin told us. "Folks just passing through. You'll meet them when we get back up to the house. They came close to being caught out in it the way you youngsters were. It's some worse, getting a wagonload snowbound."

We walked past a herd of sheep standing out in the sacrifice, the area that was always so stamped over that no grass grew there at all. Of course we couldn't see ground. It was just snow and sheep, sheep and snow. "Dogs brought 'em in," he said. "That's when I knew we were in for some weather. Just had no idea how *much* weather."

There were no less than thirty mules and horses in the barn. It was blessedly warm, and the work helped to warm us as well. We brushed the mule dry and tossed him some hay, while Ben Chaplin went around telling his hired hands what he wanted done that day.

By the time Ben Chaplin came back to us, my feet had begun to ache like a bad tooth. "Good," he said when I complained. "If it took much longer, I'd be worried you were in really bad shape."

"Where is it you're headed?" Ben Chaplin asked us.

"Texas," Maude said, and threw a look at me. I didn't need that look. I knew not to tell him where we wanted to go.

"We'll get you outfitted," Ben Chaplin said. "Plenty of time to talk about that. Nobody's going out of here till the snow melts."

We were shepherded into the cabin, which was of a good size and smelled good—it smelled of breakfast. Plates of food were set out on the table. I made a meal of bacon wrapped in a flapjack. I asked for cold milk to wash it down. It felt too warm in the cabin after working in the barn, but I was not complaining about it.

Mrs. Newcomb knew right from the start that we weren't boys, but she didn't give us away. The only way we knew she was on to us was the way her eyes laughed and her voice put a question mark at the end of our false names when she used them. She knew the trick to bringing our feet back. She made us soak them in pans of cool water that she added hot water to, little by little, until our feet were warm.

The Newcombs were fine enough company, if it came down to that. He played a mean game of gin rummy and told good stories. She had taken over the job of cooking in return for shelter, and shortly regarded Maude and me as regular kitchen help, which we did not mind in the slightest. Peeling potatoes or washing dishes was a fine trade for bedding down near a woodstove and waking to the smell of coffee on the boil.

We met the hired hands again at dinnertime. They were called Mack and Joe. They didn't talk much, but they were mannerly enough at the table. We learned they slept in the barn. There were two alcoves for sleeping, one belonged to Ben Chaplin and the Newcombs took the extra.

We would be sleeping in the front room that night, if we didn't mind sleeping on the floor. I was glad we weren't expected to sleep in the barn. I liked being able to sidle up to the woodstove and toast myself.

"I guess this is a regular thing for girls to do if they have to travel alone," Maude said as we lay in front of the open woodstove and watched the flames dance. Ben and the Newcombs could be heard snoring behind the curtains that shut off the alcoves at each end of the cabin.

"It's funny how the women know and the men don't," I said.

"Cleomie says it takes one to know one," Maude said.

"Yeah, but what does it take to know when you ain't one?"

"Sallie, your grammar gets worse all the time."

"Good, huh?" I said, knowing she didn't think so at all. But I had a notion my grammar wasn't going to be very important where we were going. It would be more important that we could ride long and hard, and survive a night in the snow. I was proud of us.

Maude turned over with an exasperated sigh and fell asleep.

The next morning we joined the men in cleaning out stalls. It was only in the late afternoon that we were freed up to go into the house to help out there.

It came as a nasty shock when Maude laid some newspaper on the table for potato peeling. "Would you look at this?" she said to me in a whisper, and set to reading.

I looked. It was a copy of the same paper we'd picked up at Cleomie's. "Oh, boy," I said, knowing we were in for some sparks now.

I yanked the paper away and folded it under my arm. "I need the outhouse," I said. Mrs. Newcomb gave this fast action a surprised look. Being glad suddenly that she knew we were girls, I acted younger than my age. In a mewly voice, I asked Maude, "Would you come with me?"

Once outside, Maude snatched the paper back and strode ahead of me. If we had been breaking snow, she could have taken us all the way to Independence. In the outhouse, we read all about Mad Maude.

"Notorious?" Maude wailed. "Notorious! What is the matter with these people? Do they think they're writing dimers? Don't they feel a responsibility to report the truth? Or don't they even know the difference between the truth and their fevered imaginations?"

"Marion said it's just how they sell papers," I said. "Don't take it to heart."

"Are you crazy?" Maude yelled. "Next they'll be telling the world we ride with Jesse James and Cole Younger. Texas won't be far enough for me to go, Sallie. It might not do for me to stop in Mexico."

"You have to calm down," I said. "Aunt Ruthie would have told you it will all come out in the wash."

Maude said, "Aunt Ruthie never said that about anything more serious than a misunderstanding with Mrs. Golightly," and let the matter drop for the time being. But I knew we would be having this talk again.

THIRTY-EIGHT

———•———

IBURNED THAT NEWSPAPER AND PUT SOME FRESH ONES on the table, while Maude took refuge in a bad mood, being snappish if she talked at all. She lost Mrs. Newcomb's good opinion, I could see, but there was nothing to be done for it. It was not till the men came inside that Maude settled herself in a corner to look boylike.

They were all in good spirits. The weather had warmed, and they had hopes of a melt. The Newcombs were interested in making the last twenty miles of their journey with furnishings they had gleaned from a relative's attic. Ben Chaplin and his men were cheered to think the winter had not begun in earnest.

Maude took up a game of dominoes with the hired hand named Joe. "That your real name?" she asked him, but of course I was the only one who knew this was just Maude's sense of humor. Joe took the question seriously and told her he was called Joe, but his name was Joseph.

Once they had begun the game, Maude seemed over the worst of the shock she'd had. If she didn't share everyone's cheerful mood, they didn't know it. Later, when we'd turned in for the night, Maude said, "What if they are all wrong? What if we are trapped here till spring?"

Thinking her mind was on that newspaper, I said, "We don't need to worry. No one can chase after us either."

"We don't know that. There might be enough of them to break snow without getting so worn out," she said. "Or they might have snowshoes."

I had pointed these contraptions out to her in the mercantile the previous winter, mostly to make a point of what I'd learned while reading *Wild Woolly*. I was sorry now for being such a show-off. Maude might never have noticed such things and known what they were for.

"We never actually saw anyone use snowshoes," I said. "Even if they tried, they certainly aren't going to be able to follow our trail; it's covered over."

Maude said, "We've come so far. If they had stopped us sooner, even after Des Moines, it wouldn't have been so bad. I still wasn't sure we were going to make it this far. It will break me in half to be stopped now."

I stewed over this as the fire in the woodstove burned down and the room cooled. I asked, "How far do you reckon we have to go?"

"Ben Chaplin mentioned it today," she said sleepily. "We're a week's ride from Independence."

This was better than I had hoped to hear. I could almost get up the gumption to do it. We still didn't sleep for some time after that, because I went on to miss Cleomie. Maude said she hoped Cleomie didn't worry about us in the snow. Or about her mule.

We woke the next morning to the sound of rain falling outside. It was not a hard rain, more of a drizzle. But rain meant warmer air. If it was warm enough to rain instead of snow, it might get warmer yet.

The less fortunate side of this turn of events was that it made for slippery going once we stepped out the door. There was not one of us who did not take a nasty fall on our trip to the outhouse, getting ourselves soaked to the skin in the icy snowmelt.

But soon after breakfast, Ben Chaplin and his boys rigged a rope from the back door to the outhouse, and to the barn and to the water pump, the only places we could want to go.

We went out to the barn and cleaned stalls with the others, leaving Mrs. Newcomb to "enjoy some privacy," as Mr. Newcomb put it. By this, we gathered she planned to take a bath. For the first time, I wished I wasn't pretending to be a boy.

The rain went on all the livelong day. The snow on the roof had been washed away by evening. The roped-off paths had turned into muddy trenches. The boot scraper was put to frequent use. The next day was the same, and by the end of it, the snow lay not much higher than my knees.

A hopeful look had begun to light Maude's eyes. If the weather continued warm, we might be on our way in another day. Talk around the table reminded us that if it turned cold overnight, all of the outdoors would be a sheet of ice.

This talk did not discourage Maude. She believed it would remain warm. She and Ben Chaplin talked horses, and she arranged to buy some supplies from him as well. She had twice gone back out to the trees with a nosebag filled with oats and sprinkled the ground for the deer. We were going to need more grain for the horse she bought.

It was well past dinner, as cards and dominoes were being put aside, when we heard the sound of riders. Ben Chaplin looked up from making his nightly mess of crumbling salted crackers into a bowl of milk, a concoction he swore made him sleep sound as a baby.

"Aw, now my crackers will get too soggy," he said.

Maude's face had turned white at the sound of hoofbeats, and she did not stand to join the hands as Mack said, "We'll take care of the horses, boss, and tell the riders to bed down in the barn. Eat your mess."

I knew what Maude was thinking. Whether they bedded in the barn, or on the floor near us, we could not avoid running into them.

We had very little time to think about this. The hands went outside, and as Ben Chaplin dug into his mess, a gunshot rang out.

Someone set up a howl, but this was only the background music to the dance being done inside. Ben Chaplin leaped from the table to snatch his rifle off the gun rack. Maude did the same, for her rifle and my shotgun were there too. A blanket covered my saddlebag, and I pulled it all over to where I sat. Marion had loaded the six-shooter, and I was anxious to try it.

The Newcombs ran for their bed. The curtain had not yet been yanked across to hide them when the door burst open and three men rushed in with a great deal of yelling and other noise. One of them knocked Maude against the wall and knocked Ben's rifle to the floor. That quickly, they had the upper hand.

Another of them motioned with a gun at the Newcombs, to make them go back to their chairs. The third man looked all around the room like he expected someone else to shoot at them.

He did not give me a second glance.

I had jumped up without thinking, without the six-shooter in my hand. I knew this for a mistake, and I felt terrible about it. I was not used to seeing Maude treated in such a manner, that was true, but without the gun I could be no help to her either.

"Anybody else here?" the first man asked Ben Chaplin. I say "man," but what came clear to me in those moments was that these men were not very much older than Maude. Fat and soft-looking, short, except for the one that was taller than anyone else in the room. That one looked like he'd been run through a wringer to get that stretched. They were all of them soaked and dripping water; that was the next thing I noticed. They were cold, which made some sense of the crazy way they had about them. They were crazed, but they were only boys.

"No," was Ben Chaplin's answer. "Nobody else."

And the boy waved someone else in.

The two hired hands came in. Joe was clearly hurt and still making a lot of noise about it. He wasn't able to put one foot down it seemed and was pretty much being carried by Mack and another man whose clothing slapped wetly as he moved. They took him straight over to a chair and set him down in it.

Mrs. Newcomb was crying as loudly as Joe. This noise

added to the general mood, which was one of upset and anger. It is true that in moments such as these, someone making an awful lot of fuss—for no reason at all that I could see, no one had knocked her against the wall—could get herself shot for no reason. I had read of it in my dimers. For this reason, I was grateful that my sister was not the weepy sort.

Maude still sat on the floor and watched all that went on with narrowed eyes. She was not too badly hurt, so far as I could tell, but her face was held stiff as a clean sheet. She looked as little like a girl as I could hope.

Mack yanked Joe's boot off, which caused Joe to yell all the more. "Oh, my," Mack shouted in an aggrieved fashion. "You've shotten his little toe off."

This announcement did Joe no good at all. He nearly fell off the chair. But Ben Chaplin acted quickly, tying a string tightly around the stump and wrapping the foot in a linen towel, which began immediately to turn red. He raised Joe's foot to rest on the table.

What followed was all confusion.

THIRTY-NINE

BEN CHAPLIN ORDERED MACK TO GET A NEEDLE AND thread. The shivering boy who seemed most in charge of things put up some argument over this and told another of the boys to follow Mack around to be sure a needle and thread was all he got.

There were accusations thrown around by all three boys. Even the one following Mack to watch him take a box from a shelf had something to say. All of the accusations concerned who did the shooting and whether any shooting ought to have been done. I did not get clear on who had done the shooting.

But then I wasn't really looking at them, or listening too closely. Because the fourth man, the one who'd helped to carry in Joe, was none other than Marion Hardly. He was looking at me with the same kind of surprise that I could feel on my own face. And when I opened my mouth to say I don't even know what, he shook his head, and gave me to know I was to say nothing.

This offended me. Didn't he think I knew better than to say his name? If I *had* said his name, I doubted anyone would have heard it, anyway.

I glanced at Maude. She had seen Marion too. Pale or not, her eyes looked ready to bite him. I couldn't really say I blamed her. She had narrowly accepted his apologies for Aunt Ruthie's death, she had not yet entirely forgiven him for the bank robbery, and here he was shooting up Ben Chaplin's ranch.

But there was already a fight in every corner, and Maude was the sort who liked to have the floor when she was making her complaints known. I had no doubt she was waiting for her chance.

It was soon to come.

The argument had not entirely died down when the boy I had guessed to be the leader decided to end it by simply moving on. "Dusty, stay here and keep an eye on them while we put the horses up," he said, loudly enough to be heard over the other two arguing with him, and over Joe's howling and Mrs. Newcomb's loud sobs. All was pandemonium.

Dusty.

Dusty looked likely enough to keep an eye on us. The others exited with a great noise of hard-heeled boots, the very kind Maude despised. But once the door slammed shut behind them, the cabin went strangely quiet.

Mrs. Newcomb fell back to loud, hiccupy breathing and a lot of sniffling. Joe dropped from a howl to merely whining. It relieved the tension in the room the minute those others had stepped out, even if they were sure to come back.

"I'm sorry about this," Marion said to us all when they had gone.

An apology was so unexpected that Joe forgot to whimper, even at the sight of Ben Chaplin threading a needle. Mrs.

Newcomb's hankie was already to the wringing-out stage, so Mr. Newcomb stepped forward to get a table napkin for her.

It had been used earlier, refolded, and put back down at the same place. I believed it to be my napkin, and as she blew her nose in it, I intended not to need it again.

"Willie is not always so short-tempered," Marion went on to say in the near quiet. He threw off his jacket, but his shirt was wet beneath it. "We were bedded down for the night not far from here when a gullywasher swept over us and drowned two of his men. It's put him in a poor frame of mind."

Everyone in the room, save Maude and me, breathed a sigh of relief. It could be seen that Marion was not trigger-happy; at least one of these men was not someone to be quite so afraid of.

"You say 'his men' like you are not one of them," Ben Chaplin said.

"I'm riding with them for a time, it's true," Marion said. "I fell in with bad company, that was plain to me right away, and I was resolved to sneak off while they slept that night. I fell asleep myself, sad to say. Then the weather hit, and I saw they were just boys who weren't going to make it if I left them on their own."

He had no sooner made this explanation than Maude said, "Dusty Har de Har Har to the rescue."

"Stop that," Marion said.

"Yes, stop it," Ben echoed. He looked at her like she was crazy.

"We know this man," Maude said. "He is a fool, but he is not much like these men he is traveling with."

Ben looked back to Marion for the proof of this statement.

"Were they following us?" I asked, figuring there were no secrets to keep.

"They were riding down on us," Marion said, "but they did not mean to follow us. When I saw the kind they were, I took advantage of some tracks I'd seen and concocted a story to lead them off in another direction. I told them I'd seen a wagonload of whiskey going westward. That was all it took."

"I might owe you thanks," Maude said, "but I hardly know whether to trust someone who takes his names from dime novels. You also said you don't ride so rough and here you are, riding as rough as I've ever seen."

"All right, but you and Sallie keep quiet, or we may all be sorry," Marion said.

"Sallie?" Ben said, and looked back at us.

I was some bothered. This was the first person who believed us to be boys for more than a minute or so, and now Marion was about to ruin it for us.

"They are girls," Mrs. Newcomb cried. "Wild girls, who've been making a lot of trouble!"

"Now that's not true," Marion said, coming to our defense, even over Maude's cry of protest. Maude stepped toward Mrs. Newcomb like she might do the woman some damage, but even this was forestalled by Marion when he snatched Maude back by the collar of her shirt. "They are girls, but not wild ones. They didn't rob that bank. I did."

Mrs. Newcomb greeted this report with a loud shriek.

"Stop that foolishness," Marion said, losing his patience.

"She didn't know about the bank," I said.

Marion turned wide eyes on me. "Then what did she mean about making trouble?"

I shrugged. "Maybe we look like trouble to her," I said, seeing Mrs. Newcomb was sobbing like a child.

Marion banged his gun on the table like a judge. "Can we have some quiet here? We have only a minute before they get back."

Ben Chaplin said, "What do you mean to tell us?"

"Only that Willie has never killed anyone," Marion said. "He wants to, but he can't bring himself to do it. Now he may be satisfied with shooting off your toe, young feller, that he's made a manly appearance. Or his boys may make him feel it's a poor job he did. There's no telling."

Mr. Newcomb said, "You and that girl, she looks ready enough, could take up your guns and shoot them as they come back in. Then we would be shed of them."

"I'm not in favor of that plan," Marion said. "We would kill three young men for no greater sin than rowdy behavior at the cost of one toe. All you need to do to get shed of them is do exactly what they tell you. Don't bother them with risky business like trying to shoot them. They'll be out of here to-morrow. Maybe with a change of horses, if you can stand it." This last was said to Ben Chaplin.

"They can have any horse on the place," Ben Chaplin said, "and it will be a bargain all around, just to be rid of them." He turned back to the business of Joe's foot, telling Mack to pinch off the flow of blood as soon as the towel was removed.

"That's it then. Just lay low and don't trouble them," Marion said. "And don't do any more talking about these girls," he said to Mrs. Newcomb in particular. "Or bank robbing, nothing. Got that?"

When she didn't answer, but looked offended herself, he added, "Or I may be tempted to do some shooting after all."

This brought forth another shriek, and she fell against her husband. He did not look all that welcoming, but at least things were in the right state when Willie and his boys clomped up the steps and came back into the cabin.

FORTY

THEY WENT STRAIGHT FOR THE STOVE TO WARM themselves. The one called Willie looked around the room at all of our frightened faces and said, "Good boy, Dusty," as if he was patting a dog.

Ben Chaplin set to stitching while Mack held Joe's heel to the table, and Joe himself began to wriggle around on his chair and howl some more. I suppose the missing toe must have caused him some pain because I've had stitches taken myself, and it didn't hurt all that much.

Then again, the spirits that Ben Chaplin claimed would help with the pain did seem to annoy Joe when poured over his toe. He wasn't much helped by drinking the stuff either.

Some people are squeamish about that sort of thing. Maude, for instance, got more bleached-looking each time that bloody towel flashed where she could see it. She had gone so pale she by this time looked a little green, something I would not have thought possible if I wasn't looking right at her.

Willie said he was hungry. The bloody towel didn't bother him one bit. Mrs. Newcomb wasn't so much bothered by the towel but looked likely to faint when Willie suggested she ought to be laying out some food.

I said, "I'm in charge of the kitchen, me and my brother, Johnnie. We have some cold pork chops and some biscuits with jelly. Will that do you?"

"That will do us just fine," Willie said. From the looks of things, he was just as happy to get a little cooperation as he was to shoot off people's toes.

I put four tin plates on the table and a platter in the middle, and put the jelly out so they could help themselves. We had cold coffee left from supper, but I had more than once noticed that coffee tended to liven people up. We didn't want these fellows livened up one bit. I dipped some cold water into mugs and set those out.

I'd have offered clean napkins if we had them, but it didn't seem we did. They would have to make do. The three of them spent these few minutes poking around the room, nosing into stuff that didn't belong to them. The saddlebags were still more covered by my blanket than not, and did not come to their notice.

They mostly talked about how good it would be to sleep in a bed. Marion, or Dusty, as I had to remember to call him, sat down at the table rather politely for a range rider.

Ben Chaplin finished up the job of sewing and, having heard the talk of the beds, made up a pallet for Joe on one side of the wood burner. He gave him a pill that looked like a nugget of dried meat.

"Here, what's that you're giving him?" Willie said like a child jealous of the Christmas candy.

Ben Chaplin held the jar up and said, "It'll help him sleep, even though he has pain. I give it to my animals, should they need it."

This caused Willie to lose interest, or maybe the food was just more of an attraction. I was chiding myself, and Ben Chaplin too. Me, for not wondering harder about that pill, which any range rider ought to do when something new turns up. And Ben Chaplin, for not thinking to pass me some of those pills. I could have put several of them into the coffee and served it without a qualm. We could have snuffed them boys out like candles.

However, having learned my lesson, I watched to see where Ben put the bottle. There might yet come a time when I could use it. I also watched Joe, wondering how long it would take those pills to put him out.

Meanwhile, a kind of unsteady peace settled over the room as the boys sat down to eat. The shortage of chairs caused the Newcombs to claim a corner on the other side of the wood burner. At first Mrs. Newcomb perched on a stack of wood like a nervous hen. She acted like she had forgotten how to sit anywhere but on a chair, or maybe she objected to the generally dirty state of the floor.

Mr. Newcomb sat with his back to the wood, resting easy with his choice. His wife could have had a cleaner corner, but it wouldn't have been nearly so warm come the middle of the night. Floor space was being treated like good bottomland, all of us staking our claim.

Joe was out cold, I noticed, in a matter of maybe five minutes.

Maude and I dragged our stuff over to our usual spots, leaving a little room for Ben Chaplin. Our eyes met, and

Maude tried to send a message that I couldn't read. There was no chance for more.

After the boys had eaten, Willie's mood seemed to have improved. He spoke to Marion. He said, "Well, Dusty, I have a couple of openings in my gang, if you want to join up."

Marion said, "I appreciate the offer, Willie. But I'm kind of a loner."

"We need a loner, Dusty," Willie insisted.

"Could be you're right about that, Willie. You're usually right," Marion said. "But I have to think on it some."

"You think you'll have thought enough by morning?" Willie asked, scratching his head.

"I'd like to get on my way in the morning, if the weather allows it," Marion said.

"I don't know," Willie said. "This looks like a fine enough place to stay till it warms up some."

"It did warm up," one of Willie's boys said. "That's how come we nearly got drownded. My cousin is dead back there."

"Now I hope you aren't going to blame me for that," Willie said, scratching some more.

"Nope," the boy said. "You ain't to blame for nothing. I'm just saying, the weather's warm enough."

"Not for me, it isn't," Willie said.

This had a bad feeling to it. Like that better mood could change faster than a rattlesnake could turn its head. "Maybe you ought to try Texas," I said in a respectful tone. "It's warm there."

Marion shot me a look from under his eyebrows. I pretended not to see it.

"Horrible dry too," the other boy said by way of complaint.

"Which is maybe a good thing," I said. "Considering."

This struck Willie awful funny. Laughter erupted out of him like someone hit him on the back.

I felt pretty good about this for a few seconds. Not only because everybody likes to feel like they say something funny once in a while, but also because I didn't like to have Willie looking only at me. Laughing closed his eyes.

Once started, he went on and on laughing for maybe two or three minutes, tears leaking out the corners of his eyes.

Suddenly the tears were real. Really real. He was crying quietly. His boys acted like they didn't even notice, so I did the same thing. Just went about my business, like, settling down for the night.

Maude heaved a deep sigh as I lay down next to her. I knew just how she felt. For the few moments that Willie's attention was on me, I had been in danger, I knew it in my marrow. Marion was right; we had to stay out of Willie's way.

"Don't stand too close to them," Maude whispered to me.

"Hey now, we'll have no whispering here," Willie said.

"We're just saying our prayers," Maude told him. And, like she was finishing up, she said, "Our souls to keep."

I shut my eyes and kept them that way till those boys started choosing up their beds. Then I looked at Maude and raised my eyebrows in question. She scratched her head hard, and I remembered how Aunt Ruthie used to move the kids who scratched their heads too hard to one side of the classroom. I understood. Willie had lice.

FORTY-ONE

I WOKE UP WHEN MAUDE DID, STILL IN THE DARK CHILL of early morning. It had been my intention to stay awake for as long as the talk went on, so that I might hear what plans were being made. I fell asleep fast and deep, as if I'd taken one of the same pills Joe took. Except that he was still out.

Marion had slept on the floor, as did Ben Chaplin, Mack and Joe, and the Newcombs. Ben Chaplin put on his sheepskin coat as soon as he left his blankets. He and Mack went out to the barn as usual, to tend the livestock, and Marion went with them.

Mr. Newcomb worked up the stove, until a wonderful heat began to come off it. Mrs. Newcomb sat at the table like she had come for tea. Maude looked longingly at the gun rack, but such was the hold those fellows had on everyone that they slept like babies while our guns hung there. No one doubted that things would end badly for someone if we had to shoot it out with Willie.

Without so much as a word to each other, the Newcombs took their coats off the hooks and stepped outside. Cold air scuttled across the floor for a moment, and then the door was quietly closed.

Maybe they planned this out as they lay in the dark; I couldn't say. Maude and I looked at each other. Were they simply making a trip to the outhouse? Were they hoping to escape? Should we do the same?

But we had lost our taste for being afoot in bad weather. We stayed wrapped in our blankets for as long as it took to know that it was up to us to get breakfast. Maude said to me in a low voice, "Not one more word to that fellow while he's here, okay?"

"Do you think he's going to stay?"

"I think we're going to be in big trouble if he does," Maude said. "Marion's in big trouble if they leave and he goes with them."

I rolled up our pallets rather sloppily, covering the saddlebags with them. Maude began to pull flour and such from the hutch where things were stored. There were still snores coming from the beds.

I pointed to the box of nuggets from up top the hutch. "Give me that. I'm going to dose the coffee." Maude handed it to me without a word.

Ben Chaplin came in at that minute with a bucket of eggs. He set it on the table and came to the stove to warm his hands. He spotted the box of nuggets. "Don't do anything foolish," he said. "I'm hoping they'll leave today."

"They aren't likely to leave if we're too hospitable," Maude said, looking at the bucket of eggs.

Ben Chaplin said, "First let's give them a chance to go peacefully."

Maude took this hard, but only someone who knew her would be able to tell. She had what Aunt Ruthie called a poker face for moments like this. Because she used it, I knew Maude liked the idea of putting Willie out of commission right away. Or at least, as soon as we could.

So did I. I didn't care if we had to feed him those nuggets till spring in order to keep him on ice. Then I thought, what good was putting those boys to sleep, really? Maybe the better idea was just to put them out of our misery.

"Is there any poison around?" I whispered to Maude. "Any rat poison?"

Ben Chaplin's ears practically rose to a point on hearing this. I doubted Maude was ready to go that far, but I might be. If Willie planned to stay around for long, I just might be. I wanted to ask Ben Chaplin about the Newcombs, but before we could talk further, one of those boys snorted and coughed and woke up.

"I'm making breakfast," Maude said to Ben Chaplin as the boys tumbled each other out of bed. "If Joe wakes up, is there anything I ought to do for him?"

"He won't wake up till sometime this afternoon," Ben Chaplin said. "Don't worry about him." Willie and his boys trundled by us like great bears coming out of the cave, hardly seeing us at all.

They stood on the edge of the porch; they didn't go all the way to the outhouse. It was only a minute that they were out there, but Maude stepped over to the gun rack and pulled back the hammer on Ben Chaplin's rifle and her own. She pulled back both hammers on my shotgun too.

Ben Chaplin saw this and went out the door, saying, "I'll

be in the barn with Mack." He spoke in a tone that meant, I'll have nothing to do with this, which I must admit did not sit well with me. *We* were not his trouble, and I didn't like to be counted among them.

Furthermore, he had not uttered a protest when it was Mr. Newcomb who suggested that Maude and Marion shoot the boys dead. He might well have gone along with it if Marion had been more agreeable.

This put Marion in quite a rosy light, as he would never allow Maude to risk her life, and I hoped she was taking that into consideration. Marion had put himself on the line for us, which was more than Ben Chaplin cared to do, however highly Cleomie appeared to think of him.

When Ben Chaplin came inside for breakfast, the Newcombs did not come with him. Maude stood at the stove, starting another round of scrambled eggs, while I served the table. I looked at Maude and then at the box of nuggets as I stirred sugar into the coffee.

But Maude gave me a disapproving look. She felt she'd agreed to Ben Chaplin's terms, and she would abide by her agreement. To my mind, she had not agreed; she had simply not argued the point. She had, after all, been the one to pull the hammers on the guns.

The chairs were filled, and I hoped the Newcombs' absence would not be noticed. Willie didn't seem to notice much. He didn't speak to anyone till after breakfast, which in his case was three helpings of everything, and no one spoke to him.

Very likely we all would have gone on without talking just as well, but for the fact that a full belly made him talkative, just as it had the night before. "You boys are good cooks," Willie said.

I gave him a nod without quite meeting his eyes.

He said to Ben Chaplin, "You there, you any relation to them?"

"Nope," Ben said. Then, thinking better of his answer, he said, "They're my neighbor's boys. Happened to be here when the snow got to blowing pretty bad."

I appreciated that Ben Chaplin said that much on our behalf, but it was a moment that got swept aside as Willie asked us, "How would you boys like to join up with a gang?"

He had that same mood on, like he was handing out presents. I remembered how quickly that mood had gone quickly from good to bad, and from bad to worse. Maude remembered too, because she had frozen in the midst of measuring the flour for another batch of biscuits. It struck me suddenly; this was more or less the same kind of feeling of being asked to marry someone she didn't want, and she didn't do well with that feeling. It was up to me to get us out of this.

"Aw, we can't," I said, trying to look flattered and regretful at the same time. "Our family depends on the money we make here, working for Ben Chaplin. They'd starve without us, and you don't want that to happen, I'm sure. You're a thoughtful man; I saw that in you right away."

There was a kind of war being fought on Willie's face, between the disappointment of being told no by a no-account boy who should be honored enough to say yes, oh yes, and thank you, and the idea of being a man who was known for having finer feelings.

"It was a good idea you had last night, Willie," Marion said, then went back to picking his teeth with his knife.

"What idea was that?" Willie asked.

"Texas."

Willie gave the beams overhead a considering look, then said, "It was a better idea yesterday than today."

I wanted to say, why's that? I bit my tongue to keep it still. Maude must have known how I felt because she laid the spatula on my arm and when I looked at her, gave a quick shake of her head. Why did no one think I had a lick of sense? Had I not already kept quiet?

"Why's that?" one of Willie's boys asked.

"Now if I thought you need to know why, I would have said, wouldn't I?" Willie said in a voice to chill the blood. It chilled mine.

The boy said, "I just asked, that's all."

"I'm pretty sure you blamed me for the flood last night."

"Now, Willie—"

There was no chance to learn how Willie's boys handled him. The rattle of wagon traces drew Willie's attention. He clopped Ben Chaplin one to the head and said, "You trying to fool me?"

Ben Chaplin said, "I am not." His glance moved to the jar of nuggets, and I knew he regretted that he had not agreed to putting them in Willie's coffee.

Willie got to the door with surprising speed and threw it open. "You good folks going somewhere?"

FORTY-TWO

MRS. NEWCOMB SHRIEKED, THOUGH WILLIE HAD NOT yet done anything to give her cause. I hoped she would not inspire him. Mr. Newcomb's voice was high and reedy when he answered, "We hoped to get an early start."

Willie whined, "It's still icy out here. It isn't safe to travel on ice in a wagon."

"We are experienced with the wagon," Mr. Newcomb said.

"Come in and set a while," Willie said in a manner that was both cordial and would not be ignored.

After a long moment during which they must have weighed their chances and found them slim, the Newcombs climbed down from their wagon. Ben Chaplin got up from the table, clearing his place.

I washed the plates, for we were short of plates, and put them back on the table.

The Newcombs looked washed out and scared as they sat down. I thought we'd have done well to serve them some beef liver. I had been somewhat peeved with Mrs. Newcomb the evening before, but I could only feel sorry for her now.

It was not a comfortable thing to bear the burden of Willie's attention.

Maude filled the platter again, more eggs and bacon, and I set it on the table. "Fresh biscuits aren't ready yet," I said. "Sorry."

"Right unfriendly of you folks to go without saying good-bye," Willie said. "You've hurt my feelings."

The Newcombs had nothing to say to this.

"Eat up," Willie said, since neither of them had lifted a fork. "I have to think about how you're going to make it up to me."

The hair stood on the back of my neck. I had no doubt it was standing on the Newcombs' necks as well. All those at the table had stilled their bodies in some way. No one drummed their fingers on a mug, no one scratched their whiskers, and no one cleared their throat.

Joe slumbered on.

Maude turned and stuck a tin mug and a spoon in my hand. The mug was filled with fluffy scrambled eggs and two slices of bacon. She pointed to the corner where I'd pushed our stuff out of the way.

I went. For one thing, I was hungry. The Newcombs were in big trouble, but my stomach either didn't know or didn't care. It started to growl the minute I had some eggs to call my own. The other thing I knew, in the saddlebags was the only gun, save Marion's, that might be turned against Willie. As I sat down there, I just hoped the business would wait until I had eaten.

Mrs. Newcomb began to cry.

In much the same way he might have said, my coffee has gone cold, I'll have some hot, Willie said, "Shut up that cater-wauling or I'll have to shoot you to get some peace and quiet."

Mrs. Newcomb only got louder.

"Now, Willie, you don't want to go shooting this woman here," Marion said, loudly enough to be heard over her voice.

"Why not?"

"For one thing, you have all these witnesses," Marion said. "Seems to me, if you want to go around killing someone, you want to do it quiet like, so you don't get yourself hung."

Willie said, "I don't plan to get myself hung, but I can't go around all quiet like. I can't make myself a reputation that way."

This surprised me. Maude had done next to nothing, and a reputation dogged her like her own shadow. But nothing Willie said served to ease the tension in the room. It didn't help that everyone had to yell to be heard, since what Mrs. Newcomb was doing now could indeed be termed caterwauling.

"Now there's the other thing," Marion said, pushing his chair back from the table a bit. He took up his cup of coffee and balanced the chair on the back legs, probably to make it look like the usual push back from the table, but I noticed he held his cup with his right hand, leaving his gun hand free.

He went on to say, "She's a defenseless woman. Killing her won't get you the kind of reputation you're looking for. You have to gun down some fast-draw sheriff or somebody like that."

I rummaged through the saddlebag as quietly as I was

able. Considering I had to work under a layer of blankets and feel around for the six-gun without anyone taking notice of me, it was just as well the talk was turning excitable.

"Where'm I going to find anybody of that description?" Willie asked, Mrs. Newcomb now forgotten. She took note of this, and her noise worked its way down to a kind of keening.

"Texas," Marion said.

"Don't let's get started on Texas again," one of Willie's boys complained. It was not the one who had spoken up about drowning, but the other one. "It's a long ride, and no guarantee that we're going to find anything but rattlesnakes and wild Indians when we get there."

I pulled the pistol to the top of the bag. I had never realized how heavy it was till then. I guessed it to be heavier than my shotgun overall, even though it was much smaller. I put both hands into the saddlebag and eased back the hammer.

Maude had meanwhile gone over by the woodpile and sat down. This put her a little out of the easy line of fire, and it also put her in easy reach of the gun rack. I admit to a jittery feeling in the general area of my breakfast, which felt like a mistake, now that it lay like a brick in my middle. But if there was trouble brewing, I couldn't sit here in the corner and watch it happen without trying to help out.

"I'm thinking of Tennessee, myself." This boy had a fair amount of nerve.

"You don't mean you're thinking of leaving me in the lurch," Willie said. He was not smart, but he was, nevertheless, quick on the uptake.

"Now, Willie, don't get like that," this boy said. "Your

momma and mine are sisters, and they won't either one of them take kindly to you shooting at me."

"What kind of gang only has two people?" Willie complained.

"The kind that is a loner," the other boy said, setting both hands flat to the table as if to say, and that's that. "For Tennessee is sounding good to me too."

"I don't want to be a loner," Willie shouted. "I am the leader of this gang. You are both coming to Texas with me!" He did a most unexpected thing. He snatched up the knife he'd used at breakfast and stabbed that boy's hand.

I saw the spurt of blood in the air, and the boy leaped up, screaming, going for his gun. Marion and Maude were on their feet, both reaching for guns, even as I pulled the six-gun from the saddlebag. Willie stood too, his chair falling as he shot wildly, all of this happening at once.

Willie was quick on the draw, for he had stabbed the boy and shot Marion before anyone else got off a shot. The only gun coming out near as soon was mine, and not because I was fast but because I'd gotten a head start, and it went off at the same time Willie's did.

And then Willie dropped to the floor.

While pulling the gun out of the saddlebag and pointing it in the general direction of all the fuss and bother, I accidentally pulled the trigger. The gun was heavy and took firmer handling than I realized. I didn't mean to be so firm with it in the trigger area, but I was not experienced enough with the rifle. I was not at all experienced with this.

The gun fired, and I felt it like a wave running back

through my wrists, up my arms, and into my neck, rocking me. It was almost as if that gun cuffed me on the head.

I was the only one who knew what happened at first. Marion and that boy were both holding on to their injured parts, and Maude's rifle was pointed at Willie, or at least at the air where Willie had been.

His cousin rolled him over and said, "He's been shot. Which one of you murderers has killed him?"

No one replied to this. From where I sat, I could see that there was a good deal of blood pouring out of Willie. It made me feel a little sick to the stomach, and I was glad Maude stood where she did. She did not do well with the bloody towel; she would do even worse with this mess. The floor would probably have to be pulled up and new wood laid.

"I'm only shot, not dead," Willie said. "But I would like to kill the one that backshot me, so who was it?"

"It looks to be that boy over there," Willie's cousin said, pointing at me.

"That's no boy," Mrs. Newcomb shouted, her eyes gone large. "They are girls, wild girls!" And then she fainted. Which was good, because it wouldn't have taken much more to convince me to shoot her too.

Willie said, "I've been shot by a girl?"

FORTY-THREE

IS COUSIN SAID, "LOOKS THAT WAY."

"Promise me," Willie said, "that you won't tell anybody?"

"Ever'body done seen it," his cousin said.

Willie coughed a long, strange cough. And then, when I waited to hear what was to happen next, he said nothing. Nothing at all.

"Well, the bullet may not have done him in," his cousin said sadly, "but that news sure did."

"You mean it?" the other boy said. His hand was bleeding nearly as good as Willie had been. I could see why he sounded hopeful. "He's dead?"

"I mean it," Willie's cousin said. "He already looks a little dead."

"You boys get over there by the wall with your hands in the air," Maude said.

"Now you don't need to take that attitude with us," the cousin said. "It's Willie here who you want to be mad at."

"I can decide for myself who I'm mad at," Maude said. "I shoot every bit as well as my sister, so I'd advise you to do what I say. I don't give out third chances, and you're on your second."

"We ain't gonna be captured by no girl," the cousin said. He was the one that was not bleeding. The other was in a more agreeable frame of mind and shuffled a few steps closer to the wall.

"She can shoot the head off a rattlesnake," I said, to discourage the cousin from making a run for it.

I had gone weak all over. I still held the pistol with both hands, but it rested on my knees and was pointed at the floor. I did not feel ready to shoot again. Marion was not bleeding especially much, but he was unusually quiet.

"She shot the eye out of a painter while it was attacking our mule," I added when the cousin did not give in right away. "It's laying out there in the snow. I tell you this because I don't think she'll let you off as easily as I let Willie."

"You killed Willie," his cousin said.

"He died quick," I answered him.

The boys continued reluctant and grumbled about unfair treatment, but they moved over to the wall. Finally Ben Chaplin said, "Well, I see you girls had your way."

Without letting her rifle drop, Maude said, "You can't blame us for what happened here."

"I have lived in these hills a long time with no talk of rat poison being put in the coffee. If you girls were the peaceable sort, not the kind who go around dressed like boys and causing trouble, things might have turned out differently."

Marion said, "That kind of talk is uncalled for. This girl saved lives today."

Ben Chaplin said, "I see three on the floor."

"Only one is dead," I said.

Marion said, "If somebody would give these girls a hand and tie up these two rowdies, I'm in need of some medical care." He did not look good.

Nor did Mrs. Newcomb, who Mr. Newcomb had just gotten to sit up in a chair. When she saw Maude's rifle was still aimed at those boys, she wilted right to the ground again to lie beside Joe, who began to snore.

Maude went over to the boys and told them to lay their guns on the floor very gently. It seemed they didn't think they ought to, so they began to raise a complaint. Maude swung the butt of her rifle up between them and, with one twist of her shoulders, swatted them both upside the head. This moved even the unshot cousin to a change of attitude.

The boys dropped their guns on the floor. This set the tone for the room. Mack got up and found a piece of rope while Ben Chaplin got out his needle and thread. He got started on Marion, who seemed glad of the chance to sit back down.

Ben Chaplin sat next to him, saying, "You don't even have a bullet in this arm. It just left you a furrow to plant beans." If Marion had any remarks in mind, he did not utter them. Ben Chaplin poured spirits over Marion's arm, bringing a noise from the back of Marion's throat.

Mrs. Newcomb was once more brought to her chair. I was beginning to feel some impatience with Mrs. Newcomb. Her antics pretty much meant that Mr. Newcomb could be no help at all to Maude. I was of no help either, and so it was easier to be rankled with Mrs. Newcomb's weakness than with my own.

Maude did not, in any case, appear to need all that much help. She looked over Mack's shoulder to be sure of the job he was doing. "Hobble their feet like a horse," she said, "for good measure." Willie's cousin tried to kick Mack, but Maude poked him in the ribs with the rifle. "If you are feeling your oats because you don't have a bullet hole in you, I can remedy that," she said.

She reminded me of Aunt Ruthie, and some place deep inside me smiled. I don't think Aunt Ruthie had managed very often to bring a smile to my heart in life; it seemed strange it could happen at that terrible moment.

When the boys were well tied, Maude came to sit beside me. She took the pistol. "Are you okay?" she asked me.

I whispered, "Will they hang me for this?"

"You defended yourself," she said. "You defended all of us. Didn't you hear Marion?"

"It was purely accidental."

Maude said, "Well, I know that. It was the kind of happening that Aunt Ruthie would have said was meant to be." Maude was right about this, Aunt Ruthie always considered bad luck to be meant to be. Good luck, she didn't trust at all.

Marion fared better for taking a few stitches, in that the bullet only grazed him, but the boy who had traveled with Willie and his cousin was not so lucky. Not only did he need a stitch or two, but also his wound needed to be washed out with lye.

"It's a puncture wound," Ben said with a sorry shake of his head. "Nothing else that looks so no-account that's likelier to kill you."

The boy was not brave about it either; he started out with

the towel in his mouth but tore it out to make a loud yell at the first touch of the solution. He carried on like a babe in arms, with Mack and Mr. Newcomb finally having to hold him down so his hand could be cleaned out. Marion sat square on the boy's legs.

Mrs. Newcomb had the good sense to retire to the bed while this was going on. I was tempted to remind her who had spent the night there, but figured if she picked up some lice, it would serve her right.

When it was done, the boy said, "I'm going home, and I'm never going to stray to the wrong side of the law again. I'm not cut out for it."

Ben Chaplin was not in a forgiving mood. He said, "That's as may be, but there is a dead body on my floor that somebody will have to account for."

"I didn't do it," he said. "That girl is the one you ought to be jawing at."

"You and this other fellow held us at gunpoint, in case you forgot," Ben Chaplin said, "and you will have to answer for that." And once more I had to be grateful that Ben Chaplin was a clear thinker, if nothing else.

"I didn't plan to shoot nobody," the boy said, and I knew how he felt. I didn't plan either, it just happened, and now my hands were shaking so hard I had to keep them pressed flat between my knees. I had not yet stood up. I was not at all sure I could.

"I'll tell you what else," Ben Chaplin said, "and this goes for everybody but Mack and Joe. I want you all out of here before nightfall. You girls pick yourself a horse, the rest of you take your own, and get on your way."

FORTY-FOUR

I WAS HURT BY THE CHANGE IN BEN CHAPLIN'S MANNER, but Maude didn't appear to be. When Willie's boys had departed, it was our turn. Maude said, "What will the horse cost us?"

"Nothing," Ben Chaplin said, "if you will just be on your way."

If he thought he'd get an argument from Maude, he had another think coming. She said, "I want you to throw in a saddle."

"Done."

But Maude was not satisfied. "You'll get the mule back to Cleomie?"

"I will," Ben Chaplin said. "And I'll put a flea in her ear when I see her too, sending me such as you to sleep under my roof."

"You've got a deal," Maude said, still unaffected by his rough attitude. I wished I could say the same. "Roll those blankets up tight, Sallie," she said, making it necessary for me to test my legs. "I will get our horse."

"I'll go with you," Marion said.

"Sallie and I can get along on our own, thank you very much," Maude said, and shut the door behind her. Marion stood helpless.

At this moment Joe chose to rise from the dead. He stood in an unsteady fashion and looked around the room. Mrs. Newcomb shrieked as if she'd seen a ghost. Ben Chaplin lost his temper entirely and shouted, "Good grief, woman, will you shut up!"

At this she went into her same loud crying act that we were all greatly tired of. Her husband hustled her out the door without so much as a thank-you to Ben Chaplin for the use of his floor or the barn for their wagon and horses.

"Good riddance," Ben Chaplin said.

"You may say good riddance to us," I said shakily, "but I thank you for your hospitality. It's not your fault things went so wrong. Of course, it was not our fault either."

He said nothing to me, but I found I didn't mind, knowing I had said the things I should. Marion said nothing too, but he could see how it was with me. He rolled up the blankets and made our things ready by the door. He made us a meal out of the bits and pieces left from breakfast and wrapped it in a napkin. I watched to see that he chose Maude's napkin, which I had not shared when setting food down for the boys.

Maude did not waste time. She was back shortly with the saddled horse. It was not built for speed. But it was a sizable creature, much younger than Flora, and more than enough horse to carry the two of us with all our belongings.

Marion carried everything out to the porch, but Maude would not accept his help in loading the horse. He asked, "You girls have supplies enough to take you the distance?"

"We will shoot something if we run short of all else," Maude said in a cool tone. "It is only a few days away now."

"That's true," Marion said. "But the weather could go bad on you again, anything could..."

If he meant to say, anything could happen, he thought better of it. So far there wasn't much that hadn't happened, and still Maude and I trudged on. We must have been something of a surprise to him. We were a surprise to me.

He gave up trying to talk to Maude. To me, he said, "That was good shooting, Sallie."

"It was pure accident," I told him. "I'm lucky it was Willie I hit and not somebody I'd feel more sorry about."

"You don't need to feel sorry, accident or no. That boy would've killed somebody before the week was out."

"You didn't look eager to kill him when Mr. Newcomb suggested it," I said, feeling a little put out about this myself. "You said he was only a boy and a rowdy."

"He was just a boy. I was wrong about the rowdy part," Marion said. "I saw that this morning. I can be wrong, now and again. Especially when the suggestion to be some other way is coming from somebody who doesn't care to bite the bullet his ownself."

"Enough talk," Maude said, and threw a leg over the horse. "Give her a hand up so we can get out of where we aren't wanted."

"I wish I was riding out with you," Marion said.

Maude did not reply to this. She gigged the horse and we were off.

"We are getting a late start on the day," Maude said. "I plan to ride till dark."

"You won't get any argument from me," I said.

"We have only a little cheese and ham left," Maude said, "and the last of the corn bread is dry and hard. But I didn't care to take anything more from Ben, even if he had offered."

"If you shoot something, I'll skin it," I promised, thinking the time was not right to mention that Marion had seen to this. Maude would be more reasonable when her belly was empty.

My belly was already thinking ahead, though. When the necessity came to hunt something up, I was hoping for a rabbit. If Maude shot it, it would be my job to clean it, and chicken feathers could be hard work.

This is how we began what we hoped would be the last leg of our journey. We enjoyed the unusual warmth of the day, and when it passed into a chilly evening, we had a fire. "Someone might notice the fire," I said, even as I sidled up to warm my hands.

"Let them notice," she said. Something in Maude had shifted; she was no longer on the run. I thought maybe I should be; I had killed a man, however accidentally, and I was made a little nervous by this change in Maude.

"We'll tell them where we're headed, and let them know we're willing to sleep in their barn if they'd rather," she added in a tone to bolster me.

This new boldness suited Maude very well, and I decided not to argue against it. No one noticed our fire, in any case, and it did us good to have it. Given the choice between going cold and going hungry, I would choose to go hungry every time.

As things turned out, and some would call it very good

luck, our greatest adventure during the next several days was eating a prairie dog for the first time. I suppose with the right kind of cooking, a prairie dog could make a good meal. For roasting them over an open fire until they are half charred, I cannot speak enthusiastically.

FORTY-FIVE

A WEEK LATER, WE WERE TIRED OF THE ENDLESSNESS OF the prairie. From all the accounts I'd ever read, we were traveling only the edge of a broad grassland more persistent than Iowa and even Missouri for grass. One that had no trees at all and took weeks to cross. I could not stomach the idea. Missouri had more than enough grass for me.

"Doesn't it seem funny to you that we never see anything but grass and sky?" I complained to Maude. "Don't you wish we would see a homestead? Don't you wish we might come across a wagon train and join up with some other travelers? Don't you wish—"

"Oh, be quiet," Maude scolded. "Isn't it enough for you that nobody is bothering us? That we're making steady progress toward Independence?"

Maybe we were making steady progress, but it didn't feel like it. It seemed we were forever wading through a sea of grass that might just about be forded when the wind would change direction and another sea would wash in.

Trees came few and far between out here. To find a stand of three to five of them was so rare as to make me want to set up camp, no matter the time of day. It was nearly as good as coming across a dressed bird.

And yet it became so much what we expected to see that when we saw something different the very next day, it was a little alarming. It didn't help that it was a cemetery of some size. Many a row of wooden markers, some crosses, and a few stones of a golden color that felt restful to the eyes. It was civilization.

But still, it didn't feel like much of a welcome.

"What do you think it means?" I asked Maude.

"Independence can't be far away," she said. But I could see the sight had unsettled her too. I wished we had come upon something else as our first sign of civilization, that was all.

"I hope there are a few people left standing," I replied as we passed the cemetery.

There were more than a few. We came upon a well-traveled road and followed it. Over an hour's time, a good many people passed us riding out.

Each time someone got a good look at us, I worried they would recognize Maude. What good were a few layers of dirt when your face had been splashed across the front page? When you were known far and wide as Mad Maude? But no one did any other than raise a hand in greeting, and some did not go that far.

When we could see the town in the distance, a pale cloud of dust seemed to hover over it. It spread out a good deal more than Cedar Rapids or even Des Moines. Its color seemed from a distance to be a fairly uniform gray. People out here did not take great care to whitewash, it looked to me.

We rode into town at about two o'clock, with Maude

congratulating herself on having a couple of hours of bright daylight left in which to find Uncle Arlen.

"Maybe we ought to find a place to stay first," I said.

"If we find Uncle Arlen, we'll have a place to stay," she said.

Her confidence had returned but mine had found a hole somewhere to hide in. Partly it was the memory of Des Moines that bothered me. But the other worry was simply the size of Independence.

I didn't like the look of it from the get-go. The streets were wide but still so busy with carriages, coaches, and riders moving much too fast, it didn't look safe to enter into the rush of it all. If we got brushed off our horse, we would be trampled or run over in a moment.

"It's just such a change from seeing nobody," Maude said when I stood reluctant. "You'll get used to it in a few minutes, you'll see."

We had to shoulder our way into the flow of horses and riders. The boardwalk looked worse to me. Crowded, and people acted like they didn't even see each other, just used their elbows to hurry on past. It made me glad I was on a horse, more polite.

I had never seen so many people together in one place before, not even in church on Christmas morning. We hadn't gone far before I was ready to turn and hightail it out of there. "Let's come back later," I said to Maude. "We can use the breather to get used to the idea of it all."

"Settle down, Sallie," Maude told me. "You are evermore the kind of person who strives for something and once it is within reach, changes her mind. But I am not changing mine, and you are stuck behind me on this horse."

The buildings were, for the most part, the unrelenting gray color they had looked to be from the distance. But every so often we saw a fancy hotel that, while it was largely still gray, sported red or orange trim about the doors and windows.

There were saloons aplenty, and these were by far the most appealing buildings, some of them dressed up like dollhouses, the likes of which could only come from a girl's imagination. The wood trim was sometimes carved in curlicues and the painted words were drawn very prettily. Occasionally the doors were painted in bright colors.

The best of these dollhouses caused us to stop and look for a time. It was a place dressed up in shades of lavender and made the mouth water for wanting to sleep there. But when I said so, Maude only made a snorting noise much like the horse was given to.

Here and there about the town were men, and even a couple of women, standing bravely in the crush of the streets, selling things to eat. We stopped beside these people pretty often, tasting their wares. When it was bread stuff, we bought only one and shared. When it was a piece of meat or potatoes, Maude said we should each have one of our own.

At first I went on worrying that someone would recognize Maude, but when one blacksmith or vendor after another did not, I let go of this worry. Either we were too dirty to be recognizable in any fashion, or nobody cared to wonder why she might have looked familiar.

We went from livery stable to livery stable, and none of them belonged to Arlen Waters. No one knew who he was. We began to realize we might just as well go looking for a needle in a haystack. There were so many streets in this city and nearly that many stables. It was a terrible discouragement.

"We don't even know for sure that's what he did when he got here either," Maude said. It was by then well past dark.

Maude was right, and I had no useful argument to give her. I had gotten used to feeling like a sardine packed tight in a can, but I had grown tired and low-spirited.

"He might have gone on, the way he wrote he planned to," Maude said wearily. "He might be somewhere else, doing something else. He might be dead. That letter could have been his last."

She was getting low too. I wanted to lift her spirits, but I was more of the mind that says misery loves company at just that moment. "I know we talked about how we might not find Uncle Arlen," I said, "but somehow I thought sure we would."

"Let's find a room to sleep," Maude said as we came to the next livery we had been told of. "We'll ask for Uncle Arlen at this place, but let's board the horse too."

We knew it would be necessary to pay for the horse's keep. Independence was some larger than Des Moines, and the back doors stood only a few feet from another back door. There were no sheds fitted to sleep a horse. It was a good thing Ben Chaplin gave us the horse to get rid of us, or we would not have had the money for boarding it.

Before we went in, I said, "We ought to ask if we couldn't sleep in the loft."

Maude considered this, then said, "No, I think we should

look for a bootmaker or the like and ask to sleep on the shop floor. That's more to my liking."

"If we're going to spend money anyway, we might go to a hotel and take a bath," I said. We had passed many hotels.

"They aren't likely to let us into a hotel, the way you look," she said.

Which made me grin. I didn't know if she'd washed her face even once since climbing onto Cleomie's mule. I had not.

FORTY-SIX

IN THE END, IT WAS NOT A BOOTMAKER'S SHOP BUT A hatmaker's that had a light burning in the back. Since we were carrying our blankets and the saddlebags, we couldn't be too picky. "Lily's Box," the fancy lettering painted on the window read.

Lily opened her door only a crack, since it was past closing time, and Maude offered her twenty cents for a night on the floor. Lily impressed me in the way Aunt Ruthie could. Not with Aunt Ruthie's spare form and stern manner, but with the lot of hair she had tumbling over her shoulders and the full figure she covered with a silky robe. There was something to be said for a woman who made an impression.

"Are you boys or girls?" Lily asked after a long, doubtful look.

"Girls," Maude admitted. "We thought we'd be safer this way."

"I imagine you are," Lily said, and let us in. "You can have a bath if you want," she said. "I can draw the curtain and get into bed so you'll be private."

I could make out a row of pretty feathered hats on wire stands as we crossed her shop. She led us to a large room, outfitted with a comfortable reading chair, a big iron bed, and a corner that served as a kitchen. Waist-high bookcases ran around two of the walls and were filled with books of all description, but I did not see any dimers.

"Why don't you sleep upstairs, if you don't mind me asking?" Maude said when we had put the pots of water on to boil.

"Hat glue smells to high heaven," Lily answered. "Best if I work upstairs and live down here where I sell the hats. Less mess, less odor to live with. Have you girls eaten?"

"We have, thank you for asking," I said. "It's good of you to let us have a bath." Maude used to be the one to say these things, but she sat on the floor to wait for the water, and had grown quiet.

"I'll leave you girls to your bath," Lily said, seeing Maude's interest was not in conversation. "Douse the light when you're done."

Lily had no sooner drawn the curtain than I reached for a newspaper left lying on a footstool. "What do you find?" Maude said after I had paused to read.

"Nothing," I said. "A receipt for pumpkin pie that reads very tasty. Tastily."

"You're reading recipes?" she said in a disbelieving tone.

"If they'd been kind enough to draw a picture, I might have tried chewing paper," I said truthfully. "There are many things about the civilized life that I miss."

Maude snatched the paper away from me. I watched

over her shoulder as she looked through pages of local news. With each page turned and no awful discovery made, my heart lifted.

But then, on page seven, there it was:

BULLETS IN THE AIR

Mad Maude Gets Her Man

A dispatch was received by the Des Moines County Sheriff's office that the same Maude March who is wanted in that city for horse thievery and robbing a bank is known to have killed her first man. That it was Willie "Golly" Griffith—

"The water's going to get cold," Lily said from behind her curtain.

Maude put a finger to her lips and set the paper aside. We weren't going to talk just then. This was fine with me. But I could tell she was in quite a state. Maude cannot hide her moods from me.

There was to be only one wash of hot water. Together we stepped into the washtub, having agreed that we should both have a moment to enjoy clean water before the dirt washed off.

We soaped our hair and dunked it, also hoping to make the best use of clean water. After that we scrubbed our skin, doing each other's backs. There was so much dirt in the water we did not sit until it cooled but got out to feel clean.

In only a few minutes we had put our undershirts back on and were determined to sleep in only those, since the stove had put out a good deal of heat. Because we could hear Lily snoring lightly, we felt we could reread the article and talk a little.

"It's on page seven, Maude," I said in a whisper. "A lot of people wouldn't read that far through." We were crouched in front of the woodstove, reading by firelight.

—That it was Willie "Golly" Griffith, a man wanted for wounding another man when a poker game did not go his way, makes no difference to the law. Dead is dead. That Mad Maude is, in fact, not much more than a girl, and grief-stricken over the shooting death of her beloved aunt, makes no difference either. She is wanted for murder. Perhaps her sad experience has turned her mind forever, because after shooting her victim, she was heard to cold-bloodedly refer to him as "a sack of dirt." She had earlier hoped to poison the man, another eyewitness tells this reporter. The evidence would seem to say the girl has become a hardened criminal. Maude March is now being pursued through Missouri and Arkansas as she tries to make the Texas border. If the Indians don't get her, the law will.

Maude slapped the paper down angrily again. "They're saying I'm crazy."

"They didn't run a picture," I said, ticking off the good points, "you didn't make the front page, and even the print is smaller."

"I hope you don't think that makes it all right," Maude said. "Did I shoot that boy, Sallie, did I?"

"No, I did," I said, and seeing the look on her face, quickly added, "By accident, like. I mean to say, it was the gun I was holding that went off."

"Don't ever tell anyone that," she said. "Not even if they catch me and hang me."

I snatched the paper away and stuffed it into the open woodstove. "I don't know why you even want to read these things," I told her. "You're only making yourself sick over it. You never even used to read anything but the wanteds, did you?"

"I never expected to be a headline before," she said.

"Maude, don't talk like that, will you? About them hanging you? It gives me a bellyache."

"All right, then, I won't say another word about it."

I shut the stove door quietly and slid down into my blanket. I said, "They think you're headed for Texas. That's not so bad."

After a time, Maude said, "You may be right."

"About what?" I was nearly asleep and dreaming off and on of sitting in a schoolroom. Funny how that used to seem like the start of a nightmare, but now I found it right comforting. If Maude answered, I didn't hear her.

FORTY-SEVEN

———◆———

IN THE MORNING, LILY PUT A LOAF OF BREAD ON THE table and began to slice it, saying, "I'm going to give you girls a piece of advice. I know you aren't asking for advice, and if you don't want to hear it, I guess you won't listen."

"We'll listen," Maude said, made meek by Lily's manner, which was suddenly easily as rough as Aunt Ruthie's.

"Don't take this stuff of the newspapers to heart," Lily said.

Maude rose from her chair so fast it fell over. Myself, I was too shocked to move.

"Sit right back down there," Lily said, setting her bread knife aside. She took up the butter knife and started to fix herself something to eat, her manner as offhand as if she had shared breakfast with hardened criminals before. "The first thing you're going to learn about people out here is they are practically all of them living down something. If it isn't a reputation, it's a failure of some kind. Usually it's the men, of course, not young girls, but they come out here for a fresh start."

Lily passed me a piece of bread she had buttered, having sprinkled sugar over it as well.

"How'd you come to be here?" Maude asked shakily, having picked up her chair and taken her seat.

"In my case, I believe we'd have to call it a failure of reputation," Lily said, passing her the butter. "Just keep your heads down wherever it is you're going, and the whole mess is likely to blow over. The further west you go, the more you'll be judged by what you show people, not by any reputation that follows you. Most everybody out here has a reputation of their own."

"Don't most people deserve their reputations?" Maude asked.

"If you're lucky, a reputation is made up of what people think of you," Lily said, "but it's just as often made up when people don't think at all."

"It's very kind of you to say so," Maude said, "but you took a big risk letting Sallie and me sleep in your place. We might have been deserving of my reputation."

"When I read that you and your gang were tearing up the pea patch in Arkansas, I had every reason to doubt that two little girls in need of a bed and a bath were going to do me any harm."

"What trouble have we caused in Arkansas?" Maude said.

Lily flushed slightly. "Never mind," she said. "Rival newspaper ran a different story, that's all."

"I should take a look at that," Maude said in a grim tone.

"No, you shouldn't. That's what I'm telling you," Lily said. "Just don't head toward Arkansas either."

We agreed that Arkansas sounded like a bad idea.

The search for Uncle Arlen did not lift our spirits. In most cases, it was a long, cold ride from one livery to another. Out of the maybe eight different people we talked to, all of them who worked with horses in one way or another, only two thought they knew Uncle Arlen once.

One of them said he thought Uncle Arlen had gone to St. Louis, and the other thought he'd gone off with a railroad crew, headed for Denver. To make matters worse, late in the day, Maude found a newspaper on the ground, and on page three, she found:

MAD MAUDE STRIKES AGAIN

Hit Like a Swarm of Locusts

The Wild Woman and her gang, numbering six in all, have struck again, riding down on the small community of Dowd, Arkansas. They robbed the bank, cleaned out the ready food supply, and changed horses at the livery, riding off again, much refreshed. Local ranchers have posse'ed up, looking to cash in on the offered rewards and the fame as well, by bringing an end to this band of despicable desperadoes. At least Missouri residents can put their heads on their pillows in safety tonight.

That was as far as I got before Maude slapped her knee with the paper and then dropped it in a horse trough. "This is good news," I said, hoping to convince Maude this was true.

I tried to convince myself. "At least we are being hunted in Arkansas. All six of us."

"Lily was right," Maude said.

"We should never have read that paper," I agreed.

"Well, that too," Maude said. "But I know what I have to do."

"What's that?"

"You stay here," she said.

"Maude!"

"No. No, we better stay together. Try harder to look like a boy."

I followed Maude at a trot, bringing the horse behind me. She walked with a man's long strides to the Lavender Door Hotel at the end of Second Street. This was the prettiest hotel of those we had seen earlier. I was eager to have a look inside of it, but Maude told me nothing more of her plan, which bothered me some. Just because she was the head of a gang was no cause to think she didn't have to tell me what was going on.

We went to the back door and knocked. I slouched in the manner of Willie and his boys as I stood there. It was to be my best performance yet, and I felt a manly frown settle over my face.

A black woman opened the door, and Maude said, "Could I please speak to Miss Lavender?"

At this the woman laughed and said, "Gosh, girl, what kind of getup is that you got on? When you come lookin' for a job, you ought to dress nice."

Maude said nothing to this, and we were ushered in without further insult.

"Oh, Miss Lavender," the woman sang out when she

closed the door behind us. Just the way she said it told me that Miss Lavender was not the right name.

We stood in a kitchen, nice and bright with whitewash and touches of color in the bowls and dishes that lined the hutch. A big family-style pine table sat in the middle of the room, worn rounded at the edges but glossy with a wax job.

The sound of piano music came from the next room, and so did the sound of laughter, girlish laughter. A short fat man put his head through the doorway. "You called?"

"These gals are lookin' to talk to you," the woman said.

"No!" Maude said. "No, I'm not. I thought there would be a Miss Lavender." The desperation on Maude's face made the man take her seriously when she said, "I need to speak to a fallen woman."

He turned on his heel without another word to us. "Kitty," he called.

A big woman came into the kitchen, or at least she seemed big. She wore heels that outdid cowboy boots, and her hair was piled on top of her head in swirls so that it looked like a brown owl to me at first. "What do we have here?" she asked.

"This'n wants to see Miss Lavender."

"Kitty's my name. What can I do you for?"

Maude told her everything. Everything. My jaw liked to drop right on the floor. Maude told her and finished up with, "I need to look like a girl again. I need to look like a different girl. I was hoping you'd help me. I don't have anyone to turn to."

"Let me get this straight," Kitty said. "You want me to fix you up, but you aren't looking for a job?"

"Yes, ma'am," Maude said. "And no, ma'am. I want to find my uncle, and I think this town is the likeliest place to do it. But if I run into any kind of trouble, I intend to get out of here as fast as my horse will carry me."

"Our horse," I said.

"Bess," Kitty said, "can you find a dress, some shoes, and some petticoats, and bring them down here?"

"Yes'm."

"Better heat some water. We're going to have to start from scratch." I went out to feed the horse and make him comfortable, because it was clear we would be there for some time.

We were both head-washed, but only I put my same shirt on again. Maude was outfitted in ladies' undies with pink ribbons. She got shampooed again with something that turned her hair dark red. It was a little shocking at first, but after Bess put some pincurls up for her and let it dry in front of the woodstove—which didn't take long, Maude's hair was still short—it looked sort of pretty.

While her hair dried, we drank cold milk and ate enough carrot bread to hold us for a time. When Maude was judged ready, she was fitted with a blue dress with more ruffles than seemed right, but then we'd been wearing boys' clothes for so long we hardly knew the way a girl should look anymore.

Maude, for her part, seemed entirely pleased with the finished effect.

While all this was being done in the kitchen, things got some rowdier in the hotel. They were having a regular party in that front room. It was late in the evening when we stood by the door to leave, and the party was still going strong.

"How much do I owe you for this?" Maude asked after

she'd stopped saying thank you so many times it was getting embarrassing.

"Not a penny," Kitty told her. "Let's just say I'm trading for good will."

"Oh, you have it," Maude said, starting to gush all over again.

"It's not your good will I'm talking about," Kitty said, "but I'm grateful to have it too. If I roll up on your doorstep when I'm old and gray, you'll remember me, I hope."

"I will, Miss Kitty," Maude said. "That's a promise."

I knew Maude would keep her word, but I couldn't see that there was any need. Kitty had that special shampoo; I didn't see why her hair ever had to go gray.

FORTY-EIGHT

A MAN ON A HORSE WAITED FOR US WHEN WE LEFT THE Lavender Door Hotel. He took off his hat when he saw us coming. The light from the windows shone on his bare head.

"Marion!" Maude said. "What are you doing here? Haven't they hung you yet?"

"You and your sister come from a bloodthirsty lot; that would be my guess," Marion said.

"How did you find us?" I asked him. To tell the truth, I was some relieved to see him. I had no idea what Maude was likely to do next. I hardly recognized her anymore.

"I've been asking around for you since I got here. I spotted you at a livery earlier today, been following you ever since."

"You asked after us?" Maude said.

"I said I was looking for two boys," Marion said. "You had me worried for a while here. But now I see what you were up to. Where you headed next?"

"We haven't found our uncle yet."

"I'll help you look," Marion said. "I hope we'll get lucky. We surely can't pass you off as a boy with you looking like that."

Which remark caused Maude to give him a look that should have singed his hair. Maybe because he had so little of it up front, he seemed immune. I went back alone to get our horse, determined that no one who had seen Maude before should see her in her fresh disguise.

And although it was well into night, we kept riding from one livery to the next.

"Well, there is nothing for it but to sit up till morning," Marion said when we gave up after finding two liveries closed for the night. "Let's us tie these horses to a post and find us something to eat."

In fact, a place stood open before us, ready to feed a hungry body at any hour of the day. Only the cook, in a dirty apron, stood ready, and he sat alone and disheveled at a table with his elbows on a newspaper. Marion ordered eggs and chili from the doorway, causing the cook to get up from his table without a word of yea or nay. But he headed for a door at the back of the room and left us alone.

In the near dark of the streets, I had almost forgotten how changed Maude seemed to be. The color of her hair suited her better than I would have thought if someone had come up to me earlier and asked, how do you think your sister would look with hair the color of a fox?

But it wasn't only the color; it was the curls. She hardly looked like the Maude I knew. It was worse than when Marion got rid of his beard. In the end, I found it easier not to look at her very much. Luckily, I sat next to her and could look across the table at Marion.

We had done almost no talking during the hours of

riding around looking for liveries, except to the smithies and stable hands we questioned. In part, I had the feeling that Maude was pretending Marion wasn't there. Maybe even Marion was pretending that. At that table, we had no choice but to talk back and forth about what we ought to do next.

Marion asked if we felt ready to give up on finding Uncle Arlen. "Not really," I said. "We might have missed a place."

"How many days are you thinking to put into this search?" he asked.

"As many days as it takes, or until I am convinced we aren't going to find him," Maude said. "We have nowhere else to go."

This statement struck me deep, and for a reason I couldn't plumb, I wanted it to strike Marion deep too. "We were orphans when we set out," I said, "and we are orphans still."

"Lots of people are orphans," Maude said stoutly. "Let's don't feel sorry for ourselves."

"I don't care to sound sorry for myself," I said, "but I would rather not be an orphan so soon."

The chili was brought to our table, and Maude said to the cook, "I could do this job of putting food on the tables, if you are looking for someone to work for you."

"It's busier most times of day," he said. "I have some help, but I could use another hand in the mornings."

"What do you pay?" Maude asked him, and when I thought she would say yes, she said, "I'm not sure that's enough for me. I have my little brother to support."

"That's for the first day," the cook said. "If you do all right, I'll pay you what I pay everyone else. Some are raising bigger families on what I pay and do well enough. But you can't wear that fancy dress to work here."

"What must I wear?"

And so they settled it while Marion and I looked at each other over our chili. "What's this?" Marion whispered when the cook had gone back to sitting at another table.

"If I work today, I'll earn the money to stay someplace tonight. As you said, now that I've returned to being a female, I can't very well share the floor with rough riders," Maude said. "At any rate, it is time Sallie was returned to being a little girl." She looked at me. "That might take a couple of days."

This silenced Marion, and if I had something to say, it could wait till I had eaten. Until the chili was set before me, I had not known I was so hungry. I had no complaints about the eggs either.

Once my belly was full, all I could think about was how good it would feel to crawl into a bed. There was no bed to be had, only the hours of sitting in the chair waiting for morning. "We could play a few hands of cards, if we had a deck," Marion said.

"Aunt Ruthie didn't hold with card playing," Maude said. "We don't know how."

So Marion told her all that she would need to know if ever she wanted to learn. That the deck is made up of four suits; hearts and diamonds, spades and clubs. "Clubs?" Maude said.

"Like a paw print," he said.

That was the last I heard. I couldn't remember putting my head down on the table. I only noticed when I woke up that I had slept until there were sounds to be heard from the street outside. The clop of horses' hooves and the low drawl of a man's voice.

Marion had gotten a deck of cards from someplace, and he and Maude were playing in silence. "Where'd you get those?" I asked.

"Bought them off a fellow who came in for a meal," Marion said.

"I don't remember that."

"You were out like a light."

Across the room, the cook got up, folding his newspaper.

"Is that a recent paper?" Maude asked him.

"Yesterday evening." He set the newspaper down and took our empty bowls. "You could be here at seven, if you want to start right away," he said.

"I will be on time," she said, and spread the paper out in front of us.

FORTY-NINE

I HAD BEEN SAYING A SILENT PRAYER THAT ANY NEWS OF Maude would have been moved further to the back, and written in very small print. If the print got small enough, she wouldn't be able to read it at all.

The first page was half taken up with a headline: DARING BANK ROBBERY!!!

"Have you robbed another bank?" I asked her.

She threw a dirty look in my direction and said, "It's Jesse James this time."

"Where?" I said, spotting a smaller story heading: BLOODY GUN BATTLE.

"Right here in Missouri," Maude said, skimming the page.

I leaned in to look at it along with her and told Marion, "Jesse James killed somebody again."

"Well, there's fresh news," he said with a smirk.

"It's all they've written about in here," Maude said.

"Read it out loud," Marion said. "I can't read upside down."

And so I began at the first column:

THE BLOODY BOYS RETURN

Jesse James Shoots to Kill

A daring holdup of the Gallatin Bank on a cold December morning ended in gunfire and spilled blood, and near tragedy for the James boys' momma. Leaving their gang of eight men stationed on the boardwalk to cover their backs, Frank and Jesse entered the bank with pistols drawn. No one stood against them and, in fact, the bags were filled to bursting with money before the shooting began. After asking him for his name, Jesse declared that the clerk reminded him of a man he despised. A few words were exchanged, then Jesse James Shot and Killed the clerk, John Sheets, and wounded another man. That it was the James boys might well have been taken for rumor but for the fact that Jesse's horse threw him as he rode out of town. The horse dragged him three wagon-lengths before Jesse freed himself! The horse ran off. Stranded, Jesse traded gunfire with courageous citizens, wounding a few, and there are reports he may have taken a bullet himself. It was Frank, onlookers tell, who defied death by riding back and rescuing his brother from an undignified end! Positive identification was proven from papers found in the saddlebags when the horse was recovered by the sheriff.

"Maybe they've forgotten about you," Marion said as Maude began to read about Jesse and Frank from another article titled, "Local Boys Gone Bad." "What with this interference, and your disguise, you won't have to worry about being recognized."

"I never believed I would feel so relieved to hear about such things," Maude said, "as a man killed."

"I bet Frank rescued Jesse so he could finally get his name in the paper alongside Jesse's," I said. Maude made a disgusted sound, but I argued, "It must get tiresome for him that Jesse gets all the attention." Meanwhile, I realized Marion was right; Maude might not be news at all anymore. I paged through the paper, skimming the headlines. "There's not a word in here about you today."

As the sky lightened outside, the room began to fill up with hungry cattlemen. Some of the help had arrived while we read the paper from front to back, girls not much older than Maude, most of them. And from the moment they stepped on the floor, they ran their feet off, carrying coffeepots and taking orders.

One of these customers came in carrying a fresher newspaper, and Marion bought it from him once the fellow had finished with it. I could see the light in Maude's eye that meant she couldn't see the sense in offering to pay for a paper that had already been read, but the truth of the matter was, the man hadn't looked like he would leave it behind.

This paper held one story after another about the James Brothers, every robbery they ever did, their days in the Confederacy. Their entire family history was written up, including their father's sad abandonment of the family to join the gold rush. Marion asked us to read every word to him.

Mad Maude did not get a mention. Again.

Maude said, "This is big news. It might well be all the papers are filled with for days."

Marion looked very much cheered by this news too. "You're small potatoes compared to Frank's daring rescue of Jesse. I'd say they're going to write about little else for weeks."

"By then they'll have forgotten about me completely," Maude said.

"So long as you don't rob any banks," Marion joked.

Maude snatched the paper out from under his elbows so fast his chin nearly hit the table. "Next time I need to get my name out of the paper, I'll know enough to write a note to the James boys."

"I never know whether to take the things you say in jest," Marion said.

"I never jest," Maude told him.

"That's what I was afraid of."

The city began to open up for business. At least the livery across the street opened up. "We might stay here a week or more, Sallie," Maude said. "I want you to board the horse across the street there. You should ask if it's cheaper to pay weekly instead of by the day."

"Where are you going to be?"

"I'll have to find a place to buy a plain cotton dress, cheap, so if it gets ruined working here, I won't mind so much. Should anyone ask," Maude said smartly to me, "our name is Waters. Like Aunt Ruthie and our momma before she got married."

"Sallie Waters," I said. "I like it."

"You and I can meet back here when we finish our business and then we'll see about a place to stay."

"Where will you be heading, Marion?" I asked him, because I figured we'd be going back to Lily's. I doubted she'd let Marion sleep on her floor.

"I might chum around with you two for a while, if it's all right with your sister."

"You can chum with Sallie," Maude said. "See if you can avoid running up the price of boarding the horse."

I was growing impatient with Maude's lack of graciousness, but decided to wait until I was alone with her to say so. "Why do you stick with us, Marion?" I asked him once Maude had gone off on her own.

"I feel responsible for the two of you being orphaned," he said. "At least that's how it begun."

"And now?"

"Now I kinda like you. Even that hardtack sister of yours," he said with a grin.

"She does grow on you," I said.

He said, "That's what I should've been afraid of."

FIFTY

I WOULD NOT BE OUTDONE. IF MAUDE COULD GET A JOB, so could I. I made up my mind to ask for work at the livery across the street. If I got hired, I would be working right close to Maude. There was that to be said for it. Maybe we would get a reduced rate for the horse too.

I think I had decided on this not only because I didn't think I'd like to wait on tables but also because it was so warm in a livery. Of course, I reminded myself, it would be a hot job when it was dead summer too.

I walked up to the first man I saw come out of the building and asked him to give me the job. He was just leaving his horse off, not working there, but he was kind enough about it. Maybe because Marion was standing right behind me.

"I think you are wrong to do this," Marion said after the fellow had walked away.

"If Maude is going to work, so am I," I said. And remembering one of Aunt Ruthie's favorite sayings, one I had always chafed at, I said, "Every little bit helps." Only now did I see that it might in some way have been Aunt Ruthie's way of paying me a compliment when I had done a share of the work.

As I say, she was a spare woman.

"Are you going to be a boy or a girl?" Marion asked before I went inside.

"I'm still a boy," I said to Marion. "Johnnie is my name."

"I thought that was your sister's name."

"If she wanted it, she shouldn't have left it laying around."

"Do you want me to come in with you?" he asked when I hesitated at the open doorway to get my boyish slouch in place.

"No," I said, and abandoned the slouch. I walked in tall.

I waited where I thought I ought to, about a room's distance from where the smithy stood holding a piece of metal to the fire. He sang a lively tune about three crows sitting on a tree, "O Billy Magee," and I didn't mind hearing all of it, even though the heat was nearly more than I could bear, standing there.

It was no surprise the smithy worked shirtless. He'd have done well to work in nothing at all if such a thing could be allowed. Watching him, I began to worry that he would never hire me. His arms looked like thick blocks of wood. His back muscles were heavy as ropes. He wasn't likely to think much of using a pip-squeak like me, even to clean stalls. Worse, I was never going to muscle up like that. I would always be a pip-squeak.

Staring at his back, I noticed he spent more time in the sun than I would have guessed a smithy would. The sun-darkened skin drew attention because of some odd white marks, not quite round but pointed at top and bottom, that were sprayed across his back. It took me a moment to realize they were scars. I wondered if he'd gotten shot up somewhere or other, if they were bullet holes, but they didn't look anywhere so neatly round as the one bullet hole I'd had a good look at.

He didn't look unhappy to see me when he turned away from the anvil, more surprised than anything. Because I had been staring at those scars on his back, I wasn't altogether struck to see them on his front. "I advertised for a man," he said, stopping his song in the middle of a line, and making me think about other than scars.

"I was hoping you'd hire me, if no men came looking for the job. I'll be thirteen soon," I added, figuring an extra year couldn't hurt.

"Well, they have come looking, but it seems I don't like to pay what they're looking for. So if you don't want more than I offered them, you're in luck," he said cheerfully. "As for me and *my* luck, I guess you'll be a man someday."

I didn't reply to that.

"It's usually part of the deal that you can sleep in the loft, but I guess that's not much use to you if you're still living at home," he said.

"I'm not living at home," I said. "Can my sister stay with me? She's fifteen."

"I don't know about that," he said. "There's a lot of men in and out of here."

"She works all day," I added. "Can we lock up at night?"

"You *have* to lock up at night," he said. "I don't want anyone stealing horses."

"Let's us try it," I said. "You pay me what I'm worth. If it don't work out, it don't work out."

"Most folks around here call me Duck," he said, putting out a hand. "My name is Arlen Waters."

We shook, but I was already thinking. "Uncle Arlen?" I said. I felt certain he must be, but now that the moment was here, I could hardly believe we'd found him.

"Are you Aunt Ruthie's brother?"

He gave me an odd look. Then he said, "Who are you?"

"Aunt Ruthie's dead," I said in answer, and seeing him take that in, I added, "I'm Sallie. Salome." I had not said my full name in so long it felt funny in my mouth. "Salome March."

"Ruth Ann wrote me last year that you girls were growing fast," he said. "I didn't really picture you right, though, not so old as you are."

I was just flabbergasted. "Aunt Ruthie wrote to you last year?"

"She wrote me once every year, whether she wanted to or not," he said, "and it was clear she didn't want to. Her letters somehow ignored the fact that I had ever written. So I quit after a time. I haven't put a letter into the mail in three years."

"We didn't know where to find you," I said.

"I should have kept on writing," he said. "I should have written to you girls."

"Why didn't you?"

"Ruth Ann and I never were close," he said. "She didn't like it when I didn't fall in with her ideas. It isn't a kind thing to say about my own sister, but she was the type to hold a grudge."

"That was Aunt Ruthie to a T," I said. "But she kept your

letters. She tied them together with a ribbon, and Aunt Ruthie wasn't one to waste ribbon."

"'Preciate it," Uncle Arlen said, and I realized he might not be much more affectionate, generally, than Aunt Ruthie. But his eyes wetted up some, maybe to hear Aunt Ruthie cared about him, in her way.

"Maude and I were worried you'd have left Independence," I said. "We figured you could have gone anywhere from here."

"I did," he said. "But the wildness of the Far West isn't for me."

"I see you did get shot full of arrows," I said, nodding toward the scars. "You mentioned it in one of the letters."

"Yep, that's why my friends call me Duck," he said. He had a sparkle in his eye. "Because I didn't."

"Well, I hope you'll tell us about it," I said.

"It helped me make up my mind about a few things," he said more seriously. "I came back here and built this place. Been open for business over a year now."

"Maude is going to be very happy to hear that," I said.

"Little Maude?" he said, and his face lit up. "Where is she?"

I noticed then, he was rather pretty for a man.

FIFTY-ONE

MAUDE MUST HAVE HAD A HARD TIME FINDING A DRESS that suited her, because she took her time coming back. Marion and I kept an eye peeled to spot her, but when we saw her, she was already working. She didn't give us a chance to tell her a thing.

"Go somewhere," she said as she first laid eyes on us. "I don't want you peering at me from some corner or other when you think I won't notice, either. Just be here when I'm done."

She was pushing us out as she spoke.

"She don't want much," Marion said in a bothered way as we found ourselves standing out in the street, like we had it in mind to sell baked potatoes.

"She has a lot of Aunt Ruthie in her," I said, mad twice over as we relayed this information to Uncle Arlen. "No skin off my nose if she thinks she's an orphan another day."

"It might be a lot for her to take in," Marion said. "Let her get the hang of this job, then we'll let her know you're here."

Uncle Arlen said, "Let's wait till noonday, and all three of us together go over to see her."

It was not a fair deal, but the minute Uncle Arlen learned I was a girl, I lost my job. He said he could not have his niece working as a hired hand. It was a small consolation that he hired Marion instead. When nothing else could be thought of for me to do, I was allowed to help with mucking out stalls. It was a small, if bitter, victory.

In the end, having such a piece of news to tell got the better of me. After a time, I saw that business across the street had slowed down some, so I went across and ordered a bowl of chili. When Maude came to my table, I said, "Uncle Arlen has the livery across the street."

I wanted to say it deadpan, but I couldn't help grinning.

"There's some good news," Maude said without cracking a smile, the way Aunt Ruthie would have. But when she turned away to set a plate on somebody else's table, she looked back at me and winked. Her face had gone pink with joy.

I had just about caught her up on what I had learned when business picked up again. I went back to mucking stalls, which I realized was a never-ending job at a livery. "You could curry a horse now and again," Marion told me in hopes that I would.

In the eyes of anyone coming for their horses, he was my boss, and it bothered him that it looked like he was working me so hard, even if I was a boy. But I had a point to make: that I could have done this job, and would do it. I admit, I hoped Uncle Arlen would soften. He could pay me in dimers if that made him feel better.

Uncle Arlen went over to the restaurant for his midday meal sometime later, which was his habit anyway. I followed him. Maude left off working and sat down to the table with us. She was breathless, and not just from running around on that floor. "Uncle Arlen?"

"Little Maude," he said softly, almost sadly. "You've grown some." They were shy with each other at first, and then began to remember things only the two of them could share.

As for her hair, I could see he wanted to say something, but couldn't decide what exactly he ought to say. It was wise of him to keep shut, although I hadn't had a chance to tell him so. We agreed to meet later, as evening came on, leaving Marion to tend the livery business.

Uncle Arlen hugged Maude as we stood from the table, and they didn't look awkward with each other anymore. Uncle Arlen tousled my hair, which felt close enough to me, and best suited my disguise anyway.

Uncle Arlen lived two streets away from his livery, in a house with two rooms up and two rooms down. He lived only in the downstairs. The place was furnished comfortably enough by the previous owner, he told us. But Uncle Arlen was not much of a housekeeper.

He helped us clear a lot of things out of the upstairs rooms, including two stuffed chairs to be taken downstairs. We moved his bed up there, and he said Maude and I could have it for our own. It was not as fine as the room we had in Cedar Rapids, but it might have been spun from gold, it made Maude and me that happy.

Marion came over to the house after the livery was locked up for the night. Maude fried eggs and toast for an easy supper. She was about dead on her feet. The same was true for me, although I tried not to show it as I set tin plates and forks on the table. Uncle Arlen didn't have napkins, but we set out clean bright blue hankies instead. It looked fair enough for a reunion.

Now that we were settled in, or maybe because she felt more private than in the restaurant, Maude was much easier with Uncle Arlen. We recounted all our adventures to him, and Maude wasn't reluctant to tell him the worst.

He said he had seen the papers but never for a moment suspected it was his little Maude they were writing about, largely because he had not seen any of those articles that mentioned Aunt Ruthie. But he wasn't sure he agreed with what we told him Lily said, that Maude March would soon be an old story. He thought Maude should go on calling herself Maude Waters, just to be on the safe side.

Marion mentioned he was thinking of following the Oregon Trail come good weather. "You mean you're thinking of leaving?" Maude said. "Why would you do that?"

"I'm still a wanted man. Worse, since I shot your aunt Ruthie, I am still a murderer."

"Me too," I said. "Nobody's sending me out west."

"Hush up, Sallie," Maude said. "You're no such thing. There is a big difference between murder and an accident, and you have both had terrible accidents, but that is all."

"In my case, they wanted to hang me for that accident," Marion said, "and they still would. I'm thinking I would be safer west of the Rockies. It's less likely I'll ever run into some-one I know. I can use that bank money to set myself up in a little business."

This sounded smart to me, but Maude said, "Uncle Arlen looks like a stout enough fellow, and he says he never wants to go west again. You aren't nearly so stout. Maybe you should consider his thinking on the matter to be good advice."

"I've been west of the City of Kansas and liked it just fine," Marion said stoutly, "and I lived to tell about it."

FIFTY-TWO

I HAD BEGUN TO REALIZE MARION WAS A MAN SENSITIVE of his pride. But he should have known that telling Maude he'd lived to tell about his adventures would sound like bragging to her.

She jumped up from her chair real sudden like and yelled her list of complaints against Marion and even, it seemed, against Uncle Arlen. Men were selfish, they were short-sighted, they were too dumb to shut their mouths in the rain.

She threw a tantrum the likes of which I had never seen, and had to admire, throwing the small pillows off the chairs and kicking table legs. Uncle Arlen and Marion sat trans-fixed. She called Marion a goose-brain, and when that did not get a reaction, she called him a liar.

"Here now," he said. "What lie did I tell you?"

"Your promises were lies," Maude said wildly.

"I don't remember any promises," Marion said in a voice gone high and a little wild too.

"It wasn't so much a promise made in words," Maude said, and stamping her foot, added, "but in deed. You are going to listen to me now, or I may go against my own grain and shoot you."

Uncle Arlen opened his mouth as if to speak but Maude said, "Don't make me swat *you* one either. You may be my uncle, but you were only a younger brother in Aunt Ruthie's eyes, and that is how I see you, too."

Marion and Uncle Arlen both looked the question at me and I shrugged. Maude was never a simple girl, nor easy to get along with.

"If we ever want to live good lives," she said, "we have to put right everything we have done wrong. Or as much of it as we can. We can do nothing about Aunt Ruthie or Willie, we may never hear ourselves spoken of kindly by Ben Chaplin no matter what we do, but there are other ways we can show that our hearts are in the right place."

"What are you talking about?" Marion asked.

"The money," Maude said. She started yanking our plates out from in front of us and throwing them into the wash water, giving us time to think. I knew Maude was right. That money could never be used to build our future. It would only ruin us somewhere down the line.

Marion and Uncle Arlen found it harder to follow her train of thought, I could tell by the concentrated looks on their faces. Marion would not bite the bullet and ask her to explain, but Uncle Arlen, who had not dealt with Maude's temper in some time, and didn't realize the storm might start again, said, "What is it you want us to do?"

"I want every penny you have left from that bank robbery," Maude shouted at Marion.

He dove for his saddlebags and brought up a sizable canvas-wrapped packet. "It's shy only of what we used to buy some supplies for you and Sallie," he said.

"We're going to send it all back," Maude said, calming down some.

"We can't very well do that," Marion said, "without giving them a pretty good idea where to find me. Us," he added, seeing the determination on her face.

"You're right," Maude said. "We'll have to send it to someone else."

"Who?" I asked. "Cleomie?"

"No, I'm afraid we've wrecked her good name with Ben Chaplin," Maude said. "Let's not do her any worse favors." She looked lost in thought, but only for about five seconds before she seized on a name. "Reverend Peasley!"

"No!" I said.

"He has his poor points, but I don't know who else we could call on," Maude said to Uncle Arlen. "It would be too much for Mrs. Golightly."

"Hard to say," Uncle Arlen said. "I didn't care much for Peasley myself. But he is a preacher now."

"I don't care if he is a preacher," I said. "He didn't strike me as the forgiving type, not way down deep. Or even the honest type."

"Who, then?" Maude asked.

"The sheriff," I said, a plan springing to mind. "He's known us forever. We have to write down everything that happened to us, everything, so he'll see how things were. He'll understand."

Marion was by then sitting with his head resting in his

hands, no doubt picturing lawmen on his tail as he mounted the Rockies. But Maude was listening. Listening as if I was telling her just what she wanted to hear. I thought carefully before I told her the best part of my plan.

"We'll tell him how our part in the bank robbery was an accident, pure and simple, and how we came to take those horses, and how we hoped they found their way home after we set them free."

"Good," Uncle Arlen said.

"What about Willie?" Marion said from somewhere deep inside himself, and if he hadn't looked so miserable, I'd have been tempted to swat him myself.

"We were there, but it was a mystery man who shot Willie," I said snappishly. "It's our word against anybody's. Mystery shooters turn up in dimers all the time." I had to stop and think a minute. He'd made me lose my train of thought. I picked it up again with, "We'll say we hitched up with a little wagon train that carried us further west and then, much to our surprise, we came across Joe Harden here, again."

Uncle Arlen nodded his approval.

I had Maude up to that point where Joe Harden's name came up. Ignoring the frown on her face, I put on my most winning voice and said, "Only he'd been shot and gasped out his last breath telling us where to find the money he hid, and we did, and now we'd like to return it and be on the right side of the law the rest of our days."

Even as Marion put a hand over his heart and said, "I've died?" Maude swatted me and said, "Sallie! You talk like you're reading right out of one of those blasted dime novels."

"Don't swear," I said. "It ain't becoming."

"I think she's got something," Uncle Arlen said.

"Kill off Joe Harden, once and for all," Marion said. "Then I am free to be Marion Hardly."

"I don't know," Maude said. "It would have to be an awful long letter."

"I'll start writing," I said.

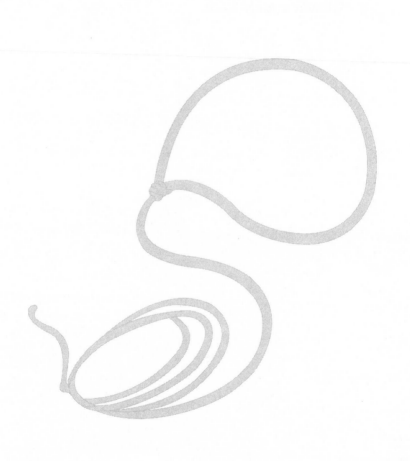

ACKNOWLEDGMENTS

———◆———

Watching Maude and Sallie find a gang of cowgirls-at-heart to champion them has been sometimes rough-riding, sometimes high-riding, occasionally rowdy, but always a rodeo ride of stellar proportions.

My agent, Jill Grinberg, is caring, thoughtful, and utterly more gracious than Maude, but she also has Maude's best qualities: she can see a far piece, she's a straight shooter, and she's a fine pardner to have by your side should you find yourself in the O.K. Corral at high noon.

My editor, Shana Corey, welcomed these girls with open arms; it's no surprise to me that Maude and Sallie rode home to her with the same unerring sense of direction that led them to Uncle Arlen.

Shana has all of Sallie's best qualities: the same quick courage and easy smile; the right combination of by-the-seat-of-her-pants and timely attention to detail (she's a planner); and a sure sense of the funny side of tragic circumstances.

Like Sallie, Shana possesses a writer's mind and heart and a great freedom of spirit with which to approach the work we do. As wonderful as it is to find these qualities in a character, it is even more special to find them in an editor.

Jenni Holm steered me toward research materials that turned out to be invaluable. Rides at a gallop, this girl, and thank you, Jenni, for putting out your hand to pull me up onto the historical horse.

I have a collage on the wall in the room where I work. In the collage, there are a few pictures of four women together, all of them pictures of contentment in different ways. In one picture they are working around a computer, in another they are hanging out in a sunroom, laughing, and in the third there are old ladies sitting on a park bench, having a chat. The pictures in that collage have been with me for a while, but now I feel like I know those women's names.

Thank you, Miriam Brenaman, for your true-life account of the rattlesnake that wouldn't die. And for bits of historical information that found its way into our conversation so subtly that I didn't know until later, when I found it useful, that I was being educated.

Thank you, Susan Krawitz, for instruction on the proper care and feeding of horses, and trail lore. These girls never would have made it to Independence without you.

Thank you, Uma Krishnaswami, for your own work, which forever reminds me that there are two sides to every story.

I'm pretty sure you all ride like Calamity Jane, and I am glad to count you among my friends.

My best friend and husband, Akila, dictated the funny, sounds-right newspaper articles while driving in heavy traffic—a high-wire feat for which I am eternally grateful. Thank you, sweetie.

Thank you, Vicki Hughes of the Ushers Ferry Historic Village—it's not only a Web site, it's the real thing (www.cedar-rapids.org/ushers).

Geno Paesano is not a cowgirl in any way, but he helped outfit Maude and Sallie for their adventures. We all thank him for telling me what I needed to know about the guns of the period.

My heartfelt thanks to all the people at Random House who put a beautiful book into your hands, with special thanks to Kristin Hall, the editorial assistant; Joanne Yates, the designer; Cathy Goldsmith, the art director; and Gino D'Achille, the illustrator.

Thank you to many unnamed librarians in the reference departments of the Cedar Rapids and Independence libraries and to Suzette, for a time at the Newberry, Florida, library, for your underpaid effort to find answers to the questions a clueless writer asks. More than that, I thank you for having the sand (aka dedication) to go even further and find information for wallpapering this book and the ones to follow it with period detail that will bring them alive in the minds of young readers.

Last, but not least, and I know she would love to hear the strains of "Ghost Riders in the Sky" playing in the background as I say this: Thank you, Pauline Macmillan, for morning cups of tea and storytelling that drifted into the lazy afternoons when I learned to appreciate country-and-western music—especially "My Mother's Hands"—and for writing encouragement of the most inspiring kind.

It was in Pauline's home that I often admired a flea-market purchase: a hand-embroidered pillow with the outline of a running horse and the words "Trouble rides a fast horse." She always said there ought to be a book with that title.

ABOUT THE AUTHOR

Audrey Couloumbis was born in Illinois. Her first book for children, *Getting Near to Baby*, won the Newbery Honor in 2000. She is also the author of *Say Yes* (2002), an IRA Children's Book Award Honor Book and a *Bulletin* Blue Ribbon Book. Before becoming a full-time writer, Audrey Couloumbis worked as a housekeeper, a sweater designer, and a school custodian. Today she lives with her husband, Akila, and their dog, Phoebe. They have two grown children. You can visit Audrey's Web site at www.audreycouloumbis.com.